I0690259

Spectrum

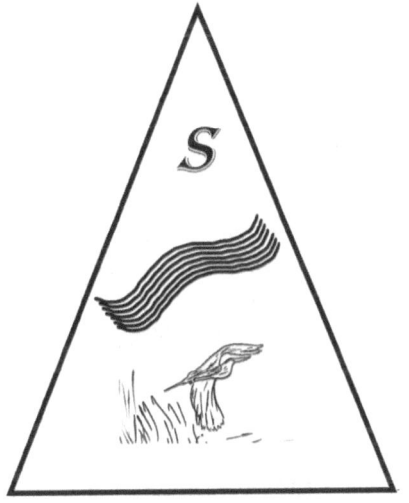

Tessa Needham

Grosvenor House
Publishing Limited

All rights reserved
Copyright © Tessa Needham, 2025

The right of Tessa Needham to be identified as the author of this
work has been asserted in accordance with Section 78
of the Copyright, Designs and Patents Act 1988

The book cover is copyright to Tessa Needham

This book is published by
Grosvenor House Publishing Ltd
Link House
140 The Broadway, Tolworth, Surrey, KT6 7HT.
www.grosvenorhousepublishing.co.uk

This book is sold subject to the conditions that it shall not, by way of
trade or otherwise, be lent, resold, hired out or otherwise circulated
without the author's or publisher's prior consent in any form of
binding or cover other than that in which it is published and
without a similar condition including this condition being
imposed on the subsequent purchaser.

This book is a work of fiction. Any resemblance to
people or events, past or present, is purely coincidental.

A CIP record for this book
is available from the British Library

Paperbook ISBN 978-1-83615-384-9
eBook ISBN 978-1-83615-385-6

To Regine for her encouragement and editing prowess.

To Melanie for her exquisite illustrations.

THE NORFOLK BROADS

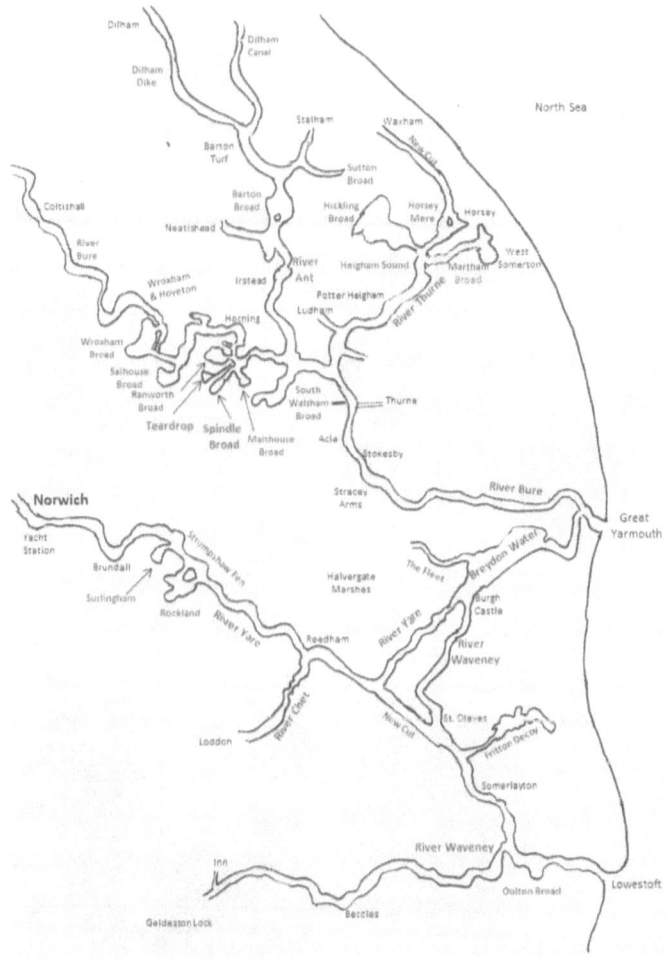

FOREWORD

Windmills in wide open skies, interspersed with puffy white clouds.

The boom of the bittern.

Starling murmurations. Thousands of birds weaving complex patterns and dancing in the air, as if to music.

But is Norfolk, the only county boasting a cathedral nestled at the edge of a National Wetlands Park?

We are at the end of the Swinging Sixties before mobile telephones were freely available, when a computer could take up any number of rooms filled with large tape recorders looking like huge owl eyes. This technology was in its infancy.

Four young Broads rangers collectively named *Spectrum* roam regularly in their rainbow-coloured motorboats, helping tourists and locals alike enjoy the Norfolk Broads in safety.

Is it pure coincidence if Christine Rogers and her three brothers share the same name as the mysterious group currently topping the record charts?

Why does their father Sam, an accountant responsible for the financial affairs of several charitable organisations in Kent make frequent journeys to the Defence Operations RAF Neatishead?

And how come Tony Dale, the number one pop sensation of the era, is seen so often in Norfolk?

The tranquillity of the reed beds brimming over with wildlife is under attack.

A vicious escapee from HMP Norwich, Jacob Wright, creates havoc, fear, and brutality.

Drug smuggling, arson and kidnapping are some of the twists and turns of our heroes' adventures.

Yes it is an adventure story but if you want to know more about the fantastic Norfolk Broads then read on ....

A TALE FOR SUMMER

CHAPTER ONE

It was 6.00 a.m. Early for many people but not for Chris and her twin Tim. She had just walked out on deck as dawn was breaking. The early morning sun was attempting to clear the mist from the reed beds, the water reflecting back a mirror image of its peaceful surroundings. It was magical. She looked into the still dark water. A bubble reached its surface causing a small expanding ripple. Could it be from a fish? Could it be from a water plant? Or could it be from methane escaping from the underlying peat! Who knows?

Hidden amongst the riverside vegetation a moorhen called. Chris turned. Her attention was caught by a pair of tufted duck. The male's clean white flanks a complete contrast to the chocolate brown of the female. At this time of year the male's tuft was extremely prominent.

The pair of them had moored overnight at How Hill before making the return journey to Spindle Hall. Sadly, the end of the school holidays was upon them. They would soon be departing for Kent.

While in Norfolk the Rogers' family lived in a beautiful thatched house dating to the Seventeenth Century nestled in its own grounds at the end of Spindle Broad.

A Broad almost oval in shape, surrounded by tall reeds and oak trees on the higher ground with the Hall situated at the top end. To one side was the boathouse and small jetty, and at the far end, a dyke edged with alder trees and reeds led out to the River Bure. The whole view from the river end made a very foreboding place, the inlet disappearing into a thick canopy of trees.

Around the house and boathouse lawns swept down to the waters edge, and at this time of the year were a mass of daffodils, tulips and crocuses.

The Rogers had owned the property for over three generations and when its rightful owners, Grandpa Fred and Grandma Blanche died, it was decided to keep the inheritance. Chris's father just could not part with it. Finances had been a little tight for a while, but the family had coped.

It was such a relief for Chris and her brothers. They would carry on spending all their happy holidays in beautiful Norfolk, and the rest of the year in Kent.

'Uggh,' Chris thought to herself, 'school on Tuesday.' She enjoyed her lessons but, looking around her, you cannot beat the scenery! Both she and her twin were passionate about the Norfolk Broads.

Nowadays Chris and her brothers never went into details about their holidays in Norfolk.

When they were very young their father's work at Neatishead Air Defence Radar Station had been kept a secret from them. But one supper time, Tim, then aged twelve, asked:

'Dad, what exactly do you do at Neatishead?'

You could have heard a pin drop.

Grace looked at her husband. Sam cleared his throat. 'I had been meaning to talk to the four of you for some time, but Tim, you have beaten me to it. You saw me arrive at the radar station during one of your bike rides I presume?' Tim nodded. 'As you know I am an accountant but I also help with air defence radar research. We handle very sensitive information, very hush hush…'

Ian interrupted: 'So you are a spy then?'

'God no! Let's say a government employee who protects our country. Now that you know, let us carry on as before, but mum's the word.'

When they had asked their dad if they could participate in the Broads Authority Ranger scheme under the name of *Spectrum* he had agreed, on the condition that once outside Norfolk they did not mention it. He had mumbled something about NATO, the Russians, the Cold War and, wanting to protect his children.

Recently too, life had got even more complicated on another front. The singer Tony Dale, a friend of the Rogers, had become a major player in the music industry.

Tony, very close to Chris's heart.

Another secret. She could not even tell her best friend June.

These musings were interrupted as her twin called from below where he had volunteered to cook a typical English breakfast.

She poked her head into the cabin, 'Mmmm that bacon smells good!'

'Quick quick, take a pew!' Tim shouted, as he placed their plates onto the table. 'Tony's latest record is going to be on the radio any minute from now.'

They savoured the moment – Tony Dale's velvety voice was superb – and just as they finished their last mouthful their walkie-talkie crackled into life.

'*Spectrum Two* calling *Spectrum One* come in please,' came Ian's voice over the airwaves.

'Ah hah, the others must at long last be up,' laughed Tim as he went to answer the call from his brother.

Ian and Mark had also been out on the Broads network over the past week.

They were on their way back from Great Yarmouth, where they had been helping the Local Archeology Society to set up a display for the forthcoming tourist season.

Incredibly, Neolithic and Bronze Age artifacts dating back about 10,000 to 3,000 years BC had been discovered in the Ormesby St. Michael area.

When Spectrum was asked to assist, Mark immediately put his name forward (one of his passions was archaeology), and Ian agreed to join him in the venture. Although reasonably confident, Mark hated doing things alone and liked at least one sibling alongside him.

Ian was only too pleased to assist. He didn't actually bully his younger brother but he was, after all, the older by 10 months! He often took the opportunity to pull rank. Something he would never get away with, with Tim!

Meanwhile Chris and Tim's time had been spent helping the Charitable Trust at How Hill which specialised in the portrayal of the Norfolk Broads' historical past. Their brief had been to prepare an appealing presentation at Toad Hall Cottage, a thatched marshman's dwelling.

The subject was *The Renowned Norfolk Tradition of Eel Catching.*

The twins, who were always interested in Norfolk Traditions, were pleased with the overall result. Their main display panel featured the method of stretching a net across the river catching the slippery eels at night on an ebbing tide. Yes, some of the rivers were tidal.

'Our bros should be back at Spindle towards lunchtime.'

Tim was beaming: 'How considerate of Ian to call when the washing up needs doing!'

'But you're drying!' she said throwing the tea towel at him.

With everything now stowed away for the trip back to the Hall, they cast off and turned the boat in the direction of Ranworth Broad and their Norfolk home.

By now the weak spring sunshine had managed to burn off the early morning mist, and the timely wind which had been of great help in dispersing the mist swiftly, was now rising in strength.

Tim seemed puzzled: 'Isn't Tony's new single the very one he recorded when he was staying with us at the beginning of the hols? Another number one for him?'

Chris laughed. 'That's right, as if it would be anything else!'

Tony Dale was fast becoming a superstar. He had a huge fan following and each new release invariably topped the charts.

Tony popped up to Norfolk as often as possible. To either record at Kipton Barns or to be with the Rogers family for a bit of relaxation.

Not to mention for the lovely blue eyes of a certain young lady named Chris.

'I wonder if he used *Spinney* for the 'B' side in the end?' Tim added.

The Rogers include music amongst their skills. Mark playing the drums, Chris and Ian the guitar, and Tim the electric organ. Their mother had trained as a concert pianist, but for Grace, Concert Halls gave way to RAF Operations Rooms with the onslaught of WW2.

Tony had immediately seen the potential of one of Tim and Ian's creations, the song called *Spinney*. Mark's idea of a drum solo in the middle of the 'A' side piece had also gone down well with Tony. But did Laurie Tony's musical director agree to use *Spinney* as the 'B' side?

'Hmmmm... let's not get our hopes up. So far Tony hasn't said a word to me about it. We'll have to wait and see!' said Chris.

♫ ♫ ♫

Spectrum One motored on its way. It was a sleek craft that always caused people to take a second look, possibly due to its colourful paintwork with wavy lines along the flanks giving the impression of a rainbow. In the bows was a very decorative ♪ for *Spectrum*, and its engine was a powerful match for the rapidly increasing wind. The best!

As they rounded a bend in the River Ant they caught sight of a small sailing dinghy battling against the elements. On closer inspection with the binoculars they could see a ginger-headed lady and two children trying their best to row the dinghy against the wind but not making much headway.

On approaching them Tim steered *Spectrum One* alongside.

'Do you require some assistance?'

The lady wiped her brow with the arm of her jumper looking relieved. One of the children, a young boy, was baling out water while the young girl was holding tightly onto her lifejacket. 'We're trying to get to Ludham Bridge where we are staying. The plan was for my husband to take the car back to the cottage and the three of us to bring the boat in, but it's a disaster. The wind is too strong for me, I am totally exhausted.'

Chris threw a tow line to the lady. Missed. It fell in the water. The boy leaned over the side to retrieve it, dropping his baler in the process. After another two attempts the line was tied securely to the bows, if a bit *Heath Robinson*.

When they reached the staithe, a casually dressed man, cap skewwhiff, was pacing up and down scanning the river.

'Daddy, Daddy!'

The children leapt up, the boat rocked dangerously. To add to the impending crisis the tidal flow crashed the stern of the dinghy into the riverbank. Chris took a firm hold on the tow line, allowing the father to grab the side of the dinghy. Phew.... a capsizing had been narrowly avoided.

Spectrum One could be proud of its swift action and quick thinking.

The children were then lifted out of the dinghy by the father. The mother, who looked very pale, was helped ashore by a couple of onlookers. Smiles and cuddles ended what could have been a dramatic start to the family's holiday.

Profuse thanks from the couple, exchange of cheery waves between the two parties, Chris and Tim continued once more in the direction of Spindle.

❧ ❧ ❧

Their short journey back home was becoming rather eventful. They neared Ant Mouth to join the River Bure when a fleet of about nine sailing dinghies appeared. They were heading towards the marker buoy, just to the left of Chris and Tim.

Tim eased back the throttle as the first dinghy reached them.

'Oh Tim it's the International Stars! Must be the first race of the season out of Wroxham.'

Designed in 1911 by Francis Sweisguth, the Star was the oldest Olympic class and an incredible boat to sail.

The pair of them watched the crafts with their tall masts speed towards them, helped by a strong following wind. What a thrill! The once still water now had white waves breaking against the buoy.

The leading Star jibed around the buoy. There was a terrific gust of wind, followed by a horrendous crack, the mast split in two.

'Oh no!' Tim shouted. 'I love the Stars but I have to say, they are very prone to masts snapping. It would make me nervous.'

More was to follow. The boat, now briefly out of control, careered towards the bank and hit it head on, getting well and truly stuck.

'Off we go sis, we've another rescue to do,' said Tim, as he steered *Spectrum One* towards the casualty.

In the distance Chris could see a well-built man – perhaps in his thirties – staring at the damage. 'Tim! It's Geoff's *Starlite*.'

'Hi Chris, Tim,' Geoff mumbled looking ruefully at his mast. 'Am I glad to see you! When I think that we had the race in the palm of our hands.'

Once more the tow line was dispatched. Unlike previously Geoff caught it first time and tied it firmly *to Starlite's* bow.

Bracing himself on the deck Geoff managed to push the boat out of the mud using his feet, whilst his ten-year old son grabbed the tiller. The boat swung round.

Chris took up the slack. By now the fleet had passed them racing back towards Wroxham.

Spectrum One, with the Star in tow, made a more sedate journey along the River Bure to Horning where Geoff had a thatched riverside cottage on the outskirts of the village.

'How long will it take for a new mast to come through?' asked Tim as he released the tow rope.

Geoff securely moored *Starlite* to the small jetty alongside his home. 'Hopefully before the month is out. At least I have a few weeks leeway before the Sailing Club's Regatta. By the way I owe you one, I won't forget this huge favour in a hurry.'

'No problem!' Chris and Tim waved and headed in the direction of Malthouse Broad, in order to reach their Norfolk home. Speedily. They were very, very late.

They ran up the grassy path to the house. Their housekeeper Jessie, a grey-haired plump lady in her late fifties, was at the door waiting for them, smiling. (She was never cross with them.)

'Sorry Jessie, it went from bad to worse.' The twins were very apologetic. 'Has the food spoilt due to our lateness?'

'No you're just fine Chris,' said Jessie, disappearing down the hall, 'I know *Spectrum* the guardian angel of our community. Dinner will be in about half an hour or so,' she called back at them as she closed the kitchen door.

Jessie kept Spindle Hall running. Sam and Grace Rogers relied on her to keep a *motherly* eye on their children. Sam Roger's now highly successful Accountancy Practice and his 'other activity', which also involved Jessie's husband Frank, kept him pretty busy.

Chris and Tim's younger brothers, Ian aged 16, and Mark, 15 were in the lounge. Both brothers were in contrast to Chris and Tim. Chris and Tim were fair-haired whilst Ian and Mark dark-haired. Mark still had some growing to do but Ian was matching Tim in height. All brothers might end up 'tapping' Chris on the head!

'What kept you?' asked Ian. 'You could have tried to message us.'

So Chris and Tim described their eventful trip home.

'Oh that's a shame for Geoff,' said Mark, 'he is so very keen to win the Series Cup especially as his son is now his regular crew.'

'Well hopefully just a minor hiccup, but yes, a costly one' Tim replied. 'On another tack, did you get the opportunity to hear Tony's latest record?'

'Yes! And he did use **MY** drum solo idea for his 'A' side!'

'Trust you to say that!' said Ian to Mark. 'Tim do you know if Tony used **OUR** *Spinney* as his 'B' side?'

'That crossed our minds as well,' Tim replied in a neutral manner, noticing a bit of competition in his brother's comment.

The door opened, delicious smells of steak and kidney pie wafted in Jessie's wake. 'Come and eat it while it's hot.'

Appetites appeased as only Jessie knew how. The four of them were now slumped in armchairs in front of the TV.

Tim shook Chris awake for the start of the TV Chart Programme.

You could almost feel the tension in the air as the DJ worked through the week's hits and eventually reached the new releases section. Ian appeared to feel it most. He fidgeted, moved around the room, sat down again.

Suddenly the DJ announced the record: 'It's brand new, yes it's Tony Dale, yes it's an incredible double-A side record. Here is *Spinney*.'

The four were flabbergasted.

Listening to *Spinney* sung by Tony was surreal.

Afterwards, complete silence. Until Ian suddenly leapt up. 'Yes!!...' he cried, punching the air with his fist, turning to Mark in the process with a wicked grin on his face.

All retaliation on Mark's side was foiled as the phone rang. Chris rushed to answer it, hoping it would be Tony.

And it was. 'Tony, you have used Tim and Ian's *Spinney*!' cried Chris.

'Hey..hey young lady, everything in good time, first of all: how are you?'

'Oh! I am sorry Tony, but we are all having a nervous breakdown here. How on earth did you manage it?'

'Let's see... what was the question again? Okay. No more teasing!' He burst out laughing.

'Well Laurie, my Musical Director, just loved *Spinney*. In fact, he loved it so much so that he decided to make it an 'A' side too.'

CHAPTER TWO

A couple of days later, after the excitement of Spinney being featured as a new release for Tony Dale, Chris and her brothers returned to Kent.

It was Tuesday, the start of the Summer Term. This April day was promising. The sun shone brightly out of a cloudless sky and the stillness of the crisp, clear morning made Chris yearn for the wide open spaces and huge skies of Norfolk and the Broads.

She reflected on the past holiday. It had had its twists and turns.

In their roles as junior rangers the four of them spent several hours a day checking waterways for any mishaps. Holidaymakers had a habit of running out of fuel or grounding their hire craft on hidden mud-banks.

Breydon Water was a hot spot where the tide ran strongly. Boats sailing along this stretch of water were required to keep to a marked channel but they didn't always comply, hence the rescues *Spectrum* inevitably carried out. Some of them quite tricky. They were now a household name, and they loved their role: helping others.

It had all started when *Spectrum One* and *Spectrum Two* were cruising on Malthouse Broad.

The local River Authority was sinking old wooden boats along the Broad's edge in order to reduce erosion. Over time they would backfill with soil enabling waterweeds to take hold and help to stabilise the banks.

Suddenly the smell of burning filled the air, a big cloud of dense dark grey smoke rising. A hire cruiser at the entrance of the Broad had caught fire. Probably a build-up of petrol vapour in the bilges had ignited.

Chris and her brothers were the first to head towards the scene, putting themselves in extreme danger: the cruiser could explode at any moment.

Luckily its occupants were already in the water. Ian threw a lifebuoy: the man grabbed it. Ian and Mark pulled him towards *Spectrum Two*. The young woman however – probably his partner – was in shock, screaming and looking more and more uncomfortable with the swimming. It didn't take two seconds for Tim to decide on the next action. He removed his shoes and T-shirt and jumped in. Very tall and fit, he had attended many life-saving courses and knew how to handle panicking swimmers.

Naturally the local newspaper reported the incident with a dramatic photo of the cruiser sinking. (Chris always had her camera on board.)

What they did not want was too much exposure, but somehow the National Press had got hold of the story. *Spectrum* was now in the limelight, synonymous not only with the Norfolk Broads but also with four heroic teenagers giving their time to help people in distress. The Rogers' name had been kept out of the newspaper, no photo of the four was taken, which left *Spectrum* clouded in mystery.

A few days later, another memorable event happened at Ranworth Broad, the Norfolk Naturalist Trust opening a Broads Wildlife Centre (beautifully thatched).

The Queen had been invited to unveil a plaque to mark the twentieth anniversary of the generous gift from a local family, who not only had given Ranworth Broad to the NNT but also Cockshoot Broad.

Chris and her brothers had been standing on a bank quite a while, their boats moored nearby. The Queen, accompanied by Prince Philip, did not look as if she would reach their spot. She was always on a tight schedule.

They had just about given up hope when they saw an aide lean towards the Queen and whisper something to her. She changed direction and eventually approached their little group.

'You would not be *Spectrum* by any chance?'

'Yes Ma'am,' they answered in unison.

'We are following your adventures. Very well done!'

The smile she gave them was delightful.

Chris came back to earth. She glanced at her watch: 'Oops! Well my girl, better stop day dreaming and get a move on. If you don't hurry you are going to be late, that will never do for a Prefect.'

She liked studying and excelled in lots of subjects and was half-way through her A-levels. But it did not stop her already longing for the next half-term.

She finally turned the corner and looked upon the grey stone building of St. James College for Girls. Two Georgian houses had been knocked into one to create the school. Its square windows gave a light airy feeling to the majority of the classrooms. She skipped up the steps, nodded to a few third years and turned into the Prefects' Room, situated just by the entrance. It was an odd shaped room with a window overlooking the road.

There were a couple of squashy armchairs the rest of the seating consisting of cushioned wooden chairs tucked under a long table.

'You're nearly late,' said the Head Girl Belinda with a grin, a confident young lady well suited to her current position.

Chris looked across the room to her two friends; June and Ginger: June, thoughtful and conscientious, Ginger, vivacious and true to the nature of her nickname with beautiful, long red hair.

The pair of them, flicking through a pop magazine, with another sixth-form pupil named Rachel, peering over their shoulders.

A sudden cry from Rachel could only mean one thing!

Chris grinned, 'Ah hah! There's not a picture of Tony Dale by any chance?'

June turned picking up her books, chuckling. 'Need you ask.' Chris opened the door and the pair of them disappeared to their classes.

It was always difficult to concentrate on the first day of term. Once more Chris's thoughts turned to Tony, and how he had come into her life. At 22 Tony was at the top of his game. He had been in the entertainment business since the age of 17, the age that she and her twin were now, having just celebrated their birthdays.

Chris and Tony had met when her father became responsible for Tony's financial affairs. All it took was one look. They were smitten. Tony looked upon Chris as a steadying influence in what could be a madcap entertainment world.

Their relationship blossomed.

Laurie, Tony's Musical Director, had warned Tony that this might be harmful to his career. Fans would be jealous. And without fans.........

These fears on Laurie's part had not materialised, because both Tony and Chris had agreed to be discreet.

She reflected about Tony's phenomenal rise to fame, regularly making number 1 in the Pop Music Charts. And this time – she had to pinch herself – it might be with *Spinney*.

She sighed. She could not wait to take her A-levels and move on hopefully to university. She felt an adult and was ready to take on the world.

'Oh well, only another four weeks and it will be Whitsun half term.' Tony should be joining them in Norfolk, she missed him so much.

She was brought back from her daydreaming by a nudge from June, as Mrs. Ramson, with a frown in Chris's direction, started the lesson. It was English literature. Chris pulled out her copy of Twentieth Century Poets. Mrs. Ramson expanded on a couple of the poems by John Betjeman. Chris was rather fond of this poet as several of his works were about East Anglia.

By Friday the weather had deteriorated and it rained on and off. The infamous April showers had appeared. The heavy clouds followed by blue sky had now matched Chris's mood admirably. Up and down. Time was dragging. Another weekend passed. The following week coincided with the official release of Tony's new record. Predictably it didn't take long to climb the Charts.

Once more before the morning lessons began, the Prefects were gathered in their Room having a good natter. Ginger was flipping through *Disc*, one of the many pop publications now available.

'Hey everyone,' cried an excited Ginger, 'listen! I have just read there's speculation that *Spectrum* might have written Tony Dale's latest hit.'

'You're kidding aren't you Ginger,' said Rachel. She almost tore the magazine from her hand. 'No you're not. Well I never. Chris have you seen this?' showing the article to her.

A startled Chris took the magazine. Mixed emotions ran through her. Her heart was pounding. How to react without giving the game away? Her friends were very, very astute.

Chris skimmed the article, composed herself and said, in a detached manner: 'Well Rachel, you know what magazines are, it could be true or on the other hand reporters trying to make names for themselves....'

'Diplomatic as ever is our Chris,' said Belinda, as the bell rang, 'Duty calls everyone.'

Chris walked to her designated class, the third form. The level of noise gradually increased as she neared the room. She stood by the door it was deafening.

With poise, she entered the classroom, dropped the register with a loud bang on the teacher's desk and shouted 'Quiet please.'

Instant silence.

As a prefect she was popular with everyone. They particularly liked her sense of fairness.

Chris sat down and started the alphabetical roll call from the register.

A hand shot up; it came from the front-row.

'Yes? What is it Sandra?' she asked the curly-headed girl with a big Cheshire cat grin on her face.

'Please Chris can you settle an argument between Barbara and me?' pointing to the girl sitting next to her. 'I have heard that *Spectrum* wrote Tony Dale's latest record but Barbara says it's not true.'

Barbara shook her head, her ponytail swishing from side to side.

It was becoming an argument.

'Anyway, what makes you think that Chris should know?'

'Because....'

'Now stop it you two,' butted in Chris hurriedly, 'As luck would have it, I have just seen this week's, 'Disc' magazine. So yes I read that *Spectrum* did write *Spinney.*'

'I told you so,' said Sandra gleefully.

Chris was not going to let Sandra carry on.

'That's enough of that Sandra, come and wait by the Prefects Room at break.'

Mrs. Baxter, Maths teacher for the third form had arrived. Chris handed over the register and with a stern look in Sandra's direction left the room.

The bell went for break. Sandra picked up her bag and rushed down the stairs to the Prefects Room to meet with Chris. She saw June and Ginger ahead of her enter the room. Sandra skidded to a halt in front of the door, not sure whether to knock or not. Indecision was resolved as Belinda appeared.

'Sandra what are you doing here?' Before Sandra could answer Chris emerged from the opposite direction.

'It's okay Belinda, I just want a word with Sandra.' Chris and Sandra walked away towards a quiet part of the grounds.

Belinda carried on into the Prefects Room. June noticed her quizzical expression.

'What's bothering you Belinda?' she asked.

'I've just seen Sandra outside waiting for Chris. I wonder if it had anything to do with first thing this morning. Chris's duty was with the third form.'

'We all know how cheeky Sandra can be,' replied June. 'Chris does have a habit of attempting to curb her cousin's enthusiasm.'

Meanwhile Chris was scolding Sandra gently. 'Sorry Chris, I know what you are going to say, but I couldn't help it. When Barbara gets the bit between her teeth.... I thought I'd just stir her up a bit.'

'This is serious Sandra. Any hints that you know about Tony, *Spectrum* and me being involved together would be catastrophic for all of us. People can react in strange ways when a celebrity is involved. Autograph hunters for instance. The Press chasing a story....'

Sheepishly Sandra acknowledged Chris's comments, but that didn't last long, her cheekiness took hold once more.

'Er Chris, will you be seeing Tony, I would SO like him to autograph his latest record.'

'Sandra....'

'Please, dear cousin. I want to have one up on Barbara.'

'And if I do, how are you going to explain it?'

'I'll think of a way Chris, please.'

'Oh, all right. I am too soft with you I am! Leave it with me at lunch-time and I'll see what I can do. But remember, mum's the word in future.'

'Ooooooo thanks Chris, you are the best!' and off she scampered.

With that Chris made her way back to the Prefects' Room where Rachel looked as if she hadn't moved an inch since this morning, still immersed in the pop magazine.

Chris leaned over her shoulder looking straight into the laughing face of Tony. 'You're not still eyeing him up Rachel, are you?'

'Come on Chris, you must admit he is rather dishy, such lovely eyes. So not a fan any longer? I thought you adored him too.'

'Of course, I am still a fan Rachel! You know I am.'

༝ ༝ ༝

It was the dinner break. Some pupils were staying put with their packed lunches but the majority were going home. The canteen only served drinks, crisps and slices of pre-wrapped cake. Chris placed Sandra's record in her bag, and left with Ginger to catch the bus.

'Chris…Ginger… wait for me!'

Their friend Mary was running to catch up with them. They waved at her, always pleased to meet up with the bubbly, kind girl. What an athlete she was, the best centre-forward in the hockey team.

Chris's facial expression had now changed from delight to bewilderment. She had just seen a very familiar car stopping not far from them.

'Hi Mary,' called Ginger, 'Coming for the bus?'

Mary nodded and turning towards Chris: 'What's up with you? You look as if you've lost a penny and found a fiver.'

Ginger was now gazing in the same direction as Chris. 'Wow, that's a beast of a car!' She stared quizzically at Chris. 'You don't mean to say that you're having a lift in this bright red Aston Martin?'

Chris was feeling so embarrassed.

'Ginger, Mary, sorry girls, it looks as if dad has sent one of his wealthy clients to take me home. Must dash! See you later.'

On seeing Chris approach, Tony, the perfect gentleman as ever, leaned over and pushed open the passenger door. Chris looked into those deep brown eyes she knew and loved so much. Her heart missed a beat. She did not kiss him for fear to be seen by Ginger and Mary.

'Where did you spring from? Are you around for long? By the way have you seen the latest article about you in 'Disc' Magazine? The record is doing well?'

'Whoa.... Not so fast young lady.'

He drove round the corner into a narrow street and stopped the car. 'Before I give my replies to Detective Chris how about a little hug? For a second out there when I called you I thought you were going to ignore me, it wasn't my little Chris any longer.'

They exchanged a passionate kiss. He slipped into gear and turned left into a tree-lined avenue.

'Well, for a start I wasn't expecting you. Secondly, remember what Laurie said. You have to be careful. What about if my friend Ginger had put two and two together? Only this morning, in the Prefects' Room, she was all over your photos published in 'Disc' Magazine.'

'Oh..., that den of iniquity,' he replied in a flippant tone.

She ignored the remark.

Tony paused, negotiated a busy roundabout, and then continued along the road.

'All questions will be answered soon Miss Marple, wait and see!'

Infuriatingly, he was refusing to elaborate.

The car went up a steep lane into a horse-shoe shaped cul-de-sac with a Norman Church at its apex.

One side of the road was a continuous row of terrace houses looping round up to the entrance of the churchyard, which boasted an ornately carved lichgate. The short front-gardens were now full of spring flowers.

The other side of the road had a small sweetie shop, a couple of detached bungalows with large gardens and the old vicarage adjoining the Church.

The Rogers lived in the detached bungalow nearest the Vicarage.

Tim had obviously heard them arrive – who wouldn't notice the unmistakable sound of an Aston Martin? – and was standing at the door. From her twin's over-excited attitude, he was obviously burning to say something.

What was going on?

Mrs. Rogers greeted Tony as if he was one of her brood, and hurried the couple along to the dining-room. Grace Rogers, a medium-sized lady, dark-haired with a few speckles of grey, exuding warmth and kindness.

Ian and Mark were already there, whispering as if trying not to spill the beans over something or other.

Mark, being the youngest, could no longer keep quiet, 'has Tony told you?'

Chris stared once more into Tony's gorgeous brown eyes, this time not so lovingly.

'Am I going to be the last to know? What exactly?' she exclaimed, exasperated.

Tony just smiled. He took a sip of water. 'Well…. the annual Command Performance at the London Paladin…. in a couple of weeks…'

She jumped up with a shriek. 'You mean?..... the one in front of the Royal family? You're in it? That's fantastic! You deserve it!'

She was hugging him lovingly now. 'So why the big secret? I am so pleased for you!'

'Oh come on Tony … put the poor girl out of her misery,' said her mum, placing the cottage pie and vegetables on the oak table.

Chris's face lit up: 'You are inviting us to see it?'

Tony took a large helping. 'Sorry Kid. No can do.'

Chris's face fell.

'It will be on the TV you know.'

He paused once more, relishing the moment, took another sip of water, and then …..

'Actually, Chris, Sir John Phillips, who is in charge of the Royal Command Performance, is proposing to include…. *Spectrum*!'

'Well sis, what do you think?' asked Tim.

'*Spectrum*? Tony, Tim, you are having me on.'

Tony explained about his London meeting with Sir John when they were interrupted by a rather flustered PA. 'The group closing the first half had cried off due to sickness. As it happens I had the recording of Tim and Ian's *Freewheelin*, played by *Spectrum* when I was last with you all in Norfolk. Sir John was impressed. In fact, he liked it very much, especially as it is an instrumental piece.'

Although now on cloud nine, Chris couldn't help but voice her concerns.

'Tony, seriously, are we good enough? It's all very well playing for fun. But that sort of audience will be expecting people like you who are household names, not a group of unknowns like us. It's all a bit scary.'

'That is why, if you four agree – and Mr. and Mrs. Rogers of course – you will rehearse at the London Paladin this coming Saturday.'

Tim, Ian and Mark enthusiastically shouted: 'We are in!'

'Okay then, *Spectrum* at the Command Performance it is,' sighed Chris. She loved the idea but was this beyond their capability?

'Be reassured, Sir John will be present and has every confidence that you will do well. I filled him in about the experience you four acquired playing at the Rushcutters Sports and Social Club last summer.'

Tony added: 'Oh Chris, I forgot to tell you. Do you remember the couple during your scary rescue on the Broads? You know the one with the burnt-out cabin cruiser?'

Chris nodded.

'You are not going to believe it. When I talked about *Spectrum* he said that he knew the name and would be grateful to them for the rest of his life. The people you saved were Sir John's daughter and her husband. How about that!'

Chris looked in amazement but then saw the clock. Reality kicked in.

'We'd better hurry Tony. Bye everybody, see you all later.'

They both ran to the car, Tony donned a pair of dark glasses and pulled on a hat with the brim turned down.

'Okay handsome who are you trying to emulate, James Bond!'

Chris was cutting it fine. Most of her classmates were already at school. In the Prefects' Room Ginger was holding court. 'We were crossing the road when Chris's name was called, and in a super sports car was the most gorgeous hunk of male you had ever seen! Well the little we could see in the distance.'

'Well it seems our Chris was a bit confused. She mumbled that it was one of her dad's clients giving her a lift home. I am sure it was bit more than a client, so I pretended to be distracted.'

A car was arriving outside warranting attention.

June, who was nearest the window, cried, 'It's them! I see what you mean Ginger, he is gorgeous. LOOK at that car. I've always wanted to travel in one of those.'

'He leaves my Tom standing,' added Belinda. 'I see what you mean about the car June,' as she too cast her eyes over the sleek lines of the red Aston Martin. 'Must cost a bomb.'

Rachel joined them. 'He looks vaguely familiar. I don't know where or when but it feels as if I've seen him before.'

Chris hopped out of the car. Tony called her back, 'You nearly forgot this for my number two fan.' He handed Sandra's autographed record to her, adding: 'In view of what you said earlier Chris, Sandra had better have a good tale to tell her friend.'

Chris laughed, 'You know Sandra I don't think she'll have much trouble.'

Tony grinned showing a set of perfectly even white teeth. Once more her heart missed a beat. He looked intensely into Chris's sparkling blue grey eyes, 'How about a goodbye kiss from my number one fan?'

'See you at dinner!' he called after her as the Aston Martin disappeared down the road.

Chris gazed soulfully at the car as it roared out of sight. Turning round she saw her friends' reflection watching her from the window, and blushed. She entered the building to find Sandra waiting for her.

'Chris, have you...., hey you're blushing! Was that Tony's new car? Did you....?'

'Shh! Steady on Sandra!' she looked around her to make sure no one was within ear shot.

'Of course it was Tony!'

Sandra looked up expectantly.

'And yes, I did get it autographed. I do hope you have a suitable explanation for Barbara, though....'

Sandra took the record and looking at the sleeve saw in Tony's distinct hand-writing...... *To Sandra, love Tony Dale*.......

'Ooooo thanks Chris,' and scampered off with her booty.

Chris smiled to herself, walked into the Prefects' Room and found everyone staring at her. She turned red as a beetroot. 'What's happening?'

Belinda was first to speak, 'Come on Chris. Who was that? Your dad's client? He was wow! I think a bit more than that if truth be known!'

'Not to mention the car,' piped up Ginger.

Luckily the end of lunch break bell rang. Phew! Chris had got away with it, again!

❄ ❄ ❄

The next morning at breakfast, Chris was rudely interrupted by Tim waving the Chronicle under her nose. And there it was in bold capitals, making the headlines was:-

TONY DALE TO TOP
THE COMMAND PERFORMANCE

She whipped it out of her twin's hand. 'Steady on Chris, Tony hasn't seen it yet.'

She scanned the article…. cont. page 3. Chris quickly turned to the relevant page…. the list of acts was confirmed.

'Tim, it mentions *Spectrum*,'

He nodded, 'I know, there's no backing out now.'

Still yawning Tony joined them. Tony and early mornings didn't go together. 'What's so interesting you two?'

'Oh nothing much. You've only made the headlines once more,' answered Tim in a casual manner. Tony lent over Chris's shoulder, gave her a peck on the cheek, 'hey you've a mention as well!'

Mrs. Rogers opened the kitchen door. 'Are you watching the clock Tim? Mark and Ian are waiting for you outside.'

Tim looked up, 'Ouch, I'm going to be late.' The door slammed. Tim grabbed his bike and with much wheel spin on the shingle drive the brothers disappeared down the road.

This left Chris with Tony.

'Are you going to be my chauffeur…. Mr. Dale?'

'Okay, - if you're ready in a couple of minutes, I'll do the school run.'

'Thanks: school run indeed!'

At Chris's school Tony parked a little way up the road from the entrance.

Softly he took hold of her hands. 'You'll be all right in the Show. I know it's been worrying you but you will be able to practise on Saturday with the boys, and I'll be there.'

'It's just that I don't want to let you down.'

'You won't. You're my star.' He squeezed her hand, kissed her on the tip of her nose, 'Go on, off to that seat of learning.'

She got out of the car, reluctantly, and Tony drove off.

'Chris!' called a very familiar voice, and then the usual scamper of feet.

It was Sandra, of course.

She was waving a newspaper. 'Chris, in the papers: my god: about the Command Performance: about you, Tim, Ian and Mark WITH Tony?'

'Sandra, lower your voice.'

'Whoops, so sorry Chris, I meant *Spectrum*.'

'Well, yes it is amazing, but if the truth be known, I am petrified!'

Sandra burst out: 'You will do us proud, I know you will!'

They went their separate ways, Chris heading for the Prefects Room, apprehensive. She guessed what the topic of conversation would be. She would have to be cautious.

Sure enough there was Rachel pouring over the Daily Telegraph with June and Ginger.

'Hi Chris, come and see…., have you heard?'

Chris didn't let her finish, 'Yes I have. Isn't it something?'

Ginger chipped in: 'What I would give to have a ticket. I had no idea that *Spectrum* was so involved in music, fantastic!'

'Yes you did,' retorted June. 'Remember what we read together in that recent article. Rachel you're very quiet not enough photos of Tony Dale?'

'Yes plenty. Funny thing is I think that I've bumped into him recently. For the moment I just can't place where and when. I am trying hard to recall....'

Ginger became involved in the conversation. 'It's funny you should say that Rachel, I get the same feeling.'

It seemed ages before anyone said anything else.

Belinda entered the room and shooed them off to their various duties.

Once more saved by the bell! Chris breathed a huge sigh of relief.

CHAPTER THREE

The following Saturday morning found Chris and her brothers outside the theatre. They looked up at the façade of the internationally known London Paladin in the West End and couldn't believe that in a very short while they would be treading on the stage of a theatre where so many stars had performed in the past.

Their father, following Tony's instructions, backed the van containing their instruments down the narrow side street until he reached the stage door. A small gust of wind whipped up a crumpled piece of paper. Chris immediately picked it up and placed it in the nearby bin her grandmother's voice echoing in her ears about tidiness, hygiene and respect of the environment.

That sparked other fond memories of Grandma Blanche. What significant changes her generation had seen over a half-century.

As a young girl Blanche would ride with her family in a two-wheeled trap pulled by Dobbin, the local farmer's horse. Dressed in her best clothes, down the Welsh country lanes they would trot to the Sunday chapel service.

By the time Blanche had reached her teens, amazing feats of engineering had arrived. Chris knew all these important dates by heart. Grandma had taught her well.

1903: American pioneers Orville and Wilbur Wright manage four flights in an aircraft, the first lasting all but 12 seconds.

Still 1903: The first electric trams run in Newport.

1908: Rise of the automobile with the Model T Ford, also nicknamed Tin Lizzie.

1957: *Sputnik* I is launched into space.

She would recite them to her and afterwards Grandma never failed to slip a bar of chocolate in her hand. Chris had been so close to her grandmother. She did miss her.

A man with bushy eyebrows – probably in his sixties – was at the stage door staring at them impatiently. Clipboard in hand, he scanned down the list of names. 'OK *Spectrum*, follow me…' he mumbled in a gruff voice.

They had a job keeping up with him. Especially as Chris could not help gazing at her surroundings. Gold leaf Rococo decorations, marble and chandeliers everywhere! He slowed down, swung open a door and announced. 'Please wait in *The Green Room*!'

She couldn't believe the shabbiness of the room they were now in. Very, very dull.

While her brothers and father were sorting things out, Chris, curiosity getting the better of her, decided to explore further.

She needed to walk, not sit. She was desperately trying to calm herself down. Pushing her way through a green baize studded door she followed a long corridor and arrived in the foyer. The lavishness of the décor jumped out at her. She looked around in sheer wonderment. Mirrors, Greek style columns, red plush velvet seats, such opulence.

Tony's arm snaked around her shoulders. 'Found you! Where is everybody?'

'In the awful *Green Room*' Chris replied with an expression of disgust. 'Such a contrast with the rest!'

'Well it all comes from a tradition in the 16th century,' he explained. 'The Blackfriars Theatre was the first to provide a room where actors waited to go on stage and they decided to paint it in…. want to guess the colour? Yep ….. green. So that when the actors were green with fear, they would blend with the walls and no-one would notice!'

Tony saw that Chris had got a little pale. 'Cold feet?'

'Look Tony, I am so afraid that it will go wrong. We have so little experience. This is such a prestigious occasion …. in front of the Royal family…. What if *Spectrum* doesn't live up to expectation? What if…?'

Tony did not let her finish. He tipped back her head, gave her a tender kiss, 'You'll be fine,' he said encouragingly.

Hand in hand they headed back to the others, but on the way to the 'awful Green Room' Tony made a point to detour past the brightly lit Wall of Fame which left Chris in awe, Bing Crosby, Bob Hope, Nat King Cole ………

She curled up in his arms. 'And one day they will add your name Tony,' she whispered with a smile.

When they arrived in the *Green Room* a tall thin grey-haired man, dressed in a dark suit, was standing by the door, chatting with Chris's brothers. The chap with bushy eyebrows was also there, very attentive, and looking almost pleasant.

The distinguished man extended a warm hand: 'Good morning Tony.'

'And you must be Spectrum. I'm delighted to meet you all again if only to repeat my thanks on behalf of my family following our one and only sojourn onto the Norfolk Broads.'

'I see that you have met some of the *Spectrum* group Sir John. May I introduce you to Chris, Tim, Ian and Mark....'

'Please to meet you sir,' said Tim, taking the lead.

Sir John was imposing and gave the impression that he didn't accept fools lightly. His eyes though had a mischievous twinkle.

'We cannot thank you enough for this fantastic opportunity to be heard. We WILL deliver our utmost.'

Sir John was not the sort of person who spoke idle words. 'It is I who should thank you, at such short notice. Tony has vouched for you, and I trust his judgement implicitly.' He paused. 'Anyway *Spectrum* I know what you are capable of. Thank God you were around when my daughter and son-in-law nearly drowned in the Norfolk Broads. I am truly grateful for what you did.'

Sir John's pager went off. 'If you will excuse me it looks as if I'm wanted. Tony can you take them around to the front please? I'll join you in the stalls when I've dealt with this little contretemps.'

With the help of half a dozen stagehands to carry Mark's drums and Tim's Yamaha, Tony led them round the back of the stalls to the wings.

Chris, guitar to hand, was speechless. Purely magical.

The Royal Box with its velvet-clad front on which the Royal Coat of Arms was embroidered in gold dominated the scene.

A slight tinkering on a piano caught her attention. It was quite funny; Chris and Tony could just see the tip of a man's head in the orchestra pit. Bald. Standing next to him was a lady and amazingly she gave them a wave.

'Mum!' Chris shouted, 'having fun?'

Grace Rogers was in her element. Her dreams of travelling around Europe giving piano concerts had faded, but she had passed on her musical skills to her beloved four children. If Chris could read music and play an instrument, it was thanks to her extraordinarily patient mother.

As always several cleaners were checking the seats making sure everything was spick and span. The safety curtain was raised and Chris was taking in her glimpse of the stage. It was massive.

'How can we fill that?' she gasped.

Tony put a hand on her shoulder.

'Don't worry. See. You'll have curtains behind you. That's the beauty of it. The stage is divided into segments to suit all sizes of acts. An artist on his own will have just a few metres from the front, yours half the space, a musical the totality of the stage.

In fact, the curtains do a grand job; they project the compère's voice forwards, but at the same time they muffle the noises of the scenery being shifted behind them.'

The amplifiers were rolled on the stage, Ian and Tim were now frantically tuning the Yamaha Electone organ. It was the most difficult moment for them as it could prove temperamental when moved any distance. The sound echoing around was brilliant.

Sir John had now reappeared and sat alongside Tony in the stalls. The stagehands, cleaners and pianist were also invited to be part of the audience.

Tim nodded to Chris. She took a deep breath and started the first few notes on her Fender Stratocaster.

The four of them played as they had never played before.

What made *Freewheelin* so special was the mixture of fast and slow, enhanced by Chris's tremolo arm on the guitar. A signature sound.

It went down a storm. The applause seemed to echo and re-echo around the auditorium. There seemed to be hundreds of people out there; instead no more than a dozen souls.

All delighted by what they had heard.

Sir John walked on to the stage still clapping.

'Bravo *Spectrum*! Just keep your composure on the night and you will have a standing ovation for sure!'

He turned to Tony, who was beaming.

'How about we all go for afternoon tea at the Ritz? My treat!'

By then a short man wearing a mustard coloured blazer and brown turtleneck knit had appeared on the stage. They had not noticed him before. He must have been listening backstage.

'Ah Laurie. Perfect timing! If you will excuse me I must dash,' Sir John exclaimed.

Tony stepped in. '*Spectrum* may I introduce you to Laurie Johnson, my fantastic Musical Director.'

The two men laughed giving each other a friendly hug. There was much complicity between them.

'Well well well …. Tony did say that you were good.' He paused. 'How would you like to record *Freewheelin* tomorrow morning?'

The four looked at each other in disbelief.

'Tomorrow?' exclaimed Tim.

‘Why not? In the music world you have to be quick. Time is of the essence. And time is money. Make hay while the sun shines. What better exposure than this Charity Performance with the Queen present?’

‘But is there something you would like us to change Mr. Johnson?’ asked Ian.

‘Call me Laurie please. No, play it just as you did ten minutes ago. You heard the applause, didn’t you? That’s enough for me. So, how about it? If you agree we would release it the day after the performance.’

Tony intervened. ‘Well *Spectrum*? What a proposal! Yes.... I presume?’

‘Yes please!’ They were so shell shocked that they could not say more. Their faces told the story: huge smiles.

Chris and her brothers had now changed into smarter clothes. Their mother, a great organiser as usual, had packed everything they might need for their London stay.

Tony had guided their steps into a very unfamiliar world. ‘Don’t forget, smart casual for afternoon tea at the Ritz, a cocktail dress for ladies and jacket and tie for us chaps!’

When they entered the hotel it felt like a fairy tale. They were swiftly ushered into the Palm Court where the Maître d’ welcomed them.

‘Mr. Dale, how nice to see you again. Sir John is waiting for you and your party.’

It was just spectacular. Glittering chandeliers, mirrors, and at the back of the room a pianist and a harpist were playing some soft melodies. On the table sandwiches, scones, clotted cream, strawberry preserve and mouth-watering pastries were awaiting them.

Sir John made them feel at ease and spoke of his love of nature, and of the Norfolk Broads, naturally.

The 'Tea Sommelier' arrived near Ian: 'Which tea would you like Sir? We have eighteen different types of loose-leaf tea to choose from.'

Ian was lost for words. 'Er …. the same as everybody else.'

Sam and Grace Rogers chuckled.

It was now time to go back to Tony's London home in Kensington, where the Rogers would spend the night.

They thanked Sir John profusely and the concierge ordered two taxis.

Inevitably, wherever Tony went, fans appeared. Chris had never realised how stressful it could be.

Fans screaming: 'Tony, Tony!' journalists pushing, girls wanting to touch him, and flash photography galore.

The following day she was first up sipping coffee in Tony's spacious kitchen. The morning sunlight streaming in through the window making her fair hair glow. The day passed so quickly.

On arrival at Eagle Studios they recorded *Freewheelin*. Laurie was ecstatic: the first attempt was perfect.

But the cherry on the cake was yet to come.

Tony, whom they thought had just come along to support them, had a big surprise in store.

'Hey *Spectrum* how about also recording my new instrumental piece?'

The four looked at each other.

'*Travellin*?' whispered Chris.

'That's right' said Laurie chuckling, 'it will go so well with *Freewheelin*!'

⁓ ⁓ ⁓

On Monday it was back to reality for Chris, the bubble had burst, school again! However, she felt pleased to get away from the hustle and bustle of the City, relieved to have done well with her brothers. They had dreaded letting Tony down, but their teamwork – and Tony's unfailing support – had thankfully been well received by Sir John. And as for Laurie's offer to put *Spectrum* in the Music industry, what an opportunity!

When she entered the Prefects Room, Rachel jumped out of her seat waving the Morning newspaper. 'UNBELIEVABLE! Have you seen it?'

'Morning. Seen what Rachel?'

June and Ginger came in: 'The photo of course! Tony Dale, who else? But wait for it, Tony with his mysterious friends. The article says it could be *Spectrum*?'

Chris almost tore the paper from Rachel's hands.

'What do you mean?' She looked at the image. Outside the Ritz. Oh dear. Chris was trying desperately not to give the game away.

'Hum, you have to admit girls, not the best of photos.'

Rachel, June and Ginger peered over her shoulder:

'I love Tony's big brown eyes, they send quivers down my spine …' giggled Rachel.

'I find the other two more interesting,' June added.

'Can't quite see the features of the blonde girl, too much flash, but the young man standing by Tony Dale, maybe he is one of *Spectrum*? Oh wow! I could go a bundle on him!' June carried on: 'I swear to you girls can't put my finger on it but the more I look at the photo, the more his face looks familiar.'

'Dream on! He does look nice. I'll give you that' retorted Rachel, 'but you'd have to go a long way to find someone like my Tony Dale.'

Chris was praying that June was not going to put two and two together. Indeed, June had met her twin brother last summer.

⸙ ⸙ ⸙

The Saturday had arrived so quickly and everyone in the Rogers family was on tenterhooks.

Tim and Chris had been up since the crack of dawn and were packing up their father's van with the instruments when Sandra arrived on her bike.

'Sandra, my goodness have you fallen out of bed?' asked Chris

'I've come to wish you all good luck; or I should say break a leg... not that I wish it on any of you!' she joked. 'And also to offer my services as an assistant, cups of tea, make-up ..... I am available right now. I could squeeze in the car, and I promise to be very quiet.'

'Well,' said Tim, 'that would be a first.'

Mark and Ian had appeared on the scene.

'Hello Miss Chatterbox!' Ian exclaimed.

'Don't be mean Ian.' Mark always behaved as a big brother to Sandra, who was an only child.

'Look Sandra,' he said, 'you know it isn't possible today. We have to find our feet and to be honest with you we have almost too much on our plate. There will be a next time, promise, and one day you'll be able to tell your friends that your favourite cousin is a star! Ah hah, I'll give you my autograph if you will have it!'

Sandra sighed, and smiled back at Mark. She knew that even if he became a celebrity he would remain her best friend.

'Come on you lot,' called Chris, 'the parents are panting to get away.'

At the Theatre they all forgot their nerves for a while having familiarised themselves with the place the week before. What a bonus it had been!

They were caught up in the excitement of taking part in a show, a Royal Show at that, in front of live television cameras.

At one time they lost Tim, but unearthed him in the lighting gallery discussing the various merits of spotlighting, quite intelligently on Tim's side much to his twin's amazement.

They bumped into Sir John, charming as usual, and looking totally relaxed. He imparted some last minute advice.

'*Spectrum*, I have every confidence in your ability to please an audience. Remember: forget about the auditorium ...... just imagine you are playing in the middle of the Norfolk Broads!'

Just then Laurie Johnson came running up to them. 'There you are, I've been looking all over for you. The photo call has been brought forward, we've got to get a move on.'

The four of them were startled. Everything was happening so quickly their heads were spinning. Now they had to change into their *Spectrum* clothes, and more importantly wear their identical big sunglasses. Never to be removed in the presence of journalists.

'For a pop group mystery goes a long way.' Laurie had emphasised.

Their outfits had been cleverly designed by Grace Rogers, symbolizing the seven colours of the spectrum.

They all wore indigo blue trousers and it was decided that the satin tops would be as follows: Tim red, Chris blue, Ian yellow, and Mark green. The idea of a boater had come from Tony, with an orange ribbon for Ian and Mark, and violet for the twins.

Tim asked anxiously: 'For the run-down of our background, what are we allowed to say Laurie?'

'At this stage it is still agreed that your names are to be kept out of the feature. You only answer as *Spectrum*. The rest...leave it to me, I will do most of the answers. Norfolk, boating, teenagers that's it. No mention of school or Kent.

If they want to know your sign of the zodiac, give it. It's good publicity. Fans love writing to wish Happy Birthday to their star. Lastly for the photo, as I have said before, you must keep your sunglasses on, the photographer might hate it because of the reflections, but tough.'

☙ ☙ ☙

Grace and Sam Rogers had seen to it that their brood was fed early enough, Ian and Mark seemed to always be hungry. Teenagers ..... The home-made pork pies had gone down well, and Grace insisted they had some fruit, after all Kent was not nicknamed the Garden of England for nothing.

Spectrum had been told that they were the sixth act and that their backdrop – much to their delight – would be a caricature of the four of them in their boats on the Broads.

The show started at 8.00 p.m., *Spectrum* standing nervously in the wings, watching the Acts before them. Sir John and Laurie had agreed that it was better to let them do this, rather than sitting in the Green Room for an hour.

The four could not believe they were rubbing shoulders with such famed artists.

Danny la Rue's impersonations of Margot Fonteyn and Sandie Shaw were an eye opener, truly different! He had the public in stitches.

As for singers, Harry Secombe, Cilla Black and the French born Mireille Mathieu left them in awe.

The curtain swung down on the fifth Act. Ventriloquist Shari Lewis with her dummy 'Lamb Chop' had done well.

Tony, who had just emerged from his dressing-room, gave them a comforting smile and a thumbs up. Chris thought he looked rather distinguished in his dark suit and bow tie.

It was their turn to shine.

Ian and Mark rubbed their sweaty hands on a towel Chris handed to them. 'Don't fret bros, you are fine musicians.'

They would never forget the moment when they heard Des O'Connor – the host…. announce: '*…..and now ladies and gentlemen, the first appearance on stage by that mysterious foursome better known to us for their exploits on the Norfolk Broads, I give you Spectrum……*'

The curtain fell back, Tim counted them in and they were away.

The concentration was so great Chris didn't have time to think about nerves. They followed Sir John's advice.

Spectrum sailed through the act, imagining they were in their beautiful Norfolk.

When the last note dropped, the four gathered at the front of the stage, apprehensively, and bowed. Thunderous applause ensued.

They bowed again, and again….

It was now the interval.

Naturally, Grace, Sam and Tony were the first to congratulate them.

Tony discreetly squeezed Chris's hand. 'I am so proud of you…and of your brothers of course!'

Sir John made a quick appearance. 'What a charismatic performance that was! You will go a long way, mark my words!'

'Such a unique sound!' added Laurie.

The four were on top of the world.

A success truly deserved.

❧ ❧ ❧

The following day, there was nothing but praise for the show in the Press.

Sir John Phillips's Royal Command Performance last night was one of the best yet and I would be very surprised if their Majesties didn't enjoy it. All the acts deserve congratulations,

45

especially top of the bill Tony Dale who with his suave and harmonious voice, brought the house down. And good news for his fans: his manager has announced a summer season in Great Yarmouth. But we must not forget to mention the find of the year: SPECTRUM the 'mystery' foursome normally involved with rescuing people in distress in the Norfolk Broads. Not only good sailors, but fine musicians too.

When I approached Sir John to learn more about them I was met with complete silence. It seems that no one will reveal who they really are…. However…… I did find out that Freewheelin is being released as a single. Look out Tony, I think you now have rivals for that Number One spot!

❦ ❦ ❦

Come Monday morning, Chris was making her way to school. Her heart was light. She looked at the cloudless skies and breathed in the cool crisp air. A beautiful spring day, the morning sun pleasantly warm.

She chuckled to herself as she remembered the words in the paper about their group topping the charts.

How quickly life was changing……

As for being Tony's rivals, she had never thought about it. Nor had her brothers.

His generosity in sharing his expertise, the recording of his '*Travellin* piece, Tony had said: 'Good team work!'

They admired him and were grateful for the new experience, but there was no question of being in competition with him.

'Chris, Chris, wait for me' called June, catching up with her. 'You looked pleased with yourself – isn't it a gorgeous day?'

They ambled along the road in companionable silence.

June sensed that Chris had something on her mind, but obviously she was not ready to share it. And she respected that, being her best friend.

As they neared the school Chris was the first to speak, 'I say June any bets on what Rachel will be talking about?'

'By the way what did you think of *Spectrum's* act?'

June laughed,

'That's one wager I am not taking! As for *Spectrum* I am going to shock you, don't tell Rachel. But I loved them more than Tony Dale's performance especially the organist tall, a sailor AND a musician. I wouldn't mind meeting him, any time, any place!'

Chris was trying very hard to keep a straight face. 'Fancy that....'

The Prefects Room was full of noise. As prophesied Rachel was holding court.

'So Rachel where do your loyalties stand now?'

'Tony Dale was so lovely' she purred 'Oh, okay, I must admit that *Spectrum* was not bad.'

Ginger stood up abruptly.

I'd have you know Rachel that the papers say *Spectrum's Freewheelin* is going straight up to the number one spot,' she blushed: 'and I think the guitarist in yellow is great!'

47

'Wow!' thought Chris, 'First June keen on Tim, now Ginger on Ian. I wonder if I should tell them.'

A joyful Belinda breezed in.

'I've just had a meeting with the Head. You'll never guess where we are going for the senior girls treat this half-term. A place which should please *Spectrum* and Tony Dale fans alike.'

Chris kept quiet. What now?

'Did someone mention Tony Dale? Please Belinda, don't keep us in suspense,' begged a rather excited Rachel.

'The Norfolk Broads for five days! So now we have a chance of meeting or at least catching a glimpse of *Spectrum* and, or, Tony Dale. How about that?'

The girls were jumping up and down with joy.

'Oh no!'exclaimed Chris, 'I have just remembered…. drat, I can't go. Would you believe it I'm going to my cousin's wedding.'

'What a crying shame,' said Belinda, 'can't you join us for a few days?'

'Don't think it's possible. The wedding is in Cornwall.' Chris hated lying to her friends.

Rachel was going to have the last word.

'Ah well all the better for us. Sorry Chris. Me with Tony, June and Ginger with *Spectrum*….' The bell went. Chris noticed that June's and Ginger's faces were quite red.

꒰ ꒰ ꒰

It was the day before the start of the Spring Bank Holiday week and those going on the trip were full of excitement and anticipation. The holiday mood was rubbing off on them all.

'Just think, June,' said Rachel, 'This time Sunday we'll be on our way to Norfolk. I've packed my sandals, summer hat and suntan cream. I do hope the weather holds.'

'What a pity you're not coming Chris,' June said.

'I agree with you, I am disappointed. Such bad luck about the dates. But family must come first. Anyway, have a super time all of you and don't forget to ask for autographs if you see *Spectrum*, OR Tony Dale!'

CHAPTER FOUR

Chris arrived home. The garage doors were open. She could just make out the top of her father's head kneeling behind a scooter. Her dad stood up, hands on hips, with a big grin on his face. 'All ready for you and the boys. Your mum has a snack waiting for you.'

'Thanks dad, you are the best, well, I mean both of you of course!' Once more she took in the sight of four spanking new Lambrettas individually painted in *Spectrum* colours.

Chris and her brothers were still in shock. On the return journey to Kent after the Command Performance Sam and Grace Rogers had acted bizarrely. It was late. The four were absolutely exhausted, but nevertheless they all helped unload the van. Sam was about to lock the front door when Ian shouted: 'Dad you forgot to put the van in the garage.'

'Did I?' winking at Grace and chuckling. 'Hum, come on outside everybody, best check to see if your old man is losing his mind.' And there was the van on the drive.

Sam handed a key to Ian. 'Why don't you do the honours and open the garage door?'

Ian couldn't understand why their father was so pleased with himself. He found the light switch, and ....yelled. Tim, Chris and Mark rushed in. And there they were. Four scooters! An amazing surprise from their parents who were so proud of their children.

Chris, Tim and Ian had already passed their scooter test. Mark was still a little too young to take it, and much to his annoyance, Ian – who else? – had got into a habit of waving his recently acquired licence under Mark's nose, brothers.

From then on, Sam would load the scooters into the van and take his brood to the disused aerodrome at Marden. This was a way for Mark to gain experience ready for his test later in the year. Sam also used these occasions to satisfy himself that his older children were proficient enough to drive on the open roads. The young Rogers had had so much fun weaving between traffic cones laid out on the old runway.

For their first '*Spectrum* scooter trip' to the Broads it had been decided that Mark would ride with Tim. Their dad wouldn't let them leave without more cautionary advice about driving safely.

Grace was apprehensive but did not let on. Still she was somewhat reassured that their journey to Norfolk was broken by an overnight stay in Essex.

Aunt Jean, Grace's sister and the twins' Godmother was waiting for them. She loved meeting with her niece and nephews and spoilt them rotten, being unmarried and without children.

'Make sure you ring us when you arrive at Jean's,' she anxiously called after them as they disappeared down the driveway.

Aunt Jean's house was situated in Brightlingsea, close to the mouth of the river Colne: another ideal location for *Spectrum* to sail in and out of the various creeks.

Everything was so different there. It was not uncommon to see a pod of porpoises, and the four were always fascinated by the fishermen harvesting the native oysters.

It took them a couple of hours to reach their destination. The traffic had been relatively light.

Jean, on hearing their arrival, had left the door open. The boys stiffly dismounted their scooters – long legs tucked up for a couple of hours didn't go down well. Unlike them Chris hopped off swiftly, being a lot shorter than her brothers. The smell of beef stew wafted through. Their mouths watered at the prospect.

'Hi Aunt Jean, great to see you and thanks for putting up with us for a night,' said Tim. Ian and Mark presented her with a bottle of sherry and a box of chocolates. 'Mum and dad send their love!'

Aunt Jean had a broad smile. Nothing pleased her more than having her niece and nephews to stay, even if it was too short a time for her. Having retired from her PR job in the Ministry of Agriculture, Fisheries and Food she sometimes felt that the days dragged on, especially in winter. So to fill her newfound freedom, she now volunteered at the Fingringhoe Wick Nature Reserve, the Essex Wildlife Trust first ever site. Situated on the banks of the River Colne it had become reputed for its nightingales.

'Come on, bring your things in and we'll eat. I shall expect a full account of your marvellous show in front of Her Majesty. You did the family proud for sure.'

She could tell something was bothering the four.

'Don't worry ….. Your mother reminded me that I am not to tell ANYBODY, not even my best friends, that you are *Spectrum*. My lips are sealed!'

Next morning, Aunt Jean, wearing a flowery apron, was standing proudly in the big kitchen, armed with a slotted spatula. 'Now you sit down and make yourselves comfortable.'

She had laid out a feast for the eyes. Toast, home-made raspberry jam, freshly squeezed orange juice, and cereals. She knew the young Rogers were always hungry.

'I propose a cooked breakfast of tomatoes, eggs, bacon, baked beans, sausages and fried bread. Any takers?'

'Yes please!' they shouted in unison.

'You're too kind Aunt Jean,' said Tim. 'What can we do to repay you?'

'It's easy. Just keep coming. And tell me about your adventures. It keeps me young!'

If truth be known it was a highlight for Jean to have a noisy household. She had been married but tragedy struck. She received the dreaded telegram from the War Office only six months after their wedding informing her that her beloved Alan had been killed in action.

'Have you got time to stop in Clacton?' Jean asked.

'Humm.....not sure Mum would approve,' Chris replied. 'Why?'

'Didn't you read last month's article in the Essex Gazette? The *Mods* and the *Rockers* fought on the sea front.'

Mark was puzzled. 'I don't understand, *Mods, Rockers*, what does it all mean?' Tim explained.

'*Mods* are gangs on scooters. They wear parkas. Whereas *Rockers* ride motorcycles, dressed in leather and denim. In other words, they are rivals. And sometimes it gets ugly. You should have seen the headlines in the national newspapers: *The Battle of*

Pier Gap. They terrified elderly residents snoozing on the beach, shouted obscenities, stole their deck chairs and burnt them .... very violent.. But don't worry Mark, lots were fined and some got prison sentences. I've heard that a number of journalists confessed to paying them for sensational reporting.'

They kissed Aunt Jean goodbye.

Once out of her sight they stopped for a brief moment, looked at each other and screamed: 'Clacton here we come!'

How could *Spectrum* resist it. A ten mile diversion to the famed seaside resort before heading to Norwich saw them re-enacting a ride along Marine Parade as 'Mods'. Fortunately, without the confrontation of any *Rockers*!

❧ ❧ ❧

Halfway into their journey to Spindle Chris and her brothers decided that their lunch-break would be Needham Lake: Aunt Jean had naturally packed them a picnic. Mark opened it. A smile of sheer delight crossed his face. Yes there was the normal egg and cress, but in addition she had included treats from their childhood, banana and raisin sandwiches and home-made jam tarts. Mark threw the bags of Smiths crisps to the others. The hunt was on to find the little blue pack of salt packaged with the crisps to season them.

It was very peaceful sitting by the lake watching the hustle and bustle of wildlife. Before long a family of great crested grebes showed up. The male would disappear suddenly, diving after a fish, the female patiently gliding nearby with her chicks. The larger humbug (their name owing to their stripy flanks) was already swimming strongly by her side whilst the little one was hiking a ride on its mother's back.

Chris was scrutinizing the elegant birds with her binoculars. So sweet, their eyes bright red, spooky........

Welcome to Norwich a Fine City sign was eventually reached. Their route now took them passed the castle built on William the Conqueror's orders, towering high above the City Centre on a man-made mound!

Its impact on Anglo-Saxon Norwich had been devastating as 98 houses were destroyed to make way for the structure. Throughout the centuries it was used as a Royal Palace, the county jail and now it was a museum, which the young Rogers had visited with their parents.

The four eased up by Elm Hill. Chris looked along the cobbled street, lined with Victorian lampposts. It felt as if they had stepped back a hundred years.

At long last they caught sight of Spindle Broad. They had made it!

Jessie and her son Matt, a tall strapping lad a year older than the twins, were standing by the two moored *Spectrum* boats when they heard the scooters arrive.

The first thing Jessie said was 'Thank God you are safe, I never trust them new-fangled things.'

Chris was pleased to see her. 'Hello Jessie! That was some ride. Fun, but I am glad it's over.'

'Thanks for preparing the boats Matt. Any hiccup?'

'Relax Tim, it's all good. We put them in the water yesterday afternoon and if I may use the pun, it was plain sailing.'

≥ ≥ ≥

Chris's alarm went off at 6.00 the next morning. She leapt out of bed and flung open the window. She gasped as the crisp morning air hit her bare arms.

In the distance she could hear the bittern booming, a sure sign of spring. Just across the Broad mallards were diving for their breakfast. A duck considered by most to be common, not worth a second glance, until you see the male's glossy green head shining in the early morning sun. Awesome, pure emerald.

'What a beautiful morning.' She lingered a little, daydreaming. Chris could hear pots and pans noises coming from the kitchen. 'Breakfast, that's what I could do with.'

By about 8.00 Mark and Tim were on the river in *Spectrum One*; Ian and Chris were finishing the half-yearly stock inventory of boat stores.

Jessie called from the house. 'Chris! Phone for you. I am sure it's Tony. He's doing one of his funny languages.'

When she picked up the telephone she knew instantly it was THE unmistakable voice that made her heart miss a beat.

'Allo. Guten Morgan, Fräulein Christine Rogers, ya?'

'Bonjour Monsieur Dale, comment ça va?'

'Hi Kid. I didn't think I could fool you …. I do like it when you speak French to me, very sexy.'

Chris chuckled.

'Does this call mean that you will be joining us for the week?'

'As it happens Laurie and Jim, my Road Manager, need to settle some last minute arrangements with the Great Yarmouth theatre before the summer show opens.

You know Laurie.... a perfectionist. He's given the band a few days holiday, so I said to myself that if the guys can have a break, so can I. We'll be coming by train and hope to be in Norwich around 4.00 this afternoon. Could you pick me up Fräulein Rogers?'

'...Erm.. let me check my diary...yes.... I CAN!'

'You little minx, you!'

'Seriously though, of course darling. Tim will be with me. Ian and Mark are at Ludham. Mark muttered something about a dragon.'

'Dragon?'

'You've never heard of the hideous dragon that used to terrorise the village?'

'Sorry Kid, I know a lot of dragons in my industry, but not in Norfolk.'

'Well to sum up the legend: one day a brave man waited for the monster to leave its den and then blocked the entrance with a single boulder. When the dragon found its cave sealed off, it flew in rage to St. Benets Abbey and thwacked the walls with its mighty tail, and then it vanished. Lucky for Ludham.'

'Wow! But surely Ian and Mark are not looking for it?'

'Ha, ha, very funny. I think it's something to do with including a reference to the dragon in the village's tapestry in the church. Mark and Ian are always keen on such things.'

'Anyway you should find *Spectrum One* at the quayside, just across the road from the station. Do you think you'll be able to get that far without being molested by your fans?'

'..Um.. I should be able to make it. Looking forward to seeing you soon darling.'

Spectrum One had now returned. Tim checked the tide tables: 'If we leave in about 15 minutes, we should make Yarmouth Yacht Station at slack water and the incoming tide should push us towards Norwich.'

≈ ≈ ≈

June, Ginger, Belinda and Rachel had just arrived at Liverpool Street Station. They knew London would be busy, but this busy, on a Sunday? Everywhere they looked was a mass of young people, seemingly agitated …. about what or whom? Curiously there were an awful lot of girls.

Rachel looked worried, 'What's happening? Could it be a CND demonstration? If things go wrong we could be hurt.'

'Don't fret Rachel,' June wanted to reassure her. 'Usually the Campaign for Nuclear Disarmament targets American or British air basis, especially in Scotland. I am sure it's something else.'

Mrs. Macdonald, their Head, usually calm and collected, was visibly on edge, trying to keep track of her charges. 'Oh there you are girls. Quickly! Everyone else is on the train. I am asking you, all this commotion because of some pop star.'

Mrs. Mac, only interested in the classics, didn't have time for what she called *'that racket we now have to put up with which seems to be called…... MUSIC! Oh for the days of the American swing bands. Glenn Miller, Benny Goodman……'*

'Pop star, what did you say Mrs. MacDonald? A pop star, which one?'

'Yes Rachel, a certain Tony Dale. Oh, do come, hurry!'

They reluctantly boarded the train. Rachel immediately heading towards a window.

'Come on Rachel,' said Ginger, gently pulling her by the arm. Just as Rachel relented a surge of screaming fans ran onto the platform. Without thinking twice Rachel shrugged off Ginger's arm and dashed back to the window, joined by Ginger and June who were almost more excited than her. They could not believe it. The good old London Bobbies were shouldering a gangway through for three men clutching holdalls.

'It's him! There he is!' Rachel was shrieking 'TONY DALE' is catching OUR train!' Rachel was now leaning out as far as she dared.

June pulled her back. 'Calm down. You are going to give us a bad name. Anyway, now you can tell everybody that you have seen him in the flesh, not in a magazine!'

The train swiftly jerked into life. The scenery gradually changed from London suburbs to rural countryside. The girls were content, reading and chatting amongst themselves. When the train stopped at Ipswich, Rachel once more did her balancing act at the window, to no avail. How disappointing.

Belinda took on her head girl voice, 'Look Rachel, Tony Dale has to be going all the way to Norwich. Don't you know he's in Great Yarmouth for the summer season? I bet you that when we get off the train you'll have a good chance to bump into him.'

The trip passed quickly. Norwich station seemed sleepy in comparison to what they had just left two hours ago. The four of them grabbed their cases and leapt down onto the platform.

Hoping.

Mrs. Mac wanted to pop to the newsagents and told the party to meet her at the exit.

Rachel was driving the girls mad, hopping from one foot to another and looking around herself like a hawk. 'He's got to come this way? It's the only exit.'

The large car park stretched almost to the river where a brightly coloured craft was tied up at the quayside.

Spectrum One, of course.

Tim nudged Chris on the shoulder. 'Hey sis isn't that your friend June heading towards us?'

Chris took the binoculars from Tim.

'Lord, you are right. Oh no! Belinda and Ginger have joined her. You know, Ginger is the one who took a liking to Ian after our Command Performance.'

'Crumbs! I think our secret is out. Wait. I can see Tony, Laurie and Jim coming out of the station. Yes! The girls are turning back. Phew: saved by dear Rachel, Tony's biggest fan. Hooray for dear Rachel.'

'Come on sis, time to don our incognito sun glasses, remember what Laurie said. That was a close shave for sure.'

Rachel, red as a beetroot, could not believe she was standing in front of her hero. After signing her autograph book, there he was, a smiling Tony Dale speaking to her as if they had been life-long friends...... incredible.

Mrs. Mac appeared, astonished to see all her girls crowding around three men.

Tony saw her approach and from her demeanor guessed she was responsible for the girls.

'Good afternoon Madam. I'm Tony Dale. May I congratulate you. Your young ladies are a credit to you.'

Mrs. Macdonald was purring, Tony's charm had conquered again!

The school trip's bus was parked near the taxi rank. The driver, a cheerful character, took Mrs. Mac's case. 'Isn't it a *bootiful* day?'

Everybody had taken their seats. Belinda was the last to step inside. She looked pensive. She was sure to have seen Tony Dale and his friends walking towards the brightly coloured boat. Could this be *Spectrum*?

Everywhere they went, be it to Wroxham, along the river to Horning, or to Ranworth Broad Wildlife Centre, Belinda had kept a vigilant eye on the boats, just in case, but *Spectrum* was never seen.

It was the last evening. Sitting in the hotel lounge June, Ginger and Rachel agreed that the boat trip along the river Bure was a highlight. Horning immediately came to mind. A name meaning *Folk who live on the high ground between the rivers*.

If their trip had taken place in early June they might have witnessed the *Three Rivers Race*. A fabulous 45-mile race along the rivers Ant, Bure and Thurne organised by the local Sailing Club.

Never mind. Norfolk gave them so many delights: waterside pubs, and thatched houses with gardens running down to the river. Windmills and lots of wildlife. They even had afternoon tea in the Ferry Inn, reputedly haunted intermittently by a ghost. The Landlord told them that the ferry on this site had been running for nearly a thousand years!

Belinda burst in, knocking a couple of chairs over in the process! 'You'll never guess what I've found out. I've

61

just been talking to the clerk on Reception. You remember that sinister dyke leading away from the opening of Ranworth Broad. Well, apparently it opens up into a lovely secluded Broad and that's where Spindle Hall is.'

They all looked blankly at Belinda.

'You do know who lives there?'

No answer.

'*Spectrum* of course!'

'On no, don't say that we were so close. Could we persuade Mrs. Mac to go back to the nature reserve?' cried a disappointed Ginger.

'Have you forgotten? Sadly, we go home tomorrow,' said June.

❧ ❧ ❧

Chris was alone in the Prefects room. Her essay on Romeo and Juliet Act 5 Scene 1 was due in the following day, she read…. *Well Juliet, I will lie with thee tonight. Let's see for means: O mischief, thou art swift….* Chris normally found it easy to concentrate and get on with it, but at the moment so much was happening in her life. She thought back over the crazy week she and her brothers had had with Tony.

They purposefully took ages to get back to Spindle. Tony having decided it was time for Laurie and Jim to get their sea legs. A detour in Breydon Water was called for so Laurie and Jim could be dropped off at Yarmouth. What fun!

Laurie coped well but Jim had never been so quiet.

The week had been relaxing. No major problems to deal with. They had enjoyed a free run of the Broads and some adventures.

Britain's past had been shaped by many incursions, none more so than the Roman occupation of nearly 550 years. These incursions sport many tales, and in the Broads it can get very, very, quirky.

One evening, Tim suggested to test out one of these eerie tales at Wroxham Broad. According to the legend, the waters transform into a Roman Amphitheatre where thousands of spectators await the beginning of the games. Apparently, some people have seen a Roman general in a golden chariot drawn by ten white stallions. And would you believe it? Lions led in chains by stalwart Roman soldiers attired in gilt armour.

They moored the boat on the far side of the Broad to the Yacht Club waiting for the supposed apparition of Flavious Magnus, Consul for the Western Roman Empire. He was presiding over the birthday celebrations of General Marcus Aurelius Carausius, who had recently declared himself Emperor of Britain and Northern Gaul.

At midnight Wroxham Broad was still. The moon had crept behind a cloud casting a ghostly shadow around the waterside vegetation. They waited. Not a sound could be heard, just a distant splash as a fish briefly surfaced, then the loud, raucous cry of an owl. Tim crept behind Tony, tapped him on his shoulder.

'Ave soldier!'

A startled Tony spun round, tripped over a bucket and promptly fell in!

Ian and Mark helpfully threw in a lifebuoy as Tony came up spluttering. He swam strongly back to the boat, but as they stretched out their hands to him, he naturally proceeded to pull them in.

So on a balmy night in early May, no ghosts, instead a joyful midnight swim.

Chris smiled to herself as she recalled the last episode.

'What are you grinning at Chris?' asked Belinda, who had just come in, 'How did the wedding go?'

'Oh fine, just fine. I have been hearing all about your encounter with Tony Dale. Fantastic! Rachel is still on cloud 9. She said you kind of saw Spectrum.'

'Yes what a shame that was a near thing. But I am not going to give up searching. It really intrigues me.'

⅜ ⅜ ⅜

The summer term was creaking its way to a close, the long summer days making Chris yearn for the wide-open spaces of the Norfolk countryside, and of course the Broads.

Regular phone calls with Tony were not the same as a good cuddle! His summer show was going down a storm. Packed houses most nights. This didn't leave much time to connect with Chris. He was missing her too.

'Are you game to go for a short week-end in Norfolk?' Sam said unexpectedly one Friday morning. 'I won't be with you much, you know, an urgent job at Neatishead. But on the other hand, you could see Tony's show. I have already spoken to him. Providing your homework is done of course.' Needless to say that all four jumped at the opportunity!

⅜ ⅜ ⅜

The following day found them at Spindle. Jessie had just brought in steaming bowls of tomato soup and some freshly baked rolls. Tony always ate a light meal before his evening performance. The phone rang, Tony was nearest.

'Oh, Laurie that's fantastic! Hey everybody, *Freewheelin* has climbed to number 21 in the charts... about tonight? I see. Hang on a mo, let me talk to them. I am sorry but the four of you won't be able to see me perform tonight.'

'We've come all the way from Kent, you must be joking!' cried an outraged Ian.

'Don't get on your high horse Ian. Laurie and Jim feel that as *Freewheelin* is doing well, and as you are presently in Norfolk, *Spectrum* could be a supporting act tonight... They also think that it will be good timing to stir up the Press again. Well, what do you say?'

'....but, what about our outfits and our instruments? I could not play with a guitar other than mine,' Chris said.

Grace got up, went into the study and came back with a big suitcase.

'Dad and I had a feeling this might happen. Your instruments are already in the van. You were so sleepy you didn't even notice. That's a first!'

What a mum and dad, strict parents but loving parents, steering them so well towards their future.

That evening the audience had the surprise appearance of *Spectrum*. Much to its delight. Not so for the Press who was left hungry. The birds had flown the theatre before the journalists could snatch a photo. The mystery continued.

～ ～ ～

It was the last day of term. The Autumn Term seemed years away instead of two very short months.

'Cheerio everyone, cheerio June,' cried Chris, 'have good hols and see you all in September.'

With that Chris disappeared out of the door and away from the friendly crowd, unsuspecting about the next couple of months.

CHAPTER FIVE

It was a beautiful sunny morning. Norfolk was showing its true colours. Chris and her brothers strolled across the lawns, still damp with the early morning dew. Instead of two boats tied at the jetty there were now four! Their father's practice was going from strength to strength meaning more money. Sam felt his younger sons were now experienced and sensible enough to handle their own crafts. *Spectrum Three and Four* had appeared a few days ago. It was amazing.

In their roles as Junior Rangers one of their tasks was to help the Nature Conservancy Council map parts of the Broads, as recommendations for Sites of Special Scientific Interest (SSSI). This Domesday-like work would lead to the Norfolk Broads becoming a Wetlands National Park. As an opener to their summer holidays *Spectrum* would help with some of these surveys.

The brief from the Council had arrived a few days previously. Now with four boats at their disposal *Spectrum* could go further afield. They had had great fun last night planning their individual routes around the Broads. The network of approximately 125 miles consisted of six navigable rivers linking several different broads – absolutely awesome.

'What a marvellous start to the holiday Tim, the weather is certainly holding.'

'It sure is, hey Ian!' he called across, 'Did you check the walkie-talkie?'

'Yes Tim, it was a faulty transistor. Matt fixed it.'

'Good. Mark, how about those lights of yours....' No answer. 'Mark!' he called again.

Mark was doing his usual. His Charles Darwin act his siblings called it. His attention had been caught by movement on a reed stem. A six-legged nymph was slowly crawling up it ready to transform into a *jewel of the air*. It was large. It was chunky. But Mark knew it was unlikely to be the rare Norfolk hawker dragonfly whose season was drawing to a close; maybe a brown hawker, or migrant hawker? Incredibly hawkers spend two to three years under water, but only survive a little over a month as flying insects.

The others headed in Mark's direction. They too became enthralled. Eventually Tim called a halt, *Spectrum* had duties to fulfil.

Mark headed into the River Ant and entered Barton Broad, the second largest of the Norfolk Broads. He looked around the vast expanse of water. Pleasure Island was in his sights, circular in shape, generally windswept, so hardly living up to its name!

In the fifties Barton Broad was on the shortlist to be included as a Nature Reserve, but the data at the time was incomplete. Now the Ant Valley's biodiversity was considered of high value. Mark was to take samples of the water for analysis. Much of the pollution could be blamed on pesticides run-off from the adjoining farmland.

During the First World War Barton Broad was used to land sea planes. As a complete contrast, for the Second World War wooden boats were sunk or moored in the middle of the Broad to stop the Germans landing their sea planes.

Mark's final destination before returning to Spindle, Sutton Broad, also has an interesting history, particularly concerning birdlife.

Black terns used to breed regularly around the Broads in the 1800s, but the Victorians wont for egg collecting and food for the pot caused the major decline of many species. The last breeding pair of black terns was found at Sutton Broad where both nest and eggs were destroyed.

Bitterns, always synonymous with the Broads, bred in good numbers until the late eighteen hundreds. Once more due to the Victorians the bittern disappeared re-emerging 25 years later when a nest was discovered on Sutton Broad. Since then bittern numbers have gradually increased.

Mark always found it interesting comparing Sutton Broad with Barton Broad. Both had been peat diggings in the thirteenth century. Barton was a huge body of water, Sutton Broad, infilled with reed swamp, was now more like a river than a broad.

Chris, Tim and Ian travelled together along the river Bure. Ian left them at Thurne Mouth with the very distinctive white windmill marking the centre of the Broads network.

Ian cruised up the River Thurne to the nature reserve on Hickling Broad owned by the local Naturalist Trust. A deafening 'honking' followed in the wake of a small group of cranes flying overhead; Ian thought of Mark in the adjoining river system and wondered if he had seen them. Cranes, once a favourite on the dinner table of Tudor England, had disappeared from the country.

Happily after 400 years the cranes were slowly recolonising.

The bickering of black-headed gulls filled the air. Ian's job was to assess numbers after their breeding season. The droppings from so many gulls nesting at such close proximity to each other were possibly polluting the broad. Ian leaned over the side of the boat and filled a glass flask so the water could be analysed as well.

He recalled an incident in the past when nature had taken on such a task. To safeguard the broad from the encroachment of algae and other pollutants a strong aquatic plant growth is a natural deterrent. One year a very wet winter followed by an extremely warm dry spring stimulated such plant growth causing an explosion of the tiny invertebrates who love to feast on the algae. The outcome, if only for a season, was crystal clear water and a reduction in the harmful pollutants.

He looked up as he heard the plaintive cry of a marsh harrier. One of the key Broadland bird species on his list to record, the others being bittern and bearded tit.

The bearded tits flit amongst reed stems. The male, handsome, with an ashy-grey head and a magnificent black moustache, the female, exquisite, with similar tawny tones but lacks the striking facial markings.

The secretive bittern, browny, barred and mottled, flies slowly over the broad, lands, and disappears into the bankside vegetation. Walking some distance it would pop up again. The marsh harrier is easier to view as it floats on the thermals, the female boasting a pale crown. Ian caught sight of the marsh harrier which dive-bombed a small section of the reed bed. He had an inkling of what the target could be, sure enough out walked a bittern. Bitterns and marsh harriers don't get along.

Spectrum One and *Spectrum Three* motored down the River Bure past Stokesby. A picturesque Broadland Village mentioned in the Eleventh Century Doomsday Book with its salt works situated on the sea shore!

They joined Breydon Water. Sometimes called the *Gateway to the Broads*; a sheltered estuary linking many of the river systems of the Broads. The area is always teeming with bird life feasting on the mudflats exposed at low tide. To their left the sun was glinting on the sea just off Great Yarmouth. A huge plus with Breydon Water is that there is no speed limit. Chris and Tim had a mini race across that stretch of water. The official explanation to test the manoeuvrability of a new *Spectrum* craft, in reality, a lot of fun!

Burgh Castle, at the southern end of Breydon Water was duly reached. The so-called *turn-tide jetty* marked the split of the waters into the Rivers Yare and Waveney.

Tim headed towards the Southern Broads, along the River Waveney, past St. Olaves to Somerleyton and into Suffolk. He stopped off at Beccles. The yacht station gave good views of St. Michaels' detached bell tower, a church where Nelson's parents were married.

Tim thought of the story his grandfather used to tell him about the tower. There were only three clock faces, the fourth one, blank, and faced west towards Norfolk. 'The other side of the river', he used to say. Grandfather always elaborated with the cheeky comment, 'who would give the time of day to them foreigners across the river!' But, always finished the tale with comment, 'all unsubstantiated of course!'

A flash of blue then caught Tim's attention. A kingfisher was flying downstream; always a delight to see, if only briefly. Finally, the Inn came into view. He had reached the end of navigation at Geldeston Lock. The Inn, not your usual hostelry, was run by Miss Banks, affectionately known as 'Esme' by the Broads' folk hereabouts. One day she might even light the inn with something other than candles!

Chris was now on the River Yare; a wide tidal river winding its way through marshland. The river once carried commercial shipping to Norwich, predominantly grain, timber and coal. Rippling reeds on either bank added to the isolation of this stretch of water. A grey heron, as still as a sentinel, standing on the opposite bank, was waiting to pounce on a fish.

Reedham staithe came into view. Yet again the Roman influence had reared its head. Reedham was once a Roman Station on the shore of a great arm of the North Sea, incredibly it was now several miles inland from the coast!

Chris was amazed to see Inspector Devenport standing on the quayside. He waved. She moored her boat and jumped ashore.

Inspector Brian Devenport, a tall bespoke man with dark brown hair, gave the impression of authority but there was a softness about him which seemed to surface whenever he encountered Chris. He used to be a judo instructor and still remembered the day when Sam bought the twins to his classes for their first lesson. Chris had taken to the sport like a *duck takes to water* and if only she had persevered he reckoned she could have become an international judo player. However, when she was 12 music became her priority. He now keenly followed Chris and her brothers' progress as musicians under the name of *Spectrum,* and was aware of Tony Dale's relationship with Chris.

'Hi there Inspector, this is a pleasant surprise. Are you waiting for me?'

'Yes I am Chris. Jessie told me I might find you here.'

The Inspector reached into his folder, drew out two photos and handed them to Chris.

The top one was of a middle-aged man with a slightly balding head and a very cruel set of eyes.

'He is one Jacob Wright, down for ten years for arson and possession of a firearm. The other one Chris is Michael Henderson, his accomplice, serving a seven-year sentence.'

She looked at the other photograph, this was of a younger man probably in his early to middle twenties but as a complete contrast to Jacob Wright, he had a baby-face look about him. His dark shoulder-length hair was tied back.

'I know what you're thinking,' said the Inspector, 'but don't be fooled by his apparent innocence, he is just as dangerous as the other one. Both men escaped from a van which was transferring them from the City Prison. They were involved in the criminal fire at Neatishead.'

Chris looked up from the photos, 'Oh I remember dad telling me about that. I think the fire burnt for nine days before it was eventually extinguished.'

Sam Rogers had been contacted shortly after the incident. Authorities thought the break-in and arson attempt had been a cover to retrieve something sensitive on which he and Frank Morris had been working on during the war and latterly during *the cold war.* Fortunately for the Government Sam Rogers, shrewd and experienced in such things, had had the item in question removed to a more secure location.

The Inspector continued...... 'I reckon they're making for the sea. We had a tip-off that they might attempt to leave the country. It is probable that some small Dutch fishing vessel is laying-off the coast around Yarmouth waiting for them.

A word of warning Chris, you are not, I repeat **NOT,** to approach them in any way, just observe and report to me.'

The Inspector reached into his folder once more. 'Here are copies for the rest of *Spectrum*.'

Back on *Spectrum Three* she waved goodbye to the Inspector. Chris now deep in thought on what she had been told turned the craft into the River Chet heading in the direction of Loddon, a name thought to mean *muddy river* in the Celtic language.

In contrast to the Yare the Chet narrows, winding through well-wooded countryside. In a short while she arrived at Loddon staithe by the mill. Loddon Mill was one of the early water mills, weatherboard clad with a pantile roof. There had been many water mills in Norfolk, usually grinding flour, but only one is now left in full working order near the coast at Letheringsett. Many mills had been destroyed by fire or demolished. Hardingham Mill was going to be actively burnt for a scene in a film but thankfully that didn't happen!

Loddon Mill, like many of the remaining mills, had been converted and was now a Post Office and a café. The homemade scones and cakes one could die for!

A grey-haired woman, short and slightly rotund, came bustling up to her.

'Hello Mrs. Hurrell, how's business?' asked Chris.

'Arr it be doin' right fine there young Chris, nice to see you again. How about coming up for tea and cake?'

She followed the old lady up the twisty path to the mill. Over tea Chris showed her the photos. 'Have you by any chance seen either of these two men Mrs. Hurrell?'

The old lady took out her specs, and carefully examined the photos. 'Arr yes Chris that young one came into the Post Office just the other day and made a phone call. He looked such a nice clean young'un, and you don't see many of them these days, such nice manners as well, though I don't go for them hairstyles that seem to be the fashion. What's wrong with a nice short back and sides I say.' She looked up. 'He's not in any trouble is he?'

'Well, I'm sorry to disappoint you Mrs. Hurrell, but he's wanted by the Police. If you see him again give Inspector Devonport a ring or dial 999, he is dangerous.'

The old lady nodded. She stuffed a bag containing a couple of fruit scones and a slice of carrot cake into Chris's hand. 'For later,' she said.

Chris returned to *Spectrum Three* and then motored back along the Chet to Hardley Cross to moor for the night. The Cross, at the mouth of the river, marked the limit of jurisdiction of Norwich and Yarmouth. In olden times the Mayors of the two towns would come in state to this spot to adjust the grievances of the watermen.

Chris turned on the walkie-talkie. There was static and then crackling and eventually Tim came on the line. 'I'm moored for the night just above Hardley Cross,' she said. 'Inspector Devenport would like *Spectrum* to keep an eye out for some escaped convicts.'

Chris relayed her conversation with the Inspector and also that of Mrs. Hurrell's possible sighting at the Mill.

'I have copies of the photos for you, Ian and Mark.'

'Okay. Let's meet at Burgh Castle tomorrow,' said Tim.

Chris turned away from the radio and sat out in the cockpit and ate her Cottage Pie. Jessie always presented *Spectrum* with meals they could easily heat up whenever they were out on the river. This time she rounded off her meal with the scrumptious carrot cake from Mrs. Hurrell.

It was a balmy night which often followed a hot summer's day in Britain. She lazed back against the aft deck. It was so unbelievably peaceful, she could hear the frogs' evening chorus, and now and then the odd splash as a fish surfaced to catch its evening meal.

Whilst Chris was relaxing and taking in the night air little did she know that her friend June had been rushed to hospital suffering from a perforated appendix.

※ ※ ※

The next morning Chris was awakened by a loud clacking. A pair of swans had landed on the river beside her craft. Their webbed feet extended like a plane's undercarriage causing a bow wash along the water's surface.

'Time for my breakfast.' She stretched like an animal. She always slept well on the boat. The air seemed so pure and sweet, especially first thing in the morning. She looked across the river and marsh. The early mist was just rising from the surface. The water was clear, the mud yet to be churned up by passing boats. The sun was a dull disk in the sky as it strove to clear the dampness around her.

She heard a sound like a squealing pig and realised that the shy water rail couldn't be far away. As she busied herself around the boat a family of greylag geese swam by, the younger ones striving to keep up with their older siblings. They hung around the stern of the boat hoping for a titbit, so Chris threw in a couple of crusts. Out of nowhere gulls appeared stealing some of the geese's bounty.

Chris picked up her clipboard listing her tasks from the Nature Conservancy Council. A couple of non-native rodents had escaped from fur farms during the Second World War; the European Coypu and the American Mink. The coypus love to graze on the succulent rhyzones of bulrush and common reed, plants that form the basis of the Broadland rush weaving industry. Unlike the carnivorous mink which enjoy munching birds' eggs and feasting on native wildlife like the scarce water vole!

Significant inroads had been made into the eradication of the coypu, but there was still a long way to go. One of its strongholds was along the Yare. Chris, now under way, was checking the banks for large burrows. The coypu's digging habits causes the river banks to collapse.

After a while she reached Brundall a name thought to mean *at the broomy nook of land*. The area around the Green was lined with several boat yards, the majority now building fiberglass cruisers. However, it was pleasing to see that a handful of the local companies were still constructing traditional wooden crafts.

Back on board, clipboard in hand, Chris filled in her survey results when the walkie-talkie crackled into life. It was Matt from Spindle.

'Hi Chris, hope the rain holds off for you. Tony's rung through. He was just checking that you hadn't forgotten you were picking him up at Yarmouth this afternoon. You know with the theatre closing for a week and his show being put on hold until next Saturday. Also some letters have been redirected from Kent by your mum. What do you want me to do about them?'

'No, I hadn't forgotten about Tony and I'll look at the letters when I get back. Thanks Matt.' Forgotten about Tony! As if she would have!

Chris turned off her radio and headed once more along the Yare towards Burgh Castle marina. Lining her route were numerous nature reserves, Surlingham, Rockland and a stronghold of the rare swallowtail butterfly Strumpshaw Fen. Swifts, swallows and house martins were skimming the water's surface seeking tasty morsels on which to feast and to feed their young.

Tim was already at the Burgh Castle marina when she arrived. The pair of them strolled around the ruins discussing the information from Inspector Devenport.

Burgh Castle certainly had a checkered history or Garariannonum as the Romans called it. The fortress built in AD.100 as a defence against Saxon raids had many a tale to tell. Gonard the Dane massacred over 4,000 settlers in AD418. Saint Fursey an Irish monk built a monastery some 200 years later, and to cap it all the Normans constructed a castle within its perimeter.

Just a couple of massive walls are all that remains now of such an iconic site.

Chris handed Tim the photos. He wasn't entirely happy with the task set them by the Police. 'Sis you take care. Promise me you'll keep in regular contact with all of us.'

She nodded.

The pair then went their respective ways, Chris to Yarmouth and Tim to meet up with Ian and Mark at Stokesby.

There was a flash of lightning followed by thunder. It had suddenly become very humid.

Chris looked up at the dark, threatening sky.

'Mmm, I didn't think it would last. Typical British summer.

Still, with a bit of luck it won't be much.'

About an hour later the air seemed to be getting more oppressive.

'I wish it would break,' muttered Chris as she nosed her boat in the gathering gloom towards the quayside at Yarmouth. A small crowd of people were gathered around a black BMW.

'Tony, no doubt, with his usual mass of fans well about half a dozen.'

His patience in that direction never failed to amaze her, his comment whenever she mentioned it was that if they were prepared to come and watch him and buy his records, the least he could do was to pay attention to them.

Chris moored *Spectrum Three*, donned the dark glasses and tucked her hair beneath a cap. The cap amused her, it had '**I ♥ the Broads**' emblazoned on it.

Tony saw her approach. 'Well everyone,' he said, 'my taxi has arrived.' The gathering cried out to him not to go. As Chris neared the scene some people turned towards her staring.

Tony seemed to be enjoying the moment. 'Not just my taxi but one of the Group about to knock me off the number one spot,' Tony continued. 'So if you want another autograph for your books try one from a member of *Spectrum*.'

Much to her embarrassment some of them held forward their books.

At that point Laurie, seeing her discomfort, stepped forward.

'Come on folks let Tony go off on his well-earned break. He'll be back next week on stage.'

Tony picked up his holdall from the boot of Laurie's car, waved to the fans and walked towards Chris laughing at her expression.

There was another flash of lightning followed by a tremendous clap of thunder and the heavens opened; the storm had finally broken after its incessant mutterings. They made a dash for the boat and Laurie to his car.

On board……. 'It's all very well for you to laugh you big big star Mr. Dale, but I'm not used to that sort of thing, nor in signing autogra …….'

She wasn't allowed to finish….. Tony took her in his arms and kissed her passionately. 'I missed you so much,' he said stroking her hair.

Eventually they broke apart and Chris started making some coffee. Tony sat down at the table where Chris had laid out the photos passed to her by the Inspector.

'Who are these men?' he asked. 'They look an unsavoury couple.'

Chris turned back from the cooker.

'Oh, they're escaped convicts. Inspector Devenport thinks they might be heading towards the coast. *Spectrum* has been asked to look out for them.'

Like Tim there was a note of concern in Tony's voice.

'Chris, I know *Spectrum* tend to do some police work, but surely this is a bit beyond what is expected of you all?'

'Possibly, but rain this heavy will cause some flooding along the marshes of Breydon Water and with a high tide due I don't think we will see much anyway.'

How wrong can you be!

She placed the mugs of steaming coffee on the table. The steady drumming of the rain on the cabin roof soon had its soporific effect. She laid back and Tony put his arm around her, within minutes the pair of them were fast asleep.

CHAPTER SIX

The radio crackled into life. A startled Chris rolled out of Tony's arms and promptly fell onto the cabin floor! It was the Inspector calling.

'Chris, I've just been talking to Tim who is with Ian and Mark on the River Bure at Stokesby. Are you still in the Breydon Water area?'

'Yes, sir, I've just picked up Tony and we're moored at the Yarmouth Yacht Station waiting for the storm to abate.' Just then there was another clap of thunder and the walkie-talkie went dead for a second: the weather seemed to be deteriorating.

The Inspector continued: 'The two escaped prisoners have been sighted in the Halvergate area, probably heading across the marshes. Can you go up The Fleet and have a look? As soon as the weather clears a bit we should be able to get a chopper up, but the roads are flooded and you happen to be the nearest. Remember, I said reconnoiter only, no heroics, it could all turn nasty. Radio in on a regular basis.'

Chris with Tony by her side, sensing the urgency, manoeuvred *Spectrum Three* into the current. The boat appeared to fly like a matchstick as it caught the strong incoming tide backed by the wind. The water level had indeed risen. They turned into The Fleet. Everything seemed so peaceful after the turmoil they'd just left.

Chris switched on the searchlight the strong beam pierced the gathering gloom.

Suddenly the tide caught up with them swinging *Spectrum Three* into the bank. They were now stuck in the mud.

❧ ❧ ❧

Jake and Mick had left a stolen car in a ditch close to Halvergate. Both were local and even in the half-light they knew their way across the marsh. They skirted the decoy and headed in the direction of an isolated cottage at the edge of The Fleet. It was in darkness. The cottage belonged to Mick's friend Charlie who occasionally visited Mick in prison. Mick had rung his friend from the Mill but had had no reply. Mick also knew that Charlie shot coypu for extra cash so there had to be a rifle somewhere. A dead coypu had a bounty on its head!

Mick wandered around the back of the cottage and came across an outhouse and tumbled-down stables. He broke into the outhouse.... Bingo! Not only did he find Charlie's rifle but also a service revolver and live cartridges.

Jake wasn't as successful. The dinghy they had hoped to use to cross Breydon Water was upturned on the bank and without an outboard! Grimly their only hope now was to find an abandoned boat or to commandeer one.

Mick appeared with the guns. He handed the revolver to Jake and kept the rifle for himself.

Once more back on the marsh, following the path alongside the Fleet, they headed in the direction of Breydon Water.

Nearing the confluence of the two waters a light pierced the gloom. Mick dived behind a tree. The reflected light briefly lit up a boat. Jake couldn't believe his luck, they had stumbled on a *Spectrum*.

Using the service revolver Jake fired at the spotlight.

'What the devil was that?' cried Chris as she and Tony ducked.

Chris moved across the cockpit to the walkie-talkie. Static and crackling preceded the call; a faint acknowledgement came down the line from the Inspector.

Suddenly a cry of pain could be heard from Tony; another shot had ricocheted off the corner of the spotlight and hit him in the shoulder. He stumbled, fell, hit his head on a protruding cleat and temporarily knocked himself out.

Chris dropped the receiver and was over to him in a flash!

Meanwhile, on the walkie-talkie the Inspector was going ballistic. 'Chris, Chris, what's happening?!'

Mick climbed on board grabbing Chris from behind. She struggled, and kicked Mick in a rather tender spot!

'You bitch!' he exclaimed, striking her across the face. Chris's knees buckled from the force of the blow.

Jake now joined in the fray. Jake never had much time for women which probably stemmed from the cruelty he had experienced at the hands of his mother as a young child. He kicked Chris in the ribs while she was down. Chris cried out then fainted from the shock of the unwarranted brutal attack.

⚡ ⚡ ⚡

A grim-faced Inspector turned to the radio once more. Was that a shot he had heard?

In the present circumstances his only hope now was to involve the rest of *Spectrum* as soon as possible.

Tim, Ian and Mark had been monitoring the interchange. They had left *Spectrum Two* and *Four* securely moored at Stracey Arms a while ago. Now all aboard *Spectrum One* they had reached Breydon Water.

The rain had eased.

⚡ ⚡ ⚡

Jake moved over to the controls of *Spectrum Three*, 'Fine boat, Mick, it should get us to the *Van de Ville* all right and on across the North Sea. Freedom here we come!'

Mick jumped ashore and gave *Spectrum Three* an almighty shove the mud reluctantly gave up its prize. The boat was afloat. Mick looked at Tony. 'Blimey Jake, this is Tony Dale!'

Jake's eyes gleamed. He looked across to Mick leaning over Tony. 'Put them below Mick, tie them up, we don't want our new found hostages to slip away.'

Spectrum Three was now under way once more and heading across Breydon Water. The sky was clearing and the moon appeared.

In the cabin Tony was coming round. Something warm was trickling down the side of his face, it was blood. His shoulder was hurting and he couldn't move, his hands were tied behind his back.

Jake and Mick were talking in the cockpit.

On the opposite bunk Chris was sitting up. She looked worriedly at Tony seeing the blood.

'I'm all right Chris,' he said quietly. 'It probably looks worse than it is.'

Chris struggled with her bindings. Mick had done a good job. Leaning back Chris nearly cried out as her hand hit a nail sticking out of the cabin wall. Seizing the possibility to free herself she started to rub the rope against the nail. The bindings were easing.

Jake, with one hand on the wheel was studying the chart. 'We must be nearly at Haven Lift Bridge, Mick. Can you see the outlet to the Yare?'

Mick looked around, 'Nope. Hey what are those lights over there?' He pointed behind them. Jake turned.

'What the heck!' Just then, over a loud hailer came the words. 'Heave to *Spectrum Three,* this is the Police.'

'Not bloody likely,' muttered Jake as he pushed the accelerator harder, the engine squealed and the boat surged forward with a tremendous bow wash.

A helicopter could be heard in the distance.

Spectrum One was also now on the scene, closing fast from the opposite direction to the police launches.

It was all happening!

The helicopter now hovering above *Spectrum* was high enough not to cause problems from the downdraught of its blades but low enough to light up the area.

Mick fired at the helicopter.

Jake, with one hand steadying the wheel, shot at the boats. The Inspector called over the loud hailer once more, 'Jacob Wright, you'd better give up, you won't get much further.'

'That's what you think.

Mick get that pop star up here on the double.'

Chris quickly laid down as he entered the cabin. Her hands were nearly free.

Mick yanked Tony to his feet and shoved him on deck.

Jake yelled, 'See who I've got with me? Go on shine your spotlight and you should pick him out nicely.'

Tony winced as the bright light caught him full in the face.

'Yes! It's Tony Dale. If you want to see him perform again and I'm sure there're a few hysterical females somewhere wanting that, you'd better give us a free passage out of the country.'

Back below Chris, now free of all bindings, moved to the forward hatchway. She levered herself out on to the cabin roof and contemplated the scene unfolding before her. Lights were highlighting every nook and cranny of *Spectrum Three*. Staying low, she crept along the gunwale to where Mick, rifle in hand, was standing with his back to her.

Bravely Chris jumped into the cockpit, her knowledge of judo coming to the fore. Using an osoto-gari she tripped Mick and the pair tumbled to the floor. The rifle in Mick's hand went flying and fired as it hit the ground. A piercing scream resounded in the night. The bullet had found its mark. Blood was now spurting from a wound high in Chris's chest her life seemed to be draining away.

Jake turned as he heard the skirmish. Tony broke free and lashed out. Jake easily side-stepped him and shot his gun missing Tony by inches. The bullet hit a boarding policeman who fortunately was wearing a bullet-proof vest. Two further policemen were boarding from the other side of Jake and easily over-powered him. Within minutes Jake was disarmed.

Jake and Mick were hustled away into one of the waiting police boats. Enraged, Jake's last words as he was pushed into the craft were 'I'll get even with you *Spectrum* if it's the last thing I do!'

Tim manoeuvred his boat alongside *Spectrum Three*. Ian and Mark leapt across just in time to catch Tony who was on the verge of collapsing again.

The Inspector was kneeling by the side of Chris, inwardly berating himself for allowing such a thing to happen. He was doing his best to staunch the blood flow and felt her pulse.

The helicopter moved in and a stretcher was lowered.

'Chris….' whispered Tony.

The Inspector stood away from Chris allowing the paramedics to do their job.

'Don't despair Tony, there is a faint pulse so fingers crossed.'

CHAPTER SEVEN

It was a lengthy night for all. Sam and Grace had dropped everything and now in Norfolk were sitting with their sons in one of the hospital waiting rooms. The duty nurse had left hot drinks and biscuits but no one was tempted.

Tony had come off lightly when compared to Chris. Sam had popped in to see him, but he was fast asleep having been sedated. He had concussion and a very sore shoulder where the bullet had clipped the edge of the bone.

It didn't take long for the news to break of Tony's adventure, if you can call it that. Not only was the hospital switchboard jammed next morning but journalists were at the door hoping to get an exclusive.

It was touch and go with Chris. The procedure to remove the bullet was tricky but it had missed the vital organs. Chris lost a lot of blood not only from the initial bleed but during the operation as well.

Eventually, Chris came to. The nurse with her wiped her brow, 'Welcome to the land of the living Chris,' she said.

Chris smiled, 'How's Tony? Can I see him?'

'Steady on, we'll have you back where you started if we're not careful. I'll have a word with the doctor and we'll see in the morning. Now you get some rest.'

The next day when she awoke sitting by her bed was Tony, arm in a sling, but otherwise unscathed. Tony leaned over and kissed her tenderly. 'You were extremely brave darling but a bit foolhardy as well. You terrified me,' he said huskily, gently stroking the side of her face.

She looked into those crinkly brown eyes she loved so well and smiled. 'I think I scared myself! I won't do that again in a hurry but what about you? Are you alright?'

'All good, and they're allowing me out today.' He gave her hand a quick squeeze and a final passionate kiss. 'The boys are panting to see you and I don't think I'll be very popular if I outstayed my time limit. I'll let them tell you the news. See you tomorrow.'

Tony swapped places with her brothers, 'Hi sis, how's things? Mum and dad send their love and should be with you later.'

Chris struggled to sit up, 'Put it this way, I've known better days! What happened with Jake and Mick? What's the big news?'

'Well to answer your first question they came up before the Magistrates Court yesterday and we went along to the Hearing. Jake and Mick have been charged, amongst other things, with the possession of fire arms. They have been committed to the Crown Court as their crimes were beyond the scope of the Magistrates Court. Their case will probably be heard within the next day or two. Hopefully that will be the last we will hear of them,' said Tim.

As they say …… how wrong can you be!

'To answer your next question sis, we've made it, we're actually number one!'

'Number 1, I don't believe it.'

'Yes, here, look there's an article in *Disc* about it.' Mark handed her the magazine. At that moment the nurse came in and shooed the boys away. 'See you tomorrow sis,' they said.

Chris laid back against the pillows and read the article and not to mention the news she seemed to have missed over the past week.

The mystery group known as Spectrum who were recently involved in another adventure on the Norfolk Broads, where Tony Dale was injured, have made Number 1. They would have appeared on 'Top of the Pops' but one of them is still recovering in hospital.

Now that this brilliant foursome has made it to the top, will we be introduced to their true identity? When we attempted to find out more from their Musical Director, Laurie Johnson, he remained as vague as usual.

Chris put the magazine down and dozed off.

❄ ❄ ❄

Back in Kent June was recovering well and looked around her at the flowers and *Get Well* messages that had been sent to her by her school friends. Something was bothering her. There was nothing from Chris. She picked up the magazine again and reread the articles concerning Tony Dale and also *Spectrum* making number 1 with *Freewheelin*.

The bell went for the start of visiting. Ginger came in with yet more good wishes and cards, but still nothing from Chris. Ginger noticed *Disc* laying on June's bed. She picked up the magazine.

'Did you read the article June? You know the one about *Spectrum* now top of the Charts. That makes the organist well and truly your number 1 doesn't it?' June nodded, 'but why so glum?'

'It's just that I haven't heard from Chris.'

Ginger raised her eyebrows. 'You're kidding me. I thought she would be one of the first. I thought your mum had contacted her?'

'There was no one in when she rang so she sent a letter.'

'I bet Chris just couldn't be bothered!' Ginger exclaimed throwing the magazine back onto the bed.

'No it's all right Ginger, leave it.'

The bell went for the end of visiting so Ginger had to go.

☙ ☙ ☙

The next morning Tony was back visiting Chris, 'Oh here's some mail which Matt has asked me to bring in for you.'

She sifted through them and one caught her attention. It had a Kentish post mark. She opened it. What colour she had paled into insignificance.

'What is it Kid? Not bad news I hope?'

She shook her head and handed Tony the letter, 'It's June, I must go to her.' She sat up too quickly. Her head swam and she was quite relieved to lie back against the pillows again.

Tony read the letter. 'There's nothing you can do darling this letter is dated a while ago so June must be well on the mend.'

'Possibly Tony, but I must ring her mother to be sure.'

'All right Kid, if it makes you feel better, I'll get the phone.'

Chris dialed the number, June's mother answered. 'Mrs. Ferguson, its Chris, how's June?'

'Humph, you took your time young lady for someone who is supposed to be her best friend.'

'I know Mrs. Ferguson, I'm sorry but circumstances prevented me, how is she?'

'She's much better than she was, thank you, but if it's not too much trouble, she would appreciate it if you could spare the time to pop in and see her.'

'I'm sorry Mrs. Ferguson I won't be able to make it for a few weeks. Can you give her my best please?'

'Humph,' she said once more, 'A fine friend you turn out to be,' and slammed down the phone.

Chris miserably replaced the receiver on the hook. Tony tried to comfort her. 'Why don't you tell them the truth?'

'You know that's impossible Tony, I'll just have to grin and bear it.'

On that point Tony had to leave. Chris laid back and tried to relax but all she could picture was June, her best friend June.

❧ ❧ ❧

A couple of weeks later Chris was discharged from hospital. Tony picked her up and drove her to Spindle Hall. When she arrived her mum, dad and Jessie all made a huge fuss of her, but of Tim, Mark and Ian there was no sign.

'Where are the boys?'

'Oh around,' replied Tony vaguely, 'Quick Chris the programme starts in a minute.'

'What programme? What are you going on about?'

He ignored the remark and yanked her down on the sofa beside him, Matt turned on the T.V. and everyone sat down, 'Top of the Pops' was on.

Gradually the programme reached the number one slot. Chris, although enjoying the spectacle looked across at Tony and her parents, why was there an air of expectation?

All was revealed.

The Presenter took to the stage. '*Before we play the number 1 Freewheelin, we have a special presentation to make to Spectrum. Unfortunately, as one of them is still recovering from the incident we all know about, we can't have Spectrum playing live, but we do have the other three members. Here are three-quarters of Spectrum.*'

Chris turned to all in amazement, 'Go on watching,' Tony said.

There was rousing applause and even some screams and onto the stage walked her brothers.

'Here comes the best bit Chris, watch....'

Tim moved up to the microphone as the presenter was saying, '*I have great pleasure in presenting you with this.*'

And much to Chris's surprise he handed to Tim a silver disc, she turned to everyone. 'Have we really won that?'

'Sure thing darling,' Tony raised his glass, 'and here's to the next quarter of a million.'

❧ ❧ ❧

Chris wandered back to school on the first day of the Autumn Term not looking forward to the reception she might get, the sky was overcast and there was a faint drizzle in the air which matched her mood admirably. Tony's words last night did their best to cheer her up but that probably won't help her. She had tried to ring June when she returned from Norfolk yesterday but had had no reply.

Just then there was a patter of feet behind her; Sandra ran up and grabbed her arm.

Chris let out a yelp. 'Oh Chris, I'm sorry, does it still hurt?' cried an anguished Sandra.

'Yes it does, still never mind, you weren't to know.'

The cousins had come to a halt by then. 'Chris did you really do all that that was in the papers, you know with those escaped convicts and everything?'

'Something like that, we'd better move on or we're going to be late.'

'You're not looking forward to it Chris are you? It's because of June, isn't it?'

She nodded, 'Anyway, come on Sandra, here goes....'

In the school building the pair of them separated, Chris stood outside the door of the Prefects Room, composed herself, her arm was still aching where Sandra had grabbed it. She took a deep breath and entered. A hush descended. She swallowed nervously. 'Sorry to hear about you June, are you okay now?'

'Yes thanks Chris,' and moved away.

Chris miserably went to her locker. While she had her back turned June looked at Chris with an odd expression on her face. Just then Belinda came in as the bell sounded, 'All on duty girls,' she called.

Ginger brushed heavily past Chris. Chris held back the cry rising to her lips and abruptly sat down.

June noticed her pallor, hesitated, 'Are you all right Chris?'

'Come on June, don't be concerned about her,' said Ginger, 'she wasn't worried about you when you were so ill,' and with that remark yanked June out of the room.

Chris started to say something, stopped, and characteristically shrugged her shoulders.

Belinda seeing Chris's colour took pity. 'Are you sure you're all right?'

'Yes, thanks Belinda. It's just that I hurt my arm during the hols and Ginger knocked it just in the wrong place.'

'I see, well anyway you've a free period now haven't you, so you might as well stay here. I'll cover your duty.' Belinda closed the door quietly. Chris dozed off.

June and Ginger were walking along the corridor. 'You were a bit hard on Chris, Ginger, she didn't look at all well.'

'Look June, save your breath, you're just making excuses for her.'

'Ginger, she's your friend as well.'

'Was my friend you mean! If she was concerned about you as much as you seem to care for her she would have had the decency to make contact ...'

'She couldn't,' muttered a voice behind them.

They spun round and saw Sandra, 'What do you mean Sandra?' asked June.

Sandra looked around her, 'er nothing,' she said and started to go away. Ginger pulled her back, 'Come on Sandra, give.'

'I can't. Chris would be rather annoyed if I did, not to mention the others, especially Tony.'

'Others, Tony, Sandra just what are you getting at?' asked Ginger.

Sandra once more tried to leave them.

'Half a second Ginger,' said June, 'Things are suddenly falling into place, the likeness, the mystery male.'

Sandra turned back, 'Oh no,' she said, 'They'll slay me.'

'No, they won't because if I'm right we all owe Chris one heck of an apology.' Sandra looked up at June. 'We won't tell Sandra, I promise we won't tell anyone else.'

'Will somebody let me in on the secret as well?' said an exasperated Ginger. 'So, I'll also know what I'm supposed not to tell.'

'Correct me if I'm wrong, Sandra,' said June, 'Ginger, when I was in hospital do you remember what hit the headlines?'

She thought for a second, but only a second, 'Of course the biggest headline of the lot was Tony Dale being shot, but what's that got to do with Chris?'

'Am I on the right track Sandra?'

She nodded.

'Well, Ginger, think again, who was with Tony Dale?'

'*Spectrum* of course, but I still can't see what you're getting at!'

'Oh you are dim Ginger,' said a frustrated June. 'Who else was hurt?'

'The girl of *Spectrum*.' Light started dawning. 'Oh no, is the girl Chris? Sandra is it Chris?'

Sandra looked from one to the other.

'You're going to have to tell us everything now,' said June. 'We promise not to tell another soul.'

'Promise' said Sandra.

'Promise,' said Ginger and June.

'Yes, it's true, Chris is the girl and Tim her twin, whom you know as well June.' (June nodded). 'Mark and Ian, her other brothers are *Spectrum* and Tony Dale is the unknown male who gives Chris a lift to school on the odd occasion.'

Ginger laughed, 'If only Rachel knew how close she's been to her idol without realising it. Anyway June, you and I have a lot of apologising to do.'

'Thanks Sandra. Is Chris fit yet?'

Sandra shook her head. 'She shouldn't really be back at school.'

'Oh, I see. Well Sandra you'd better be off,' said June 'and thanks. We promise once again not to spread it around.'

With that Sandra scampered off and June and Ginger turned back towards the Prefects Room. They quietly opened the door and saw Chris asleep in the chair. June gently shook her shoulder.

'Hi June, Ginger, what's up?'

'We're sorry Chris,'

'Yes,' echoed Ginger, 'we're very sorry.'

'Sorry? Sorry about what?' Chris said warily.

'Sandra......'

'What has that cousin of mine been saying now?'

'She told us the truth Chris of who you are, and also why you couldn't get to see June.'

'She had no right, wait until I see her,' said Chris, rising, if a bit shakily, from her chair.

June gently pushed her back. 'No, don't Chris. She didn't volunteer the information, we persuaded her and we promise we won't tell a soul.'

'Yes, Chris, we promise,' said Ginger.

And that is where we leave Chris, June and Ginger until the next time

CHRISTMAS AT SPINDLE

CHAPTER EIGHT

Chris walked to school on a crisp September morning. There was a little wind and every now and then it whisked up the leaves and for a short while there was a flurry of brown and gold, just like a miniature whirlpool.

It had been a challenging start to the Autumn Term after the events back in the summer holiday.

'I wouldn't want to go through that time again,' she muttered to herself and hurried a bit as she noticed it was nearly 9 o'clock. She turned the corner into Rock Avenue and saw her young cousin.

'Hello Sandra, how are things?'

Sandra pushed a strand of auburn hair away from her face.

'My, you look happy, I wonder why?' said Chris.

'You know very well. It's true, isn't it? It's not a joke that while mum and dad are away I'm staying with you at half-term?'

Sandra was now in full flow. Chris tried to butt in..........

'We will be at Spindle Hall, won't we? Will Tony be there?' her voice gradually reaching a peak with excitement.

'Keep your voice down. Do you want the whole street to know about *Spectrum*?'

'I can't help it Chris. It's absolutely brilliant that I'm going to Norfolk again after so many years. To be in the company of *Spectrum* and Tony for a whole week is a dream'…. (And what a story to wave in front of Barbara, if only I was allowed to.) She thought.

'Sorry Sandra, no Tony. Fantastic news for him though, he has just started a tour of North America promoting his latest album.'

Her face fell. 'Cheer up, you'll still have us and the Broads.'

By now they had reached school, Sandra disappeared along the corridor to her classroom while Chris, as usual for first thing in the morning, entered the Prefects' Room to go to her locker. For once there was no one in the room. She took out the various text books required for the day, and paused. Sandra's comment had reminded her that she wouldn't be seeing Tony for nearly two months. She sighed. Closing the locker, deep in thought, she left for her lessons.

꒳ ꒳ ꒳

The weekend arrived. Instead of Kent they were at Spindle. Sam had been called to an important meeting at Neatishead and had suggested that they might as well all go to Norfolk as the weather seemed to be holding.

Just after lunch Chris was sitting on the jetty by the side of Spindle Broad, her feet dangling above the water line. Her mum had gone to Ranworth to help with the Church's Autumn Flower Show and the boys were off on some adventure with the local sea scouts. The sun was shining, warm for the time of year. The reeds along the Broads edge had grown tremendously over the summer and now slightly obscured her from the sun's rays. Yellow and white waterlilies were still in bloom and the odd water lily leaf, slightly below the surface, had tiny fish making the most of the warmth in their mini pools. Whirligig beetles appeared to be chasing each other in never ending circles on the water. Migrant and brown hawker dragonflies, true to their name, were hawking around the Broad to catch some tasty morsel.

She felt completely relaxed. Relieved that June and Ginger were in the know at last. Two very good friends like two solid rocks with whom she could now talk to about her life with *Spectrum* and more importantly her love for Tony.

❧ ❧ ❧

It was the first day of a new week, a wet one at that. The weekend had come and gone. With mock examinations on the horizon Chris was a wee bit guilty in not having done any revision. She entered the Prefects Room. The buzz of conversation was the half-term holiday. June smiled at her. She was still a little in awe of what her friend had achieved. She was also a bit chuffed at now being part of the pretence in keeping Chris's secret.

'Hi Chris,' said Rachel. 'Belinda and I were just weighing up the opportunities for half-term. No school trip to look forward to this time. How about you? Are you going away as you did in the spring?'

'Yes I am.' She looked across at June. 'Actually June, Ginger and I are off together for the week.......'

The door burst open... It was Ginger... She always had problems getting up in the mornings, especially on Mondays! 'I heard that. Have you told them where yet?'

she teasingly said, taking off her coat and splattering raindrops over everyone.

Ginger can be impetuous.

Was Chris's secret as a fully-fledged member of *Spectrum* about to be revealed?

June and Chris held their breaths…

'We're off to Norfolk, we're boating on the Broads,' said an excited Ginger, just refraining from jumping up and down.

Phew…. secret safe.

'Oh, you, lucky people,' said an envious Rachel. 'Are you going on a *Spectrum* hunt, you know, exploring that creek up from Malthouse Broad which we later found out led to Spindle Broad?'

'Well, you never know whom we'll bump into,' answered June.

Belinda was also a wee bit envious, but trying not to show it.

'Don't forget the school's Guy Fawkes' Party. Are you still going to help build the bonfire with the wood from your uncle's orchard?'

'Rest assured Belinda,' said Chris, 'we'll be there, complete with bonfire builders.

❧ ❧ ❧

A few days later Chris and her friends arrived in Norfolk. The trees aligning the driveway to Spindle Hall were now bereft of leaves; it was like walking on a golden carpet as they approached the house. The front-door was open. The boys dropped the cases. Sandra looked around her memories were surfacing of her last visit. She was then just ten years old. Jessie appeared.

'Hi Jessie, do you remember me?'

'Of course, I remember a scallywag like you, but my! You've changed. So tall.... So elegant.' Sandra did a pirouette and almost stumbled, much to the others amusement.

After lunch Sandra and Mark caught the bus into Norwich. The cousins shared similar passions and were kindred spirits. They were both roughly the same age. Mark was eager to see the new exhibition in the Cathedral. One of the dinosaurs usually at the Natural History Museum in London was touring the country and was on show in the area for a couple of weeks. Sandra was only too happy to accompany him. He was so clever at finding unusual activities.

The rest of them wandered in the direction of the Broad. Like the front of the Hall the only greenery now were the holly trees boasting a good crop of red berries ready for Christmas decorations.

Tim, with a cheeky look in June's direction said: 'What would you and Ginger like to do, as our honoured guests?' and gave them a long sweeping bow.

They laughed. 'Maybe look at the boats,' said June.

'Matt usually leaves one in the water for half-term.'

Ian quickly butted in. 'And it's mine, *Spectrum Two*,' he said, almost puffing out his chest in the process.

'What about the Christmas holidays?' asked Ginger. 'Are you still about then?'

'Well, it depends on the weather. If the snow comes early and the Broads begin to freeze, we normally have them all out of the water. On the other hand, if the weather is set for a mild period, then we might have them all in.'

They reached the boathouse where *Spectrum Two* was moored. June and Ginger had their first real close-up view of a *Spectrum*. The colourful wavy lines on the side of the boat reflected in the still water of the broad.

'Come on you two' said Ian. 'hop aboard.' Ian held out his arm for Ginger and Tim for June. This didn't go unnoticed by Chris.

June and Ginger were given a guided tour of *Spectrum Two* by the proud skipper.

'I say you lot, do you fancy a spin?' called Tim who was still on the quay standing by one of the mooring ropes.

'You bet,' replied Ginger enthusiastically.

Ian took the controls and Tim cast off for'ard whilst Chris cast off aft. *Spectrum Two*, now with all on board, motored quietly along the creek. Ginger and June looked at each other.

'What's up with you two, something wrong?' asked Chris.

'We were both thinking how ominous this waterway looked when we first saw it back in the summer. It's quite unbelievable how gorgeous it is where Spindle Hall is situated, but this….' June once more looked at the dark forbidding trees which seemed to reach endlessly into the sky. 'It's so, eerie.'

'Yes I can see that to an outsider it does appear sinister and unrelenting, but I suppose I'm used to it. All things considered, that's helpful from our point of view as no one will come up the creek.'

'But suppose someone was feeling a bit venturesome surely they could easily sail up it?' said Ginger.

Tim shook his head. 'They would have a slight problem. You see, there's a chain under the water at the end of our creek and unless you know your way across, you wouldn't be able to get very far.'

At that point Ian did a quick manoeuvre which caught June unawares. Tim reached out just in the nick of time to stop her falling. She recovered her balance. 'Was that where it was?' she asked breathlessly, for more than one reason! He nodded, acting cool, though his heightened colouring told another story!

They had now reached the River Bure.

'Well crew,' Ian said, 'which direction? Do we go left to Horning and Wroxham or right to Thurne Mill?'

'Let's go to Horning,' said Ginger, 'I'd like to see all those pretty thatched houses along the river bank again.'

They motored along the river, a grey heron flying across their path, or as Norfolk people would say, a hanser. It landed on the opposite bank taking up its normal stance, waiting for some unsuspecting fish or eel to swim by.

Due to the peaty ground, some of the houses they were now passing were standing at peculiar angles, one was leaning forward while another had sunk so much that the top storey was now used as the ground-floor! By the Swan Inn, they were hailed.

'Hi folks,' shouted Inspector Devenport.

Ian steered the boat alongside the quay. Tim jumped ashore with the mooring rope.

'Tim, I'm glad I've managed to catch you all,' said the Inspector.

'Are you in Norfolk for Christmas?'

'Yes, we are.'

'You couldn't by any chance do me a favour?'

Tim looked at him with a wry smile. 'It's not the Policemen's Christmas Party for the children by any chance?'

'Umm yes, good guess Tim. I know how important it is to keep your true identities a secret, but can you think of a way to join in the fun and maybe play the odd tune or two? I'll no doubt be dressed in the white beard and red jacket,' he said, raising his eyebrows.

'Of course, we'd be delighted to' replied Chris. 'How about if we dress up as your elves, complete with animal make up face effects. Tim, Ian are you game?'

'That's fine by us,' they said in unison, as a constable arrived on the scene, breathless, a look of worry on his face.

'Sir, you are urgently wanted on the radio.'

'Thank you, Constable.' A small wave, and both swiftly dashed away.

Ginger and June were once more in awe of Chris. They hadn't fully appreciated that *Spectrum* were held in such high esteem.

Spectrum Two slipped its moorings and carried on its way once more; they neared the first entrance to Wroxham Broad and turned into it.

'Well girls,' said Ian, 'you have the Queen of the Broads.'

'It seems so peaceful,' said June as she looked around her at a Broad surrounded by alder and willow trees. A cormorant, dark coloured with a white patch under its chin was perched on a depth gauge. Its wings outstretched, possibly drying them or to aid digestion of its latest meal. A pair of swans, with a couple of first year young, glided serenely towards the nearby reed bed. Every so often a tern wheeled and dived into the broad to catch a fish. Such a sight!

Chris pointed at a building on the opposite bank. 'That's the Clubhouse of the sailing club,' she said, 'and those pens over there are usually full of sailing yachts and motor cruisers. Woe betide any motorboat which gets in the way of a sailing yacht on Regatta Day.'

'How big are the boats?' asked Ginger. 'My uncle has a Wayfarer dinghy. Are they the same size?'

'Well, there are some Wayfarers which reach 16 foot,' said Tim. 'You would be surprised at the variety of dinghies and yachts now available on the market. The Sailing Club has a few of the Classes. The International Stars for instance, are about 20 feet long with a wide expanse of sail, probably the largest keel boat used at this Club for racing. A slightly smaller Class is the White Boats, built of timber. The Yeoman is the fiberglass version of the White Boats. These boats, as the title implies, have to be painted white and usually have names of butterflies or moths.'

'What do you mean by calling it Class?' said June. 'It sounds like that they should be in school.'

Tim chuckled. 'I suppose it does seem a bit like that. No, it just means that all the boats/dinghies in a specific Class are of the same specification.'

'Oh.....'

'However, the younger members of the Club are more likely to be found with Enterprises, Top Hats or Mirrors. A fun dinghy which has just come on the market is the Laser. You could say it is a small dinghy cum surf board with a single sail about 10 feet long; a nice nippy craft. Unfortunately it has a habit of capsizing.'

'Especially at Easter!' added Ian quizzically.

June and Ginger looked at Tim. 'Oh it's only because I was on one at Easter and the wind blew at the wrong time, caught me unawares and I sort of catapulted off the rig into the water.'

'It's all so fascinating,' said June. 'I hadn't realised there was so much to sailing.'

'Many five and six year olds start their sailing in an Optimist, a pram dinghy about eight feet long with a single sail,' said Chris. 'This craft has been on the market for many years. I tried one once but it was a bit of a tight squeeze for me!'

Ian, seeing Ginger's look of amazement said: 'when we get back to Spindle, if you like, I'll dig out some more information about sailing craft both past and present so it won't just be a string of names.'

'Oh yes, I would like that very much, thanks,' said Ginger, trying to be nonplussed, but her face showing something entirely different.

June and Chris exchanged looks behind Ginger's back. 'One down and one to go,' she mouthed to June discreetly.

Tim carried on, 'however it's not all about sailing, there are motor cruisers as well. One that always causes some amusement is called *Mamma's Mink*. You could imagine a wife hoping for a fur coat but ending up seeing a boat!'

Their attention was then drawn by a majestic looking craft, as June and Ginger were having their first glimpse of a wherry, sailing quietly past them with hardly a ripple breaking the surface. Its black sail stretched the whole length with the single mast towering above, appearing to reach the top of the trees.

'Wow!' was their reaction.

'That's the Albion,' said Tim. 'It is 124 years old, one of only two commercial wherries still in existence. Wherries used to be very common along the Broads network. In fact for a while the only form of transport for both passengers and cargo. The cargo could consist of such delights as sugar beet and manure.'

'But there are only a couple of people on board. How can so few people sail such an impressive craft?' asked Ginger. 'Also, how can such a tall boat get beneath bridges? From what I've seen on the Broads it will have to pass under so many of them.'

'Mmmm.... let me explain,' said Tim. 'The mast swivels on its foot so that it can be lowered by one person. In fact, the largest wherry ever built, the Wonder, used to take coal out to steamers off Yarmouth. In the mid-nineteenth century commercial traffic was at its height with some 300 wherries plying for trade. Some captains were not amiss to doing a bit of smuggling on the side.'

'That's amazing!' said a smitten June.

'The smaller wherries used to transport garden produce from Ludham to Yarmouth. Two of them had very amusing names' Chris added, 'Wasp and Cabbage!'

Ginger was still taken with the Albion. 'Is there a reason for the black sail?' She asked. 'All the sailing boats I've seen so far have white ones.'

'It's quite a saga. Originally, they were white,' answered Chris. 'But they used to get too dirty, so they were coated with herring oil, which turned them red. It proved a disaster. Rats found the red coated sails very tasty, munching them and making lots of holes. The next move was to paint the sails with tar in order to avoid any more problems.'

The light was beginning to fade so Ian turned the boat around and they made tracks back to Spindle. However, Tim's attention had been caught with something else which he hastily pointed out to the others. Binoculars in hand he had seen a group of marsh harriers flying overhead.

Ginger for once dumbstruck looked at the fantastic sight. Tim handed her the binoculars.

'No…. no Ginger, the other way round,' he jokingly said.

'Oh right.' Ginger was looking through the big lenses instead of the small ones. A natural mistake frequently encountered when faced with binoculars for the first time.

Chris handed another pair to June so she too could enjoy the spectacle. She held them the right way round!

'They're beautiful,' said June. 'I like the way they glide. How come there are so many?'

'Well….' said Tim. 'From now until early February many raptors spend the days feeding in the fields and the nights roosting in the depths of a reed bed for safety. At one time in the Broads it was always hen harriers in the winter and marsh harriers in the summer. Now we are more likely to find marsh harriers all the year round in Norfolk, and a scarcity of hen harriers.'

'I see,' said June.

It was quite dark by the time they reached Spindle. Matt had left a couple of lights on to help in the mooring of *Spectrum Two* and to go to the house.

Dinner was brilliant, everyone chatting about the superb day they all had and Jessie having excelled – as usual – at her role as *the Chef*. Her fish pie was scrumptious, but the blackberry and apple crumble and custard got all the votes. Not a crumb left.

Afterwards, true to his word, Ian invited Ginger to his cubby-hole.

Sandra and Mark had also disappeared. Knowing Mark they were probably consulting some reference book about the different kinds of dinosaurs that had been in existence in prehistoric times.

In the lounge Chris was quietly strumming her guitar. June looked up from the magazine she was reading.

'Chris is *Spectrum* going to make any more records?'

At that moment Tim came into the room and hearing her question said 'Ah... funny you should ask... we very much hope to. *Freewheelin* is now dropping out of the Charts and Laurie has been pressurising us to produce another piece promptly.'

Chris laid her guitar to one side. 'Actually June, the next one we hope to do is another of Tim and Ian's compositions, do you want to hear it?'

'Oh YES!'

Tim sat down at the piano and started playing, June by his shoulder, both glowing with pleasure. Chris picked up her guitar and joined in.

The last note faded out. Tim turned bashfully towards June.

'What do you think?' he asked. 'It's obviously more up-tempo.'

'Oh Gosh, this is so beautiful and different from *Freewheelin*. Would you mind if I asked to hear it played by all of you, so that I have the complete picture?'

'That is an excellent idea! Anything to oblige, Miss:' said Tim.

'Let's find the others.' He went to the door and called them. Ian and Ginger were the first to appear.

'We'll have to go and unearth Mark, I expect he's already in the Den. Knowing Sandra, she will have persuaded him to let her play on his drums.'

In the Den they found Sandra beating her heart out.

'That's terrible,' said Tim. 'I don't know how you can stand it Mark?'

No answer. 'Mark!' he yelled, and tapped him on the shoulder.

Mark spun round.

'Sorry Tim, what did you say?', and proceeded to take out his ear plugs.

The others laughed. He shrugged his shoulders.

'Fancy playing our new number to June and Ginger?' asked Tim.

'Rather! Sandra…. come on Sandra…off!'

Sandra moved away from the drum kit and sprawled on the floor. 'I enjoyed that, even if all of you think it was terrible.'

June and Ginger sat on the giant beanbags and looked around them. The walls were decorated in warm apricot, the dormer windows had bright print curtains, and in the alcoves were pictures of sailing craft on the Broads. There was also a sofa and a couple of armchairs. You would have thought that the electronic gear seemed out of place, but somehow it blended with its surroundings. Pride of place had been given to the silver disc *Spectrum* had won for *Freewheelin*.

'Do your neighbours ever complain about the noise?' asked Ginger as Tim ran his fingers along the keys of his electric organ.

'No, the room is soundproofed. Is our audience ready?'

June laid back on the cushions with a contented smile on her face.

'This is super! I say Ginger, our own private performance of *Spectrum*.'

Tim was right. The contrast between *Spectrum*'s two pieces was terrific. *Freewheelin* was silky smooth and ideal to smooch to. Their latest sound was a different kettle of fish. This was definitely one to start the evening with, extremely lively and culminating in a fabulous drum solo.

'Wow.......' said Ginger. 'That was BRILLIANT! It was so wild! My ears are still ringing. What are you going to call it?'

'We haven't been able to find the right title yet but thanks Ginger! You've hit the nail on the head!' exclaimed Ian.

'Tim, she is right, it has to be something .... WILD. How about *Ringing Wild*?'

'Maybe .... *Running Wild*?' suggested Mark.

'That's it kid brother!' said Tim. 'Let's put it to the vote. Who is in favour of *Running Wild*?'

'Yeah!' four voices shouted.

For once all were in agreement! *Running Wild* was now ready for the discerning public to judge.

꙰ ꙰ ꙰

The next day was delightful as they walked in the woods around the Hall even if the beginning of the path was a bit damp from the early morning dew.

The girls stood silently basking in the warmth of the autumn sunshine. What breadth of wind there was helped gossamer and seed heads float through the air, the seeds eventually falling to the ground to spring once more into life the following summer. A bumble bee landed briefly on Chris, no doubt for a bit of extra warmth before hibernating.

Birds were singing defying the fact that winter was just around the corner. A cheeky robin perched on a nearby bush sang as if to say 'Christmas is nearly here'.

The rushes in the damp grass were neatly clipped, no doubt by some passing deer. A grey squirrel, ever watchful for danger, was busy picking up a discarded acorn. Every so often leaves, now golden in colour, would float down to the ground and blackbirds sifted through them to find some tasty morsel.

In amongst the leaf litter, poking their heads up into the autumn sunshine, were the fruiting heads of fungi, one of which was the distinctive *Fly Agaric* with its bright red cap and white warts. Ginger hoped a little pixie might appear sitting on it, but no luck! Poisonous and infamous for its psychoactive and hallucinogenic properties, the *Fly Agaric* became the first ever flytrap when mashed in milk. Flies attracted by the delicious scent would fall in the deadly liquid and drown!

The sun eventually disappeared behind a cloud and the temperature dropped, so it was back to the Hall for hot drinks and tasty scones.

The rest of the week flew by and soon it was time to leave Norfolk.

'See you at Christmas Jessie,' said Chris, Tim, Ian, and Mark, all giving her a big hug.

Ginger June and Sandra presented her with a small present: 'Thank you for looking after us so well.'

Jessie dabbed her eyes. 'It was a pleasure, as usual.'

Jessie hated it when they returned to Kent, the days seemed so dull without them. It wasn't the same in the cottage in the grounds where she, husband Frank and son Matt lived. They all missed the hustle, bustle and excitement when *Spectrum*, Sam and Grace were around.

For *Spectrum*, and of course Sandra, June and Ginger, the return to Kent heralded Guy Fawkes' night just around the corner.

For Chris, sure, Guy Fawkes' night was going to be a lot of fun.

However....

Her inner thoughts for the 5th November were only about Tony's return from his concert tour in America.

She longed to see him again.

CHAPTER NINE

Luckily November the 5th dawned bright and sunny.

Commonly known as Guy Fawkes' Night, the commemoration of the failed 1605 Gunpowder Plot had now become a hugely popular social event.

Fireworks symbolising the gunpowder and a bonfire with an effigy of Guy Fawkes placed at the top, provided a lot of fun. Families would hold displays in their gardens and neighbourly competitions of who could build the largest bonfire took place.

This year Mrs. MacDonald, Chris's Headmistress, thought it would be rather nice to involve the whole school for this celebration and welcomed the proposition of Chris's Uncle Nick's field as a venue with open arms.

Mrs. MacDonald made the announcement in the assembly and explained that Guy Fawkes was caught guarding explosives beneath the House of Lords, shortly before the attempt to blow up Parliament. A history teacher, she was always fond of details, pointing out that the conspirators were Catholics whose aim was to assassinate Protestant King James I.

She even added the gory description of Guy Fawkes's death. Just before being hanged he fell from the scaffold and broke his neck. After that, his lifeless body was quartered, as was the custom.

Early in the morning Chris, Ian, Mark and Tim arrived on their scooters at *Marygold,* Uncle Nick and

Aunt Jackie's farm. Sandra was riding pillion behind Tim. Meg, Sandra's mother and Grace's sister, was always wary of letting Sandra do such things. But Tim had reassured her: 'No antics on the road, it's a promise!'

It was also Mark's first scooter trip having just passed his test. Another reason for a cautious drive!

A tractor was parked in the yard its trailer piled high with wood ready for the bonfire. Nick, burley and tanned from a lifetime working the fields, jumped down from the cab. Chris gave him a quick hug. 'We're so grateful uncle, that we've been able to use *Marygold* for my School's Guy Fawkes evening.'

'My pleasure,' he said, running his hand through his thinning once jet-black hair.

'I understand that you two,' looking at Chris and Tim, 'have successfully passed your driving tests,' he said.

'Passed first time!' they proudly replied in unison.

'Both of you have nagged me long enough to drive a tractor again... Catch!' Uncle Nick threw the keys.

Tim was the fastest.

'Th....thanks,' mumbled a surprised Tim.

Nick and Jackie were well aware of *Spectrum*. Childless like his sister Jean, they keenly followed Grace's children's rise to stardom. An optimist, he was ever hopeful that one of his nieces or nephews might eventually take on the family business.

His farm was a traditional Kentish fruit farm.

Kent, the Garden of England, had excelled in fruit growing since the Romans first introduced the apple.

Nick had orchards of Cox's Orange Pippin, Bramley and Conference Pears. Sometimes he had the odd flock of sheep from a neighbouring farm grazing amongst his fruit trees.   Like many others in the area he also grew hops for beer. Although the majority of the picking was now mechanised, in his grandfather's day London Eastenders would traditionally holiday away from the smoke of the capital to take part in the annual harvest, and breathing in the clean air of the countryside. It was also interesting to note that the hop pickers were paid in tokens for each day's work. At the end of hop picking the tokens were then exchanged for real money. The story goes that this was to ensure that the hop pickers would have some cash to take home with them instead of spending it all on ale!

The iconic oast houses used for the drying of the hops are to Kent as windmills are to Norfolk. These conical buildings, usually two storeys in height, would have hops spread out on the upper floor. Hot air rises from the wood or charcoal fire below to dry them and a cowl in the roof turns in the wind allowing excess heat to escape.

The first oast houses date from the seventeenth century but many of them have now been either converted into homes or demolished. It is a great shame that such a symbolic building of the brewing industry has gradually disappeared from the countryside.

Rachel was the first to see them arrive at the field and ran to meet them. Tim and Ian climbed out of the cab whilst Chris, Sandra and Mark jumped down from the trailer. Ian, a little envious that his older brother had had the opportunity to drive the tractor, was itching to get behind the wheel.

'Hi Chris, you made it back then, and with the wood, great.'

'Did you doubt us?' said Chris jokingly and proceeded to introduce her brothers as June and Ginger joined them.

Rachel, impetuous as ever, half listening to Chris's reply was only really interested in one thing. 'Did you see anything of *Spectrum* whilst in Norfolk?' she said excitedly.

Chris smiled, little did Rachel suspect that the four of them were standing in front of her.

June piped up. 'Oh, we went for a boat ride, did some exploring, but unfortunately no *Spectrum*.'

More people arrived to help unload the wood, thus ending any further conversation.

The bonfire took longer than expected to build but by early afternoon the tractor and trailer were duly returned to their uncle.

'See you later,' called Chris. Nick waved.

Spectrum, plus Sandra of course, were now back on the scooters and rode the short distance home to a rather belated lunch come tea.

As they turned into their road there was a rather familiar car parked outside the house. Chris was off her scooter in a flash. Tony had heard them and had the front-door open. She ran into his outstretched arms.

He gave her a warm embrace and a quick peck on the cheek.

'How's my number two fan?' he said to Sandra. 'Any more records for me to sign?'

'That's a fatal question,' said Mark, 'You'll never get any peace now.'

Sandra ignored him. 'Are you around for long Tony?' she asked.

'Just the weekend; I then have a concert tour interspersed with several recording sessions from now until Christmas. Talking of recordings Tim, Ian, how's that follow-up coming along? You know how impatient Laurie can be. He wants it recorded before the months out.'

'It's another instrumental as you know. There are just a few tweaks to do,' said Ian, 'mainly the end piece, Mark's drum solo. However, Chris's friends, June and Ginger, seemed to enjoy *Running Wild*, which is what we have decided to call it.'

'Come on everyone, it's time we were on our way,' called Sam standing by the front door. Their dad was acting as chauffeur for the boys and Sandra. Sam and Grace were going to spend the evening with Nick and Jackie.

Tony dressed in black and with a bobble hat, which amused Chris no end, was determined to go. He insisted that he hadn't seen a decent firework display in years. He reckoned the lack of visibility should be enough to hide his identity.

They arrived as the bonfire was lit. To begin with the flames shot high and then calmed. The effigy of Guy Fawkes didn't last long. Many of the younger children were having fun with their sparklers drawing circles and shapes in the air until the metal stick spluttered and died.

Sam, Grace, Nick and Jackie enjoying mulled wines were chatting with Chris and Tony. Tim and Ian had hooked up with June and Ginger and were watching the display with them.

The first rocket lit up the dark sky followed by the inevitable 'ooohs' and 'ahs'. A roman candle shot red then yellow then green flared into the air just like traffic lights. Catherine wheels were even attempted. One was successful, the other one nearly spun off its prop.

As the last firework hit the velvet blackness, all that was left was the after-glow of the bonfire. The crowds started to disperse. A light in the distance pointed the way to the village hall and the evening's entertainment plus, of course, hot soup and jacket potatoes!

Chris and Tony were wandering back to the car hand in hand when they bumped into the others. A starstruck, June and Ginger were introduced to Tony.

'I can't believe it, I never thought I would ever meet you in person,' said Ginger.

Just then Sandra appeared with Mark in tow. 'Are you coming into the disco?'

Chris looked at Tony, a silent communication passed between the pair. 'No, I think we'll give it a miss this time Sandra.'

'Go on, Tony won't be recognised, especially with that hat,' remarked Sandra.

Tony gave a jaunty nod of the head giving the bobble a really good shake!

'Joking aside Sandra, I don't think we should.'

'Oh, I suppose your right,' she said a bit disappointed.

Ian had been enjoying himself in Ginger's company and did not want the evening to end.

'A disco.......mm.......' he muttered, 'that's sounds fun. Tim shall we lead the ladies in?' and bowed towards Ginger. Ginger, entering into the spirit, curtsied back to him. 'That is very kind of you young sir,' and graciously took his arm.

Tim, much to June's embarrassment, did the same to her, 'May I have the pleasure,' he said and held out his hand. A very flustered June took it. Chris grinned at her friend's discomfort.

'See you all later,' she called after them, as she and Tony went in the opposite direction.

They reached the car when Rachel came running by. She stopped as she saw them.

'Hi Chris, not discoing tonight?'

'No, unfortunately we have to be somewhere else.'

As Chris was speaking the night sky cleared and the moon peeped out casting a bright sparkling silvery glow which lit up the trees and also shone brightly down on the trio. Rachel looked at Tony. Then the clouds drifted over the moon once more and everything was plunged into the ghostly half-light.

'Oh well, anyway, it's a shame you won't be joining us. See you on Monday Chris.'

As the car disappeared into the murk Rachel pondered. Chris's partner looked very familiar, almost if she knew him. 'Don't be silly,' she muttered to herself.

Sunday passed quietly and Tony went back to London in the evening.

Sandra's parents had rung to say they wouldn't be back from Africa until the New Year. Her father was advising the Botswana Government on managing their mineral wealth. Botswana had achieved its independence from the U.K. in 1966 and remained part of the Commonwealth.

It wasn't all work for Chas and Meg though. They had been fortunate enough to have a trip on the Okavango Delta. The third largest river in Africa made up of many crystal clear channels fringed with thick beds of papyrus. A myriad of lakes and sandy islands completed the picture. The Okavango River starts life from heavy thunderstorms over the Angolian highlands and takes six months to reach Botswana. The delta eventually disappears through evaporation and not into a sea or ocean.

As you can imagine the wildlife is amazing. Hippos feast on water plants, Nile crocodiles sun themselves on the sand banks, antelope ever watchful paddle in the shallows, and fish eagles look down from their lofty perches. However, Chas and Meg had a shock of their lives as a bull elephant took a distinct dislike to their dugout and attempted to charge it……

Mark couldn't let this part of the story pass him by. A very down Sandra was soon chuckling from the antics of Mark as he made out to be the charging elephant.

꒳ ꒳ ꒳

The next day was one of those typical November days. It was cold, it was overcast and it was raining a horrible damp drizzle, in no way could one keep dry. Chris shook her fair hair and a cascade of raindrops fell on to the floor.

'Hello everyone,' she called to the other Prefects, 'What an absolutely foul day, it was just as well it wasn't like this on Saturday as we would never had raised a spark from the bonfire, let alone a rocket off the ground. How was the disco?'

'You missed a brilliant one there,' said Rachel, 'Why didn't you stay? Your brothers certainly enjoyed themselves, not to mention their partners,' and looked across to June and Ginger. The former blushed.

Chris smiled, 'Yes Tim and Ian did say it was pretty spectacular.'

'Talking of discos and parties,' said Rachel, 'has the format been decided yet for our Christmas celebrations Belinda? You were going to speak to Mrs. Mac.'

'That's a point, it's not that far away when you look at the calendar,' said Ginger. 'In fact some of the Department Stores already have a Father Christmas. I can't understand why the kids don't catch on, when there is only supposed to be one Santa Claus, and yet they see one in every other shop.'

'Actually Ginger,' said Janice, 'my niece took my brother and sister-in-Law on a Father Christmas hunt to see how many she could find in one day!'

'Joking aside,' said Belinda, 'Mrs. Mac has given the go ahead so it's a matter of finding a disco outfit and booking them. We could use the one we had on Saturday or someone else; any ideas?'

'It's a shame we can't book a live group,' commented Rachel.

'Who had you in mind? Not *Spectrum*? For a start you've got to find out who they are, and if the Press can't, what hope have we?'

Rachel smiled. 'Yes, I suppose it was a pretty far-fetched idea, a disco outfit it will be then.'

⁂

Later that week Laurie rang them in connection with the recording of their new record. After much toing and froing, and a lot of pressure on Laurie's part, it was decided that they would travel to London on the following Saturday.

'Chris,' said Ian, 'do you think Ginger and June would like to come? We shall have Sandra with us, seeing as we can't get rid of her for the day,' he said tongue in cheek. Sandra ignored that remark.

'It's a thought Ian. Hopefully Tony might be around, I'll see if he can join us.'

Tony's housekeeper answered the phone. Chris gave the password, all very M.I.5.ish she thought, but could see sense of it. If Tony's fans knew the number he wouldn't get any peace.

A very sleepy voice came over the line, 'Hi darling,' followed by what sounded suspiciously like a yawn.

'Tony, have I woken you or something?'

'Well, you could say that love, we've been recording all night and most of the day.'

'Sorry about that. Laurie's been speaking with us. He might have mentioned that we're coming to London this weekend to record *Running Wild*. We thought of asking June and Ginger to join us. You might have noticed they appear to be linking up with Tim and Ian.'

'Mm……. I thought so.'

'We are aiming to stay overnight.' Chris hesitated…... 'Any chance of staying with you?'

'No problem, you know there's plenty of room. I could book somewhere for us to eat in the West End on Saturday evening.'

'Thanks darling, see you at the weekend.' Chris replaced the receiver and went back to join the others, secretly very happy with the outcome. 'It's all okay with Tony and he will be joining us.'

'Oh goody,' said Sandra.

The following weekend they travelled to London. June and Ginger hadn't fully recovered from their surprise trip which Chris had suggested a few days earlier. Ginger being Ginger had great difficulty in not spilling the beans to the other prefects. Yesterday at school Belinda's friend Mary was talking about her hockey trial for the county team. She was very excited. She had been selected for the *Probables* and was due to play on the Sunday.

This of course spurred on the others to talk about their coming weekends. Fortunately June was on hand to restrain Ginger from letting the cat out of the bag.

When they reached the Studios, *Spectrum* were whisked away, Sandra, June and Ginger were left in the very capable hands of Jim Adams, Tony's road manager, who took them on an extensive tour of the recording studios.

The three girls were fascinated at all the individual cubicles overlooked by a master control room. Jim explained the reason for the barriers: 'To ensure that the singer's voice or voices are not drowned out by the musical accompaniment. It also aids the Producer sitting in the control room and the Sound Engineer to get the right mix. Most of the singles these days are multi tracked so it's doubly important that the right sound is achieved.'

They were now in one of the control rooms. Ginger looked in amazement at the desk covered in various switches better known as faders. The countless tape machines seem to stare back at her, the blank reels looking like enormous owl eyes.

Jim looked at his watch, 'If we go along to Studio 2, we should catch the action and you will see how we set about recording music to disc.' He led them along to the viewing gallery. Chris looked up and waved.

Laurie called them to order and very soon she and her brothers were engrossed in what they were doing. So too were the others. They didn't hear an extra person join them until a voice spoke in June's ear.

June jumped and spun round to see Tony standing by her side.

'Are they nearly finished?' Tony asked Jim.

'We just have the final run through to do,' he said.

A couple of minutes later Laurie gave the thumbs up – a broad grin on his face. *Running Wild* was ready for the charts.

'How did it go Chris?' Tony asked and gave her a quick kiss and cuddle.

'Fine, you've surfaced then?'

'Cheek! Yes I have, and I've booked the *Checkerboard* for us all to eat tonight. It is a restaurant which is slightly off the beaten track but has marvellous Italian food. At the weekends there is usually a cabaret. It could be a comedian or a singer, you never know but one thing is certain there is always dancing.'

Tony was right about off the beaten track. The venue was in the cellar of one of the Banks. The clientele was primarily Italians which showed what a reputation its food had for the local community.

The girls were dressed in smart cocktail dresses and the boys in dark suits. For once Chris felt relaxed in Tony's company. He was right. They were left to themselves with no one coming up asking for Tony's autograph or for photos.

They had a super evening; the cabaret was a magician and they were duly *spellbound* by his act.

Ginger kept on pinching herself. To be in such a plush place, in such exalted company, it was awesome. She wanted the evening to last forever.

'Ginger, put that drink down! Let's go and boogie again,' said Ian, and took her hand.

Sandra, being the youngest, hadn't experienced such a venue before and felt a wee bit out of her depth. However, she hadn't realised how thoughtful Tony could be.

'Come on Sandra,' he said, 'it's about time we had that dance,' and led her onto the floor.

Chris leaned over to June, 'Having fun?'

'It's incredible Chris. I can't thank you enough for the opportunity. To be in such an amazing place,' June said gazing at a room decorated in silver and black in Art Deco. '…… and …. Tim,' but she wasn't allowed to finish as Tim claimed her for yet another twist.

The entertainment concluded with Engelbert Humperdinck's The Last Waltz.

All evening Chris had been checking on the safety clasp of her bracelet. It appeared to be rather loose. The gold bracelet, encrusted with diamonds, was very, very precious. Tony, the romantic, added a charm to it every year on the anniversary of their first meeting. The first year was Eros. Now she was looking at a guitar which Tony had given her on his return from America.

As she and Tony left the dance floor the bracelet slipped from her wrist. It was a blessing in disguise. Chris bent to retrieve it, a camera flashed. Fortunately before any more photos could be taken the manager stepped in and their party was hustled away.

The next morning blazened across several of the Sunday papers was Tony with the caption…

TONY ENJOYS NIGHT OUT, BUT WITH WHOM?

Caught in the flashlight is Tony Dale. He was seen dancing cheek to cheek with a beautiful young lady in Checkerboards last night. But who is she? Speculation has it that it was SPECTRUM. Checkerboards remains nonplussed …..… this best kept secret of Spectrum appears to continue.

The twins were at breakfast. No one else had surfaced yet. Tony's housekeeper had laid out cereals, toast and marmalade. The coffee percolator was bubbling away.

Chris read the article and passed the newspaper to Tim.

'I'm not sure how much longer I can keep this guise up Tim,' she said as she poured another coffee. 'It can only be a matter of time before we are recognised. Tony's used to this sort of thing but I shudder at the thought of fans chasing us everywhere and chanting our names!'

'I know,' said Tim,' putting his mug down. 'Come on sis, relax, let us enjoy it while we can.'

CHAPTER TEN

The sixth form, in their final year at school, has several free periods of extra study for their upcoming A Levels. Chris had Twentieth Century Poets in front of her and was reading through John Betjeman's *East Anglian Bathe* highlighting Horsey Mere.

> *Oh when the early morning at the seaside*
> *Took us with hurrying steps from Horsey Mere*
> *To see the whistling bent-grass on the leeside*
> *And then the tumbled breaker-line appear ......*

She paused, thinking of the analogy of poetry and lyrics in music. Both had rhyming lines. The success of the latter tied to the tune whilst the other to the inflection in the voice of the reader.

Her musings were interrupted by Rachel who had lost interest in the *Journey of the Magi* by T. S. Eliot and was flipping through a pop magazine. She had reached the page of forthcoming new releases.

'Girls! You have to see this!' she cried out, holding up the magazine.

'Why what's so interesting?' asked Diana, pushing her long hair out of her eyes and marking her place in Jane Austen's *Northanger Abbey*.

'It seems the race is already on for the Christmas No. 1 and that *Spectrum* could be in the frame. Apparently a follow-up to *Freewheelin* is being produced.'

Rachel now had the attention of nearly everyone in the room. Janice was the only one who appeared disinterested. She was into trad jazz, Chris Barber, Kenny Ball. Acker Bilk.

'*If music be the food of love, play on....*' quoted Belinda fittingly. She had just started reading *Twelfth Night*.

'I hope it's another instrumental,' said Diana. 'It's so refreshing to have something different.'

'If it is instrumentals you are after, there is always Kenny Ball,' interjected Janice.

But nothing could deter Rachel, she was on a roll. 'It's bound to be good, instrumental or not. I'm going to preorder it this weekend from *The Music Box*.'

'It is,' said Ginger looking up from her study book, *The Life and Times of Shakespeare*, 'very good INDEED!'

'How do you know that?' asked Rachel. 'According to *Disc,* nobody has heard it yet.'

'Aar, umm......' Ginger dried up, but fortunately June came to the rescue, once more.

'Er.... Ginger, I think you meant to say that with the following *Spectrum* has, it could only be a success.'

'Ah.... that's right,' agreed Ginger, looking a little flushed.

The bell went for the end of the period. They picked up their books. Chris, June and Ginger walked to their next class. There was no one else around.

'I know Chris. I know I nearly let the cat out of the bag,' said Ginger.

'I don't think Rachel suspected anything. All this talk about Christmas has reminded me that it's not that far away. What are you up to for the annual festivities?'

Chris couldn't believe their expressions. Ginger, normally fiery and bouncy looked down in the dumps whilst June was as miserable as sin.

'What an earth is wrong? Why so glum? I thought you usually looked forward to Christmas?'

June sighed. 'Well Chris for Ginger and me Christmas is a non-event this year. Our parents are going to be away. Mine will be in Canada on business and I might be staying with my aunt and uncle in Sussex. But nothing has been confirmed yet.'

'As far as I am concerned' said Ginger, 'I was going to be at my grandparents in London. However, Grandad is not well at present and needs to have an operation. A lot of uncertainties....'

'Oh I see. Look if you haven't any firm arrangements and it's up to you entirely there is plenty of room at Spindle. You know you would be welcome. Do you fancy coming to Norfolk instead?'

'You bet!' they said as one voice.

'Great! But you'd better check with your folks first. Oh, by the way, just one thing. *Spectrum* might be called out. Do you think you'd mind getting involved in our work on the Broads?'

June and Ginger, a huge smile on their faces, hugged Chris. 'Rather!'

'OK. That's settled. You'll be fully fledged members of *Spectrum* at this rate.'

Chris was so happy to be of help. She valued friendship and possessed such a warm heart.

⚜ ⚜ ⚜

As predicted by Rachel, the following week saw

Spectrum's new single hit the record market. It was constantly played on the radio and by the end of November it had climbed into the Top 40.

'What did I say, Chris, I knew *Running Wild* would be as good as *Freewheelin*. I reckon it will be the Christmas Number 1,' said June.

'I agree,' said Rachel. 'The more I play it the better I like it.

What about you Chris? Do you think it is equally chart-top worthy?'

'Oh, yes, um, I think it is as good as *Freewheelin*. But to me *Freewheelin* will always remain something special.'

She looked a bit surprised, 'How come Chris?'

'Oh, because of it being their initial release and has such a distinct blend of music.'

'Really? Anyway I hope they're going to record more tracks. *Spectrum* has such a unique sound,' said Rachel. 'I adore them. Wouldn't it be fantastic to see them live?'

Chris shrugged her shoulders, 'I'll have to disagree with you Rachel. I would prefer to see Tony Dale live.'

'Crumbs, what am I thinking of? I was going to mention it first thing this morning but I completely forgot,' exclaimed Belinda pushing her book aside.

'You obviously haven't heard, HE IS coming here next week? It's an extra date on his tour.'

Chris looked startled, June and Ginger confused, and Rachel was jumping about the room in excitement.

'Where an earth did you hear that?' asked June.

'It was on the local news this morning just as I was leaving home. The tickets will be on sale this weekend.'

During the mid-morning break June quizzed Chris about Tony appearing at the *Imperial,* their local theatre.

'I'm flabbergasted June. I know that Tony's road manager, you know, Jim, pulls strings at the last minute, but I'm as much in the dark as you are.'

Later on that evening, a frosty Chris asked Tony the exact same question during their usual phone call.

'Don't be cross darling... I was informed this morning, and you, I mean *Spectrum*, should receive a phone call from Laurie within the next hour.

The reason why he said yes to the *Imperial* is brilliant! They have been trying to book us for a while, putting forward that there was a spare date just before the start of the Christmas Pantomime.

Laurie wants *Spectrum* to appear and perform its new number *Running Wild*. He feels that it will give *Running Wild* a nice boost in the Charts.'

'Oh....'

'Tony....' continued a worried Chris. 'I've been meaning to mention this to you for a while. I love you to bits as you know, but this seems to me like a conflict of interest. You are so generous but you must think of your career too. As they say in the music industry, we are now rivals, especially for the Christmas No. 1.'

'Bah...That's life!' replied Tony with his usual good humour. 'Anyway, I can't think of a lovelier person to be in competition with.' And he blew a loud kiss down the line.

Sam and Grace were just as thrilled as their children. To be appearing in their local theatre was a prize indeed. It was very special for the Rogers family. Many years ago, just after leaving musical college, a young Grace had performed her first piano concert in front of a paying public, at the *Imperial*. Unfortunately, as the saying goes 'the rest is history'. Her promising career was cut short by World War Two.

𝌆 𝌆 𝌆

It was the start of a new week. June had the kettle on to make their early morning coffee; white for her and Chris, a strong black for Ginger. Ginger was slumped in one of the only two comfortable armchairs in the Prefects Room doing her best to wake up. As we know, mornings and Ginger don't always go together!

A disgruntled Rachel came in, tossed her bag onto the other seat and sat down at the table.

'What's up Rachel?' asked Chris, 'I thought you'd be on top of the world with Tony Dale coming this weekend.'

'That's the point,' she said throwing her arms in dismay. 'I couldn't get a ticket.'

'You couldn't get a ticket? But you had it all planned,' exclaimed Ginger.

'You were going to be first in the queue.'

'Well things went wrong. My bus, No. 12, always on time never turned up. The next one came along full...... By the time I arrived at the Theatre, all tickets had been sold.'

'Oh no, I am so sorry to hear that Rachel,' said June. 'If it's any consolation, we are in the same boat. Ginger and I couldn't get tickets either.'

Chris suddenly stood up, reached for her coat and pulled out one ticket. 'Look who has been successful.' she said with an enigmatic smile.

'Oh, you lucky thing!'

Rachel's face looked thoroughly dejected.

Chris plunged her hand in the left pocket of her coat this time, and produced not one, not two but three more tickets, holding them up high in the air, with a huge grin.

Rachel, June and Ginger looked on in amazement, almost speechless. 'WOW!' was the universal comment.

'However, I can't use them.' The huge grin faded. 'They were for my brothers and me. Uncle Nick and Aunt Jackie, the farm where we had our firework evening, has a major problem with the Christmas turkey production. Several of the farm labourers have the flu. The first order is due with the wholesalers this coming week. A Rogers call to arms, so we're all at *Marygold* this weekend helping with the packing.'

Chris gave June, Ginger and Rachel each a ticket. The fourth one was for, who else, but Sandra.

'Chris, I don't know what to say,' said Rachel, obviously moved. 'Many, many thanks. We owe you big time! Thank you again.'

Rachel carefully tucked the ticket into her bag and left the Prefects room.

In fact the excuse was partly true. There was a problem at *Marygold* with the turkeys. Sam and Grace knew how important this time of the year was for Nick so had agreed to assist even though they would be missing their children's debut at the Imperial.

June put her mug down. Shrewd as ever. 'I think I can guess where the tickets came from but, you missing Tony Dale, on our doorstep! Come on Chris.'

'Ah. Tickets compliments of Tony naturally! But, yes June, it's not being advertised until the evening, but we're appearing as *Spectrum*.'

'But don't *let the cat out of the bag* either of you. Sandra is in the know. It's to be kept strictly under wraps until the night.'

Ginger only half-listening, was still dumbstruck. She couldn't take her eyes off the ticket in her hand.

'I don't know how you keep up with it all Chris. Appearing in shows, studying for GCE, recording music. It is just amazing,' said June.

'Yes it does get a bit hectic at times.'

Chris did find it a problem but couldn't let on to her friends let alone Tony or her brothers.

༈ ༈ ༈

The *Imperial* was buzzing. A famous pop star in their midst! What an incredible opportunity! People outside the theatre were spilling onto the road. Police were on hand to keep control and traffic moving.

The three school friends met in the foyer. Rachel's dad had dropped her off whilst June and Ginger had arrived by public transport.

Rachel was unusually overawed, even more so when entering the auditorium. None of them had realised that the seats were bang in the middle of the front row.

'Unlucky for Chris not able to keep these tickets, they couldn't be better placed. June, Ginger, I'm going to enjoy this and with *Spectrum* appearing as well, Chris is missing a good show.'

Sandra slipped into her seat next to June, and whispered, 'Chris is waiting for you, behind the pillar. If you can nip out with Ginger you can see them backstage before it starts!'

Rachel, still enthralled in what was going on at that moment picked up her programme and suddenly said, 'I'm just going to get some sweets.'

'With your programme,' teased Ginger. Rachel gave a slight smile and left them.

'Come on Ginger,' said June, 'we are waiting for you.'

Ginger looked startled. 'Waiting for me? For what?'

'They are all waiting for you backstage,' said Sandra, 'you've a good twenty minutes to see them.'

'Oh, right,' said Ginger suddenly realising what was happening.

And there was Chris. 'You look great!' exclaimed June, suitably impressed.

Chris was already dressed in her outfit of indigo blue satin trousers and blue top. As yet the boater hadn't been added but the dark glasses had, in case Rachel saw her.

They slipped through a door by the side of the orchestra pit. The commissioner who was standing guard backstage looked at the three of them and waved them past.

'It's a bit like Fort Knox,' said Ginger.

'Yes, it has to be, they never know where Tony's fans will get to next.'

'I think Rachel's gone in search of the stage-door, Chris,' said Ginger.

'I don't think she'll get far, but never mind I'll see what I can do for her later.'

By then they had reached a door marked with the number 6. Chris knocked and called, 'Are you decent in there? I've a couple of young ladies to see you.'

Tim opened the door, 'Hi June, Ginger, come on in.'

Ginger looked at Ian. He had a yellow top, plus, of course, the indigo blue trousers, and the boater. 'You look fabulous Ian,' which was all she could muster, for the moment!

This didn't last long. We all know Ginger.

'Can I try on your dark glasses Ian?'

Ian obliged.

'What do you think? Do they suit me?' asked Ginger, looking at her reflection in the mirror moving her head from side to side.

Before any judgement could be made by anyone, the five-minute call came over the Tannoy. Ian took back his glasses. It was time to go and enjoy the show.

Chris led them back through the maze of corridors until she had them in the auditorium once more.

June and Ginger returned to their seats. Rachel was already in position.

Ginger couldn't resist it. 'Did you find, sweets?' teased Ginger with a twinkle in her eye, but before Rachel could answer the house lights dimmed and the show began.

Spectrum was the second act on. The opening performer, a comedian, was good. He did his best to achieve some interplay with the audience but it was obvious they were only interested in what was to follow!

When *Spectrum* appeared Ginger and June couldn't believe how professional they were, Ginger leaned over, 'It's hard to believe June, that's Chris, Ian, Tim and Mark up there and we actually know them!'

'I know, I can hardly believe it myself.'

After the interval the inevitable screams welcomed Tony Dale on stage. He began with a lively medley of rock and roll numbers with some people dancing in the aisles. Then it was time for his latest, *Love in the Moonlight,* which quietened the audience. A smoochy ballad sending shivers down one's spine. As Tony's velvet voice reverberated around the auditorium he walked slowly to the front of the stage and winked. June and Ginger did their best not to laugh, but poor Rachel didn't know quite how to react.

Up tempo again, this time the girls were joining in the fun, clapping and swinging to the music. And then it was all over. Much stamping of feet, whistles and screams ended a brilliant evening's entertainment with several curtain calls.

June and Ginger sat down, not so Rachel who was hastily gathering up her belongings. She was determined to get the autograph. Yes Ginger had been right. Rachel had attempted before the show to do just that.

Suddenly a tall gentleman in a braided uniform stood in front of her. It was the commissioner.

'I believe you wanted to meet Tony Dale? Please follow me.' He turned.

Rachel was speechless. The others were just as stunned.

'Can, can my friends come as well?' stammered Rachel.

'Of course.'

He took them along a corridor, which ended in a red-studded door with a gold star, knocked and a voice bade them to come in. Much to Rachel's surprise she found herself in Tony Dale's dressing-room. Jim, his road manager, was with him.

There was no flicker of recognition of June, Sandra or Ginger from Tony. He was his usual professional self.

The commissioner left them.

Rachel, again speechless, limply handed her programme to Tony for the treasured autograph.

It didn't take long for Tony to put Rachel at her ease. She then became the chatterbox we all know her to be.

Tony duly signed June, Sandra and Ginger's programmes, keeping up the pretense, asking their names.

Rachel produced her camera. 'Tony, can we have a photo with you please?'

'No problem.'

Jim became the photographer.

Just then Laurie poked his head around the door, 'Tony, oh sorry, I didn't realise you had company. Can you go to the stage-door? There's a few fans waiting for you, and that's an understatement, I think the whole town's turned out.'

'Okay coming Boss.'

'Thanks for seeing us Tony,' said Rachel.

'My pleasure, if you'd like to go with Jim here, he'll take you round to the front so you won't have any difficulty in leaving the theatre.'

Jim led the four of them back to the foyer where Rachel's father was waiting for her. Rachel's broad grin told him everything.

'It's no use me asking if you had a good time, I can see you have,' said Mr. Jones.

'Dad, it was brilliant, I've actually met him. I've met Tony Dale and look he's autographed my programme.'

Rachel's dad gave her a quick hug. He turned to the others. 'Do any of you require a lift home?'

Before June or Ginger could answer Sandra piped up, 'No it's fine thank-you Mr. Jones. We are all sorted.'

'Oh right.'

'See you Monday,' said Rachel, and followed her dad into the November night.

June and Ginger faced Sandra: 'Come on Sandra, spill the beans.'

Just then Jim came back into view. 'So girls ready for a fabulous party?' he asked

Jim led them into a large room where a buffet was laid out. Some of the delights were cheese and pineapple on sticks, warmed sausages rolls, chicken vol-u-vents, slices of quiche, devils on horseback and even a lobster mousse! Pride of place was a glorious Black Forest gateaux. Wine, soft drinks and an amazing alcohol-free punch were also available. Soft music was playing in the background.

Laurie, more conservatively attired than usual in grey slacks and a crumpled sports jacket was smoking a massive Cuban cigar whilst talking to the *Imperial*'s Manager. A tall gentleman, probably just turning sixty, with a receding hairline dressed in a dark lounge suit with a carnation in his lapel.

Laurie was feeling chuffed. He had two of the best musical acts on the market signed to him with two chances of the Christmas Number 1 under his umbrella. Yes, life was good at present.

As soon as they appeared Tim and Ian claimed June and Ginger and Sandra went off in search of Mark.

Chris waved to them from across the room where she was relaxing in an overstuffed armchair.

Tony appeared at her side. She looked up into those crinkly brown eyes. 'They let you loose then?'

'Cheek! Laurie was right, I think the whole town was there. My pen nearly ran out of ink.' He gazed across the room where June and Tim were engrossed.

'What do you think of Tim and June's relationship darling? It looks as if they have hit it off!' he said.

Chris followed his gaze. The pair of them were talking animatedly and Tim had his arm around June's shoulders. 'Well they certainly seem to be enjoying themselves,' said Chris.

'Come on lazy bones,' he said, and pulled Chris to her feet, 'I need feeding, I don't know about you?'

The pair of them wandered over to join the others.

CHAPTER ELEVEN

The last week of term was nearing its end, and the school was full of the Christmas spirit. Everyone was busy decorating the hall for the evening disco. Chris was balancing precariously on top of a ladder, with June hanging on to the bottom. She was putting the finishing touches to the tree when Belinda called across the room.

'What a cheerful place now. Well done everybody!'

Chris surveyed the decorated hall. Every prefect had taken part, a great team effort. Yes. Chris was pleased with their result after so much hard work.

From her vantage point she saw Rachel enter.

'Hi Rachel,' she called, 'Are you bringing anyone tonight?'

Rachel looked up at her, grinned and said: 'Ah hah, you'll have to wait and see, and what about you? Are we going to meet that handsome escort of yours? Or is he a thing of the past?'

This time it was Chris's turn to grin and say: 'Ah hah, you'll have to wait and see.'

She climbed down the ladder, June muttering to her: 'don't tell me that you are planning to come with Tony, are you?'

Chris laughed. 'You'll have to wait and see.'

It had been decided that Ginger and June would go to the Rogers for tea and change for the evening afterwards. Tony arrived duly at 5pm. Grace was always pleased to see him, a well-mannered young man who made her daughter so happy. Dressed in white flared trousers, matching jacket and a white open-necked shirt with navy blue lapels, he looked most handsome.

Chris waltzed into the room. She stopped in her tracks, stunned.

'Is this really YOU?'

Tony's face was definitely not the same as before: he was now wearing a goatee beard!

'Well, what do you think darling? Do I pass muster?'

Giving the inevitable showbiz twirl.

'And more to the point is my new disguise good enough to deceive the infamous Rachel?'

She fell into his arms. 'Mmmm, let's see.' She tapped his cheeks to verify that the false beard was well attached, and kissed him passionately.

'That beard tickles, but I'll make do with it for the time being.'

Chris was also wearing flared trousers, pale blue with a sequined sparkly top completing the look. Her beautiful blond hair and blue eyes was the perfect match for the colour scheme.

Tony had admiration and so much love for the vision he had before him.

Through the open door an effervescent Ginger dashed in, followed by a much calmer June. 'Wow! I guess it is you TONY? What a transformation!'

She was still in awe at being in the company of someone so famous.

'Are you sure it's not too big a risk for you to accompany Chris tonight?' asked an anxious June. 'Most of the girls see your picture in their favourite magazine day in day out.'

'You don't think I'm going to let Chris roam around unescorted, do you?' he answered, putting his arm tenderly around Chris's shoulders.

'Anyway, Chris told me that I look at least ten years older with my beard... so don't worry, everything will be hunky dory!'

This time chauffeuring duties were split between Sam and Tony with Sam returning at the end of the evening.

On arriving at the school, they were pleasantly surprised by the ambiance. The headmistress had obviously authorised quite a few changes to the lighting system.

A lot of red bulbs were dotted around the hall, which gave a warm glow to the large room.

Amazingly, a few spotlights had a spinning wheel installed in front of them containing a hole in order to provide a strobe effect. The perfect disco!

They found a table in one of the candle-lit alcoves, Ian and Tim going off in search of drinks.

To complete his disguise Tony donned a pair of horn-rimmed glasses, just like Superman.

'If anyone identifies me as Tony Dale, I give up!' he said, making faces at Chris.

As she burst out laughing Rachel showed up, as if by magic.

'Having a good time?'

She stared at Chris in silence. Evidently, she was not going to move an inch till she had been introduced.

Chris cleared her throat. 'Rachel ......um this is Cliff.'

Tony stood up and shook Rachel's hand. 'I'm pleased to meet you Rachel, Chris has told me a lot about you.'

Rachel went pink with embarrassment. Those deep brown eyes were extremely captivating! It sent shivers down her back. She was dumbstruck! Lucky Chris to have such a boyfriend, even if he could be a bit too old for her especially with that horrible beard! Their conversation came to an end. Ian and Tim had returned with a tray of drinks.

'Hello Rachel,' said Ian, 'Would you like a Coke, 7-Up, or something?'

'Er....um.... er....no it's all right thanks Ian my boyfriend Neil is getting one for me.'

Heading in their direction was a tall fair-headed lad weaving his way through the many twisting and gyrating dancers, with two drinks held aloft.

Ginger was already opening her mouth to quiz Neil when all of a sudden Tony's latest hit was on the turntable.

'Oh Neil,' Rachel shouted, 'my FAVOURITE! We must dance to this.'

He deposited the two drinks in haste. Rachel was pulling him onto the dance floor. Clearly, he had little choice.

Tony was laughing. 'I don't know what she'd do if I suddenly sprung up onto the stage and started singing it live! Well my darling, how about we go dancing to this fabulous song, sung by a fabulous singer?'

⁂

The day after they broke up Chris and her brothers, not forgetting Sandra, travelled to Spindle. Tony returned to London as the build up to Christmas required his presence on television, and more studio recording was also on the cards. He would join them all shortly before Christmas, for a much-needed break.

Ginger and June weren't coming until after the weekend.

'We'll pick you up at Norwich railway station,' Chris said, 'but make sure you're wearing extra warm clothing.'

'Oh. Why?' queried Ginger.

'You'll have to wait and see, won't you?' she replied with a broad smile

June seemed none too pleased. 'To quote Rachel's description of you, Chris, you can be so infuriating at times.'

Chris shrugged her shoulders and gave them a friendly wave.

The following Tuesday saw June and Ginger outside Norwich Station. They had put down their cases and were hopping on their feet to keep warm. Of Chris and her brothers there was no sign.

'Where an earth are they?' asked June. 'This north wind is whipping through me. On days like this, one realises there is not a lot between Norfolk and Siberia!'

Ginger looked around the car park and then across to the river suddenly catching sight of Chris waving. 'I can see now why we had to get an early train and wear warm clothing. Look, they're over there just tying up. It looks as if we're boating to Spindle.'

June grinned and picked up her suitcase. 'At least we can wave back today. Shades of the Spring Bank Holiday. Only now there is no Tony Dale behind us. It is so nice not to have to pretend. I don't know how Chris can keep her two secrets, and for how much longer?

When the fans discover she's not only Tony Dale's girlfriend but also a member of *Spectrum*, the journalists will never stop hounding her.'

Ian leapt ashore as they approached. 'Come on then, give me those cases.' He gave June and Ginger a quick peck on the cheek and disappeared with the luggage.

Chris said a hurried hello and took them swiftly into the cabin to warm up.

'Sorry about the rush,' said Tim poking his head through the hatchway, 'but the tides are all wrong in Breydon Water and if we don't get there quickly it'll be a hard slog across that stretch.' He then went back on deck.

'That sounds wonderfully technical and adventurous,' said June, a bit miffed about the lack of affection from Tim!

'Well, we knew it would be tight,' said Chris, 'but you know us always ready for a challenge!'

At that moment Tim came back down below. 'I think I forgot something,' and swept June into his arms, kissed her affectionately and pushed a strand of hair out of her eyes, 'come on young lady, let's go and blow the cobwebs away.'

'Where's my coffee?' called a voice from above. 'How about looking after the skipper then?'

'There you are Ginger,' said Chris moving a mug over to her. 'Try out your sea legs and see if you can carry that up to Ian without spilling.'

Ginger was only too pleased to oblige. She picked up the mug and gingerly made her way up to the cockpit to Ian where Tim, with his arm around June's shoulders, was pointing out various landmarks.

'Tim,' asked June, 'what are windmills used for? Because whenever you see pictures of Broadland there is always a windmill.'

'Windmills were a way of draining the fens so that they could be transformed into grazing marshes,' replied Tim. 'However, steam eventually took over powering the pumps and look!' Tim was pointing, 'Strumpshaw Pumphouse and chimney, a fine example of a Victorian steam drainage pump.'

On the opposite bank was rather an impressive building. 'Is it still steam powered?' she asked.

'No, it is now converted to electricity although in the 1940s diesel was used. In fact many of the windmills were in danger of being lost forever, but the Norfolk Windmill Trust has been preserving as many of them as they can for posterity.'

Back in the cabin, Chris cleared away the coffee things. She joined them as they reached Burgh Castle and Breydon Water. They soon knew they were in that stretch of water. *Spectrum Two* had caught the turn in the tide and with the wind against them it was quite a choppy crossing.

For once Ginger was silent, looking pale, if not a little green.

They eventually reached the other side and the calmer waters of the River Bure. Motoring under the new concrete bridge at Acle, Tim turned to June.

'Are you superstitious?' he asked.

'Hum, is this a loaded question?'

'What I mean June is that there is a legend about the bridge we just passed under. The Norfolk folks swear that before it was rebuilt, Acle Bridge was haunted. In fact, Grandad used to say that it had been THE PLACE for executions. Not all of them legal you understand. Apparently, criminals were left dangling over the side, continuing to hang in ghostly shapes.'

Tim saw June shiver.

She caught sight of his worried look and laughed.

'OK, OK, a chilly story indeed! But on a more mundane note, I am beginning to feel like your tale, chilly!'

Tim, quick on the uptake, squeezed her into his arms. Any excuse to warm her up!

They were just coming to the windmill by Upton Dyke.

'Is that Thurne Mill?' asked Ginger.

'No, it's not, we don't in fact pass Thurne Mill on this trip, but we can come down to it one day during the week if you like?' By the time they reached Thurne Mouth it was getting dark.

'Not long now,' Ian said to Ginger and June, and in a very short while they arrived at Spindle, and Mark and Sandra were on the quay to meet them.

'Hi all, welcome to Spindle,' said Mark. 'Did you enjoy Breydon Water?' he added in a mocking tone.

Chris gave him a reproachful glance.

'Sorry Ginger, June, only teasing. By the way sis message from Tony. He should be here tomorrow evening towards 6.00 p.m.'

☞ ☞ ☞

The next day dawned crisp and frosty, Chris came in from the garden just as her two friends appeared for breakfast. 'Morning all, brrr it sure is nippy out there today.'

The large kitchen was thankfully warm no doubt due to the radiant heat provided by the Aga cooker. All seven tucked merrily into waffles, toast and home-made jams, washed down by hot coffee and tea.

After breakfast Ian and Tim disappeared into the Den. Manager Laurie had reiterated to them: 'You need eight to ten tracks for your first *Spectrum* LP. Remember, time is of the essence!'

The release date had not yet been established, but Laurie, with a big smile on his face had intimated: 'Shortly after the New Year break?'

Pressure was on!

The girls decided to spend the day in Norwich wandering around the shops and looking at the sights of the City itself, a City which at one time had a church for every Sunday and a pub for every day, within the old City walls.

As they left to catch the 9.30 bus Jessie called after them.

'Don't forget the Carols around the City Hall Christmas Tree this afternoon.'

'We won't, but thanks for reminding us Jessie,' answered Chris.

Alighting from the No. 10 in Castle Meadow they were met with a sight which took their breath away. The castle was looking amazing with laser images projected onto its façade.

'Wow!' was the exclamation of all.

They spent a good while in the Castle museum, especially amongst the nature tableaux. Ginger and June did their best to identify the various animal and bird calls.

'I'm so confused,' said June, 'all the birds sound the same,' as once again the bird's name she pressed on the printout lit up a definite *NO*.

'Hey, I've got one right,' exclaimed Ginger, who had just recognised the boom of a bittern.

They ambled through the archaeology section and eventually to the Keep where they looked down a very deep well. 'That's where they used to throw the bodies,' said Sandra with glee.

June and Ginger shuddered.

As the castle once served as the County jail, prisoners who did not survive instruments of torture such as the scold's bridle, (an iron muzzle in an iron framework that enclosed the head) were disposed of in the well. Prisoners were often kept in windowless damp dungeons chained to the wall waiting for the assessor to arrive to hear their pleas. If you had money though you were entitled to your man-servant and kept away from the paupers and housed in your own private cell.

From the Castle they crossed to the pedestrian roadways which had rows of brightly lit angels strung across them. The shops were decorated with fairy lights and seasonal greetings. The biggest department store, run by a local family, had placed Christmas trees balancing precariously over the main entrance doors. From afar it looked a bit like a mini Harrods, sparkling brilliantly. The main attraction being its windows dressed with snowy scenes of polar bears and penguins.

The tree in front of the City Hall shone cheerfully in the gathering gloom of the December afternoon. As you can imagine the area was packed with people. The carols started and the girls joined in with as much gusto as everyone else. It was such a great forerunner for the festivities to come.

'Everywhere is so Christmassy,' said June, 'It makes you feel happy just to look. All we need is the snow to make it a white one.'

'Last August,' said Chris, 'the City Council put a Christmas tree by the Post Office and loads of pretty lights across the streets. Even the shops displayed Christmas Greetings in their windows. Just imagine the tourists' reaction. They thought that Norwich had gone mad, how could they have got their dates so wrong?'

'For a television programme?' June queried.

'Good guess! Roald Dahl's Tales of the Unexpected: such fun to watch the filming. The cast were in fur coats with the sun streaming down. Make-up people were running like busy bees mopping their perspiration. I remember one actress who looked particularly uncomfortable, she was melting like an ice cream, the poor soul.'

The girls moved on to the older part of the City around the Charing Cross area passing a nut barrow roasting chestnuts. The smell was compelling and very tempting.

They looked in many of the little shop windows in Pottergate and eventually reached the Maddermarket theatre, the history of which June and Ginger found fascinating.

In the medieval times this location was a market selling scarlet dye called 'madder', hence its name. Theatre enthusiast Nugent Monck opened it in 1921 as an Elizabethan style playhouse, with no curtain falling when the show was finished, the actors simply walking down the centre aisle.

'Its audience capacity is about 300 I think' added Chris, 'and the Maddermarket owns the largest collection of costumes in the whole of East Anglia. You can hire them, and the props too. Like several theatres the Maddermarket has its own ghost. A friar. He is said to walk across the stage in the middle of a performance, hide wigs and jam doors. Once he rescued a young actress from a falling light fitting and hugged another actor who had forgotten his lines. Children have also asked after a show why there was a friar in it!'

From there they wandered down the cobbled streets of Elm Hill with its authentic gas lights, decorated with tinsel and overhanging the narrow street, though of course now lit by electricity. They eventually made the Cathedral which, as it was quite late, was floodlit.

June had always had a vague interest in church architecture and deep down was disappointed that when they were in Norfolk at half-term they didn't get the chance to visit the cathedral. Now they had the opportunity.

The four of them entered by the west door passing the outdoor crib and Remembrance Tree; the daily organ recital was in progress. June and Chris sat in the pews for a bit of quiet reflection. Ginger and Sandra were not in a habit of sitting still. They picked up a leaflet and started exploring the majestic building dating back over 900 years. The pair entered two of the four chapels. St. Saviours which was dedicated to the First World War and St. Lukes dedicated to healing. Budge the cat, who had adopted the cathedral as its second home suddenly jumped down from behind a stone monument startling Sandra! Budge, with one of those disdainful looks that only cats are capable of, calmly strolled away.

The two girls paused by the Dispenser Reredos, one of the Cathedrals greatest treasures. This altarpiece with engraved scenes from Christ's Passion survived destruction for over four hundred and fifty years by being hidden as the underside of a table.

Exiting the cathedral they strolled down to the river. Some leaves were still falling from the trees and the four of them idly kicked their way through the carpet of brown. When they reached Pulls Ferry, an ancient right of way and ferry crossing, June was complaining she was frozen. The friends looked at each other, and did an about turn. Yes, it was high time to return to Spindle for some hot chocolate and mince pies.

They had about a mile walk from the bus stop but turning into the driveway of the Hall the girls were met with an amazing transformation. A couple of the trees were now aglow, the front of the house had flashing coloured bulbs along its roof line and by the front door was a solitary reindeer pulling a brightly lit sleigh.

Ginger stopped in her tracks. 'It looks incredible,' she said. 'It's almost as if the illuminations have continued all the way from the City.'

An extra car in the driveway had caught Chris's eye.

The hall was just as festive with a Christmas tree and, yes you guessed it, more lights. Jessie, always a stickler for traditions had hung mistletoe from the roof beam. Mistletoe was a sacred herb of the druids and thought to be a magical sign of new life in mid-winter.

The tree was flanked by a Father Christmas and a snowman. With Frank up the ladder and Matt hanging onto the bottom the final touches were being made to the décor. Matt turned as they entered. Sandra was in the lead. The light caught her reflection. 'Wow, she's turning into something special,' he thought.

'Come on son, hand up those bulbs.' Matt turned back to his dad, the moment had passed

Jessie had heard the door and came out of the kitchen wiping her hands on a tea towel. There was some flour on the apron, she had obviously been baking. She looked straight at Chris, and seeing the expectant look. 'Yes, Tony is in the Den with the others. Now don't be too long all of you as dinner is nearly ready.'

The boys were around the piano. There was obviously a bit of an altercation going on. Tony was lounging on one of the chairs watching the scene with a little bit of amusement. He was completely relaxed. It was good to be in Norfolk where he didn't have to put on any sort of act for the fans and could just be himself.

His eyes lit up – you can guess who has just entered.

Chris saw Tony's expression and went straight to him. She hadn't realised that her brothers were having a slight disagreement.

Sandra bounced in behind her. Ian stopped in mid-flow. He had been pretty vocal up until that point. Mark had been trying to be the mediator.

'Oh...hi Sandra, Chris, you're back then!' Mark exclaimed.

Which, when you think about it, was a pretty nonsensical comment!

'Where are the others?' he continued.

Chris disentangled herself from Tony. 'They're just changing and wrapping, I believe, some surprise presents.'

She was now aware that there was something not quite right with her twin and Ian.

Tim was sitting at the piano and Ian had his guitar in hand, both glaring at each other.

'What is up with you two?' She asked.

Mark explained. 'As you know sis, a middle section of a song can be pretty prominent, completely different from the beginning or the end. Tim wanted something soothing and relaxing for this creation, as the tune was a ballad. However, Ian was of the opinion that there should be something lively!'

'Okay.' Chris, now taking on the mediator role, 'let me hear what you both have in mind.'

Tim's was a classical piece which was now out of copyright and could be used.

Ian was more into a bit of heavy rock which, as he put it, could wake up the buying public!

Chris picked up her guitar, looked at the music. She played Tim's suggestion first and then Ian's.

There was a bit of a serendipity moment. Chris, not knowing that June and Ginger had joined them, was still playing Ian's version.

'Hey I like that!' cried Ginger, not guessing that she had just sealed the fate of a track for the new LP.!

Ian turned to Tim with a wicked grin on his face.

'Okay, I concede. That's the version we will use,' he reluctantly said.

With that the tension eased.

On seeing Ginger, Ian's mood changed and with a big smile said: 'What is this I hear about a surprise present?'

This time it was Ginger with a huge grin: 'What makes you think it's for you? You'll just have to wait and see,' she said playfully.

The door opened. 'Come on everyone, dinner is ready,' said Jessie.

CHAPTER TWELVE

It was bright and sunny the following morning and the weather forecast held good for the next couple of days. 'Right Ginger,' said Ian, 'how about that trip to Thurne Mill I promised you?'

'You bet!' Ginger was really getting into boating now. She was determined to take up every opportunity which came her way, to gain knowledge and to better understand the waterways.

'That sounds like a good idea,' said Tim. 'With *Spectrum One* and *Two* still in the water we could take both boats, so that if we did decide to go further afield we can stay overnight.'

June shivered at the thought. She liked her warmth, especially in bed! Unlike adventurous Ginger she was still to get into this boating lark. However, she knew she had to make the effort as her feelings for Tim were growing.

'Don't worry June' said Chris, 'you'll be as warm as toast once the heaters are turned on in the cabin. Just think what it would have been like in 1962 when the Broads and rivers froze. What was fantastic was you could skate for miles along the rivers. A couple of wherry captains weren't so happy as they were stuck in the ice on Oulton Broad for a month. Just imagine the loss of income they would have experienced to be out of action for so long.

People even did ice boating.'

'Ian didn't you show me an old photo of an unusual yacht,' said Ginger. 'You know, the one looking like a plank on runners with sails. Wasn't that on the ice?'

'Yes, you are right,' he said. 'You're thinking of dad's seventeenth century print of the Dutch flat-bottomed sailboat. Nowadays the yachts sit on a triangular frame supported by three skate blades called runners. The front runner is used for steering. There are regular regattas, and with the yachts averaging 72 mph the course is usually a frozen lake or river. At one time 90 mph was recorded.'

Jessie then appeared with a bag full of goodies for their meals whilst they were away. Tim looked at the mountain of food presented for their boats stores. 'We are only going for a few days Jessie, but thanks a bunch.'

Tim and Ian each gave Jessie a hug. 'We know you have a tendency to worry so we swear we will radio in on a regular basis.'

The two boats cast off with Ian, Ginger, Mark and Sandra in *Spectrum Two,* the others in *Spectrum One.*

Ever cheeky Sandra couldn't resist the last word. 'Jessie, with us out of the way should give you a great opportunity to practise your Gracie Field's number which I've heard so much about.'

Jessie waved and smiled but didn't quite blush. She was known to break into that well-known Music Hall number, *The Biggest Aspidistra in the World* after a few sherries. Jessie still had heaps to do for Christmas. More mince pies to make, the cake to be fed with brandy and then decorated. The list went on and on.

Grace and Sam were due to arrive later in the day. Sam and her husband Frank were to go to Neatishead for a short meeting. Grace will happily join her in the kitchen and her sausage rolls were superb.

❧ ❧ ❧

Travelling along the River Bure in the direction of Thurne mouth, all that could be heard was the slapping of water on the hulls as the boats cut smoothly through the still river. Everyone was silent, each with their individual thoughts. The tide was speeding them along.

Passing Ant mouth and South Walsham Broad, open meadowland came into view. St. Benets Abbey, another icon of the Broads emerged in the vast landscape which stretched endlessly into the distance.

St. Benedict gave his name to the Abbey. He was an Italian and the Father of Western Monasticism. Hermits and monks lived in modest dwellings as early as the ninth century. Even to this day the Bishop of Norwich is still the Abbott and conducts an annual outdoor service there, arriving in style standing on the foredeck of a wherry. Quite a sight.

Norfolk is very fond of its folklore, especially those involving ghosts. St. Benets Abbey is no stranger to such tales, but its story is very gruesome. Read on if you are of strong heart!

The monastery survived an attack from King Canute in 1016. You would have thought that this was enough for the brethren, but no! The next encounter was William of Normandy. One of the monks, Brother Veritas, always had visions of being the Abbot of

St. Benets. With promises from the Conqueror of being made Abbot and saving his brethren from the sword, he agreed to unbolt the oak studded entrance door. The Abbey was then easily taken by the invaders.

Great surprise followed the event as Brother Veritas was duly robed and crowned as the new Abbot of St. Benets.........it didn't last! Suddenly the soldiers grabbed Brother Veritas. With hands bound, and still in full cape and mitre, kicking and struggling, he was hanged for all to see, for his treachery! Every year, on the 25th May, this sickening sight is re-enacted.

At lunch-time June and Ginger had their first glimpse of the two windpumps standing guard either side of the entrance of Thurne Dyke. The white one, such a landmark, stood out in the cold December day. Whenever the sun peeped out from behind the clouds it cast a welcome relief over the stark outline of the mill.

'There it is Ginger,' said Ian, 'Thurne Mill, the centre of the Broads network, and one of the most emblematic and photogenic sites of the Broads.'

Ginger stood in the cockpit and just looked. She took in the amazing sight of this iconic mill. 'Ian it's unbelievable. Wow, it was worth the journey. Thank you.'

The two boats motored down the short dyke. Over lunch Tim kept both June and Ginger enthralled. Built in 1820 the canvas mill sails drained the nearby marshes. To furl and unfurl the sails to keep the pump working proved heavy on manpower. Consequently in 1855 a new pump was installed, the sails now turned automatically in the wind. By 1926 a steam turbine was doing the job. Shortly after this event the mill ceased operation. It became derelict for many years but has now been restored and leased to the Norfolk Windmill Trust to secure its future.

'Can we go in?' asked Ginger.

'Unfortunately not,' said Tim, 'the best way to do that is to attend one of the Trust's open days.'

They spent a little while wandering around the village which boasted the smallest Post Office on the Broads, an Inn and the thatched Norman Church. St. Edmund has a very interesting squint or crack through the west wall, assumed possibly to be a Lepers Hole. However as the opening lines up with St. Benets Abbey across the fields, historians think it was to create a kind of sacramental connection between the two.

The village name of Thurne is of Saxon origin and thought to mean *thorn bush*.

Dusk was falling, June was watching the setting sun: 'Look!' She cried.

The others stopped in their tracks and turned to where June was pointing. A dark swirling mist seemed to be approaching. The so-called cloud moved closer accompanied by a cacophony of bird song. It was an incredible sight. It weaved and danced as if to music. Complex patterns appeared. First a spiralling ball, then sweeping, twisting lines and so it continued.....

'It's a starling murmuration,' said Mark, as more birds flew in from opposite directions joining the original flock. It was like iron filings being drawn to a magnet as the starlings, now numbering thousands, merged into one and continued to create complex patterns in the darkening sky.

Suddenly, without warning, the birds swooped down into the reeds and silence reigned.

'That was outstanding,' said a gob smacked Ginger. 'I've never seen that before. What triggers it?'

'Well,' answered Mark. 'With the starlings grouping together there is safety in numbers. Any airborne predator finds it more difficult to focus on a single target when faced with a churning mass. The birds can also huddle together for warmth and communicate whilst roosting in the reed beds.'

'It's not just here in the Broads,' continued Tim. 'Starling murmurations occur all over the country, even in towns. Brighton always has a spectacular one over its seafront.'

It was only a short distance from Thurne to Ludham where they decided to spend the night moored in Womack Water.

Tony always fancied himself as a dab-hand at cooking and offered to do the dinner. He shooed everybody off *Spectrum One* onto *Spectrum Two* while he created his masterpiece. Well, actually he really combined a couple of Jessie's meals!

Ian, who had been acting as *sous chef* to Tony, rejoined them on *Spectrum Two*. 'Sorry to disturb you all,' he said, 'But our chef is waiting for us to sample his concoction. I think he's named it something like, *Jessie's savoureux repas*! '

They crossed from one boat to the other to be greeted with a most succulent smell. They crammed into *Spectrum One's* cabin and squashed around the table. Tony dished up. They were about to start. 'Wait!' Tony cried, 'something's missing?'

Tim hastily got up. 'And I know what it is. Sorry Tony I forgot.' He disappeared out of the cabin. They heard a splashing and then Tim reappeared with a dripping object.

'Oh the wine,' said Ian.

'Chilled to the right temperature, courtesy of Womack Water,' added Tim.

※ ※ ※

June woke the next morning to the delightful smell of freshly brewed coffee. She had slept well and couldn't believe how cosy she had been in her sleeping bag. Maybe this boating lark is not so bad after all!

Pulling on her tracksuit, June padded into the main cabin. Tim, with his back to her, was frying eggs and bacon. Chris was laying the table setting out the delights of home-made marmalade and crusty white rolls. She saw June and went to speak but was silenced as June crept behind Tim tapping him on the shoulder. 'That smells delicious, Tim, am I late?'

Tim spun round, spatula disappearing into the sink. 'No young lady, you are just about on time,' and gave her a very hearty good morning kiss.

Next on the scene, stifling a yawn, a rather tousled figure, came through into the cabin. 'You do keep the most unreasonable hours.' Bleary eyed or not Tony still had to do the proper thing. Chris was also given a very long and welcome good morning embrace.

He sat down at the table. Chris pushed a cup of black coffee under his nose.

'That might go some way to waking you up darling,' she said.

They had just finished breakfast with June volunteering to do the washing-up when the boat rocked as Ian and Mark boarded.

'Hi Folks,' said Ian, 'Look who has found us! I have a feeling we might be a wee bit busy over the next few days.'

Inspector Devenport had followed them on board.

'Oh morning Inspector,' said Tim, rather taken aback. 'It sounds a bit ominous if you have tracked us down,' and handed him a freshly brewed coffee.

'Mm, well I called at Spindle last night and Jessie told me I would find you here. As Norfolk Broads' Rangers you are always very helpful to me, especially when I'm short-staffed as I am at the moment with flu and Christmas just around the corner. We have had reports of strange lights over Horsey Mere. It might not be anything at all, but it has been reported by more than one person and thus warrants investigation. It leads me on to the question, would you mind extending your trip for a couple of days to see if there is anything in the reports or if it is just the ghosts from the past of the Children's Mere?'

Tim looked at the other members of *Spectrum*. It was obvious from their expressions.

'We'd be pleased to,' said Tim.

The Inspector finished his coffee leaving them with the parting words: 'Remember, report anything out of the ordinary immediately.'

Spectrum was used to taking on such requests from the Inspector, but on this occasion there were others to consider.

Tim turned his attention to Tony, June, Ginger and Sandra, the latter having followed the Inspector in.

'If you four don't want to come along, we shall quite understand and can easily drop you off somewhere where you can be picked up. As much as we would like your company it could turn into something more adventurous than we all anticipate. After all it may just be a hoax and a touch of the Christmas spirit. The choice is yours.'

'On my part, after what I experienced back in the summer, I think I'm ready for another adventure, Captain Tim,' said Tony with a mock salute. 'Anyway, I do not want Chris out of my sight,' and gave her a quick cuddle.

'You're not going to get rid of me that easily cousin,' said Sandra.

'In for a penny, in for a pound,' Ginger wanted to be included, smiling at Tim. She would not let something like this pass her by ...... especially with Ian being involved.

The only hesitation was from June. Tim took her into his arms.

'I know it's quite out of your comfort zone, but I would really like you to be with us .... me.... but I'll understand if you would prefer not to. *Spectrum* has tons of experience in such things and the Inspector would not ask us if he did not trust our actions. True last August went a bit pear shaped but that was the exception.'

June thought for a moment. Her feelings for Tim were growing. She knew his work on the Broads was important to him. If their relationship was to survive she would have to be involved.

'I don't fancy being at Spindle by myself, so I'm game.'

Tim kissed her on the tip of her nose. 'Good.'

From then on it was all systems go and in a very short while they were underway heading up the River Thurne in the direction of Hickling and Horsey.

While Chris and Mark were at the helms of the respective boats, Tim and Ian instructed the others in the use of the walkie talkies and also the elementary running of the boats in case of an emergency. For Tony it was a refresher course. Jessie was duly radioed and told that they wouldn't be back for a day or so as they were going *ghost hunting*!

Prompted by June, Chris started to explain the reason for the Inspector's comment about the ghosts of the Children's Mere......

'It all dates back to Roman times. If a child should die its tiny body was weighted and gently lowered into the depths of Horsey Mere. However, their spirits live on. During the night of the 13th June the skies supposedly darken towards midnight. The reeds along the banks brighten as if a myraid of glow worms come to the fore. Music is heard and the water rolls back revealing a beautiful grassy meadow. Down the mossy banks come children dancing, clapping and smiling in the sunlight. Lions follow and the children play without any fear. After a while the vision gradually fades, the Broad becomes a broad again and all signs of a Children's Paradise is extinguished.'

'How moving,' said June, 'and is that what the Inspector thinks is happening even though it's the middle of winter rather than summer?'

'That's an interesting scenario. Well, we'll soon find out,' said Chris.

The boats had entered the narrow waterway of Heigham Sound which was full of wildfowl.

Mark was in his element. He was thoroughly enjoying himself helping Sandra identify the birds, many of which overwintered in this part of Norfolk. There was teal, the country's smallest duck boasting dark chestnut heads and green speculums; pink-breasted wigeon with their beautiful whistling call and waders like the curlew and black-tailed godwit. The geese on the adjoining grassland were mainly pink-footed, interspersed with a few rare Taiga bean geese. This species really excited Mark as it breeds in the Arctic and occasionally winters in the Broads grazing on the fields of sugar beet remains left, especially for them, by the local farmers.

Whenever a peregrine falcon or marsh harrier flew over, the golden plover were up in one big swarm all swooping and swirling in unison. A breathtaking sight.... When the coast was clear they descended once more and resumed feeding.

The two boats travelled up Meadow Dyke into Horsey Mere. June looked appreciatively around her at the banks wild with thick beds of reed, 'What a pretty Broad. I'm so pleased I decided to join you.'

'It's even better in the summer,' said Tim, 'and it's only about 1½ miles from the coast; we'll come here in the spring if you like, when it will be warmer and far more interesting.'

They passed Horsea Island, which was rather small and made up basically of reeds with some heather, bracken and alder trees on the firmer ground towards the centre. In fact, the Island was a fine example of succession; how nature reclaims land from water. As they looked towards the narrow inlet leading up through the reed bed there was what looked like the remains of a fire.

'That's odd,' said Chris pointing. 'Maybe there is more here than meets the eye.'

'Possibly the ghosts having a BBQ' said Tim tongue in cheek, and then his tone changed, 'or maybe something more sinister.'

The light was now fading. 'We'll have a closer look in the morning,' he continued.

Spectrum One and *Two* had reached the north-west side of the Mere and moored just below Waxham New Cut for the night.

Tim was checking the mooring ropes and looked across to *Spectrum Two* to see Ginger with Ian doing the same. Ginger was determined to learn all she could about the running of a *Spectrum* and Ian was only too pleased to oblige. Ginger stood up from the stern lines, a light caught her attention.

'Ian!' she called, 'what's that?' and pointed.

The light appeared again and this time Tim saw it as well.

Ian turned round, 'Curiouser and curiouser, maybe there is some truth in those reports after all.'

'Come on,' said Tim, 'let's launch the rubber dinghy and go and have a look.'

Tony was quite worried, after the dreadful incident back in the summer. Chris sensing his mood, put her arms around his neck and kissed him. 'It'll be okay darling, lightning is not supposed to strike twice!'

He sighed heavily. 'No I suppose not.'

Chris gently eased herself into the waiting dinghy which Tim was holding steady and they quietly paddled away. Tony watched the ghostly outline until it merged into the blackness. The boat rocked gently as a breeze brushed the waters surface. It was strangely comforting to hear the lap lap of the Mere on the sides of the hull. He looked up at the starlit night just as the moon peeped out from an invisible cloud casting an eerie shadow around the reedy banks. He suddenly shivered and hastily went below to the warmth of the cabin to join the others now all on board *Spectrum One*.

The long wait had begun……

⁂

Spectrum Rangers reached the far side of the island to where the embers of a fire had been spotted. The moon came out again and lit the area briefly.

'What was that?' whispered Chris as she noticed something glinting in the dark.

'I don't know,' said Tim.

They left the dinghy hidden in the bushes.

Spectrum moved silently through the bracken, creeping on their bellies to avoid any silhouette breaking the skyline. They could just make out a man drinking by the side of the now relit fire. His colleague was down at the waters edge signalling frantically across the marshes. An answering flash came back from what they knew to be the open sea. The interchange went on until the man turned back to his mate who appeared to be the younger of the two. They' laughed obviously satisfied with their reply.

⁂

Meanwhile back on *Spectrum One* the time seemed to drag. The girls had been playing a game of cards. Ginger had won. Sandra, with now nothing better to do, became fidgety and decided to go out on deck. She passed Tony on the way who was sitting in the closed cockpit.

'Where are you going Sandra?'

'Just for some fresh air, it's so stuffy in the cabin.'

'Well don't go far young lady. Just stay around the boat.'

Sandra slid open the hatch to be met by the barrel of a gun. 'Get back,' said a gruff voice. She slowly backed away. For the first time in her life Sandra was extremely frightened.

She collided with a bewildered Tony who put a protective arm around her shoulders. 'Who the Hell are you?' he exclaimed.

Before any answer could be given, a second, much younger man followed the gunman in. He grabbed Tony by the wrists forming a very effective armlock. Sandra was unceremoniously pushed to one side.

'For Christ's sake,' said Tony struggling, and seeing the now terrified Sandra, 'leave the girl alone.'

The first intruder, probably in his fifties, glanced into the cabin and flicked the gun. 'Right below.' Tony was released, shoved into the cabin followed by Sandra. A silent communication passed between the two of them. Where are June and Ginger?

The younger of the two grabbed Tony once more. 'Ouch! You're breaking my arm!'

'That's not all we'll break unless you give us some answers:' said the man with the gun. 'Anyway who are you, the Cap't or something?'

Tony inclined his head.

'Right *Spectrum*, where are your other two members? I'm not having six months planning come to nothing

177

because of the interference of **YOU** and a bunch of schoolkids. I've got a boat to catch.'

At that moment there was a scraping noise on the cabin roof. 'What was that?' said the youngster looking up apprehensively.

'Probably geese:' interjected Tony. However, his thoughts turned back to June and Ginger.

The noise continued. Could it be them?

June and Ginger had heard the disturbance on deck and headed towards the bow. They climbed out through the fo'ard hatchway. There wasn't time to grab their coats. The pair of them stood on the bank behind some of the reeds shivering in the cold December night.

Freezing or not they had to do something or other to get help.

'What about the radio?' whispered Ginger, 'Do you think we could get to it to call someone?'

'That's a bit dangerous,' replied June, 'but it does seem to be the logical thing to do.'

It wasn't a case of tossing a coin – we all know who was going to risk it!

Ginger moved along the cabin roof and quietly dropped into the cockpit through the open door. She peeped into the cabin and saw the back of a man with a gun pointing at Tony and Sandra. She turned to reach for the radio but never made it. The young one, who had been loitering in the shadow of the hull, grabbed Ginger from behind and pulled her into the cabin. She stumbled and Tony caught her.

'Well, that's three down. Dave search the other boat for the remaining one.'

The dark-haired lad who couldn't be long out of his teens, did as he was told.

After what seemed ages, actually only a couple of minutes, he returned. 'There doesn't seem to be anyone else around or on the other *Spectrum* craft Wilf.'

The older one handed his gun to Dave as he reached into his pocket and pulled out a small radio. 'We've three of S, but can find no trace of the fourth member, over.' They couldn't hear the reply. Wilf grunted, put the radio away, took control of the gun and kept it pointed.

'Tie 'em up Dave, we're moving out. The job is nearly complete.'

This comment puzzled the three captives.

The two men then left leaving them trussed up like spring chickens. Tony felt it was a bit *déjà vu* only this time there was no blood trickling down the side of his face or a sore shoulder! Just a few bruises and an aching arm!

❧ ❧ ❧

Back on the island the swaying reed stems helped to conceal Tim, Ian, Chris and Mark. They watched, and waited. Nothing seemed to happen for a while; the two men just sat either side of the fire until the radio crackled into life. The signaller picked it up. They could hardly hear what was said, but caught the answer, 'you'd better leave be, we've made contact and the rendezvous has been agreed for midnight.'

He turned off the radio, chucked his can of drink away and picked up a webbed belt lying at his feet. He opened one of the pouches. 'It's hard to believe Bill,' said the signaller, 'that just this one pouch is worth nearly a quarter of a million.'

'Drugs!' muttered Chris and moved her left leg which had started to cramp; unfortunately, as she stirred so a twig snapped beneath her foot. It echoed around the still night sounding just like a gunshot.

Bill spun round, whipped out a revolver. 'What was that?' Chris held her breath.

'Oh, put that down,' said his partner, 'It was probably some animal on the night prowl. Don't be so jittery, you're making me nervous.'

He reluctantly put his gun away and the two men's attention was once more on the pouch.

Tim was coming to the conclusion that they were now way out of their depth and back-up was required, urgently.

However, events continued to deteriorate. A motorboat arrived.

The two men became four.

The signaller spread out a map on the ground for the benefit of the new arrivals. 'The Black Swan is laying off here.' He pointed at the map. 'We're to take the pouches to the mill where they will be picked up and the exchange will take place in just under an hour, so we'd better get a move on.'

The moon had now re-appeared from behind the clouds and cast bright shadows lighting up the surroundings.

The man named Bill turned again to where Tim, Ian, Chris and Mark were concealed. He obviously wasn't altogether convinced with his mate's explanation. There was a lot of money involved in this deal and he was not about to give up his share. He took out his gun once more and approached their hiding place.

'Right! Now!' shouted Tim.

The three boys descended on Bill knocking him to the ground and the gun went flying.

The skirmish alerted his colleagues who all jumped up ready to join in the fray.

The light from the moon picked out the fallen weapon. Chris seeing the possible danger to her brothers grabbed the gun.

In the most assertive voice she could muster cried, 'I'll shoot and I mean it.'

This didn't seem to deter the rest of the gang as they started to move towards their fallen comrade. Chris fired a warning shot above their heads. It halted them. Fortunately at that moment out of the corner of her eye she saw two dinghies beach,

Or you could say the cavalry had arrived!

The relief Chris felt was overwhelming, she didn't know how she would have reacted if the criminals had continued towards her. She dropped the gun. Tim was at her side. She started to shake and crumpled to her knees.

Tim kneeled beside her and put a protective arm around her shoulders.

'It's okay sis, it's all over:' he said.

The four men were handcuffed and frog-marched to the two police launches.

The Inspector approached them, looking just as concerned as Tim.

'How did you know?' Chris started to say, but her twin interrupted.

'There's a pick up waiting by Horsey Mill and a boat called the Black Swan laying-off the coast.'

The Inspector turned to the radio just as a familiar outline appeared on the horizon.

'To answer your question Chris,' he said, 'you'd better ask your friends about that.'

⁓ ⁓ ⁓

Back on board they exchanged stories where it turned out that June was the heroine.

'To my horror I heard them catch Ginger. The moon was shining so brightly I was convinced I would be spotted. I must admit it was rather chilly hiding in the reeds in just my sweatshirt and jogging bottoms. My heart was beating nineteen to the dozen. Nothing seemed to happen for a while. Then suddenly I heard an engine start and with relief saw their dinghy disappear across the Mere. As soon as they were out of sight I rushed to *Spectrum One*.'

Tim was impressed.

Tony took up the story. 'We radioed the Police HQ and thank God they arrived pretty quickly. Two launches were already on the river and the Inspector at Stalham. It was all pretty impressive. Hats off to the British bobby!'

Spectrum One was now moored alongside *Spectrum Two* for what remained of the night.

Sandra was keyed up and couldn't get to sleep. She had always been envious of her cousins' exploits and oh so wanted to be involved. However, having experienced one, it was scary and now she wasn't so sure. But we all know Sandra, this didn't last. She soon dropped off, no doubt dreaming of her next adventure!

Ginger was lying in her bunk. She too was having difficulty nodding off. Her mind was racing. If this was the life she would expect whilst around Ian she was going to have to accept it. Her consolation was that escapades like this were few and far between.

Back on *Spectrum One*, June woke the next morning to find the boat was already moving. Suddenly she remembered the events of the previous evening. June couldn't believe she had been part of such an undertaking. True it had been both exciting and terrifying in equal measure but it might not be at the top of her *wish list* to experience again.

She went into the cabin to find it deserted; in the cockpit she heard the soft murmur of voices. At the wheel was Tony with Tim and Chris either side drinking coffee. A concerned Tim spotted her.

'Morning June,' he said extracting himself and giving her a cuddle: 'are you okay after yesterday?'

'I'm fine Tim, thanks. Am I very late?' she asked.

'No not really,' said Chris, 'but we wanted to get back to Spindle early to get ready for tomorrow.'

'Tomorrow?'

'It's Christmas Day tomorrow, had you forgotten?'

'Of course it is I still can't get over what has happened. It's just like something you usually read about.' She looked across at *Spectrum Two* following in their wake.

'Anyway,' said Chris, 'you beat Ginger and Sandra up, they haven't surfaced yet. Come on June, I'll make you some breakfast.'

'Don't forget more coffee for the Skipper and his mate,' called Tony.

'Right-oh, Cap't sir,' said Chris doing a mock salute and beating a hasty retreat to the cabin before they could retaliate.

⛵ ⛵ ⛵

They arrived back at Spindle in the early evening just as the phone was ringing. Tony went to answer it. In a short while he rejoined them in the lounge. 'That was Laurie, the Christmas Chart is out.'

'Who's number 1?' asked an excitable Sandra, 'You or *Spectrum*?'

'Well.....' Tony hesitated. 'Sorry kids, but I'm number 1.'

'Congratulations Tony,' said Chris. 'We couldn't really have expected two hits in a row,' and she hugged him.

'But guess who is No. 2?'

'Whee I said it would be a hit,' cried Ginger and did a victory dance spinning poor Ian around.

The next morning when Chris woke up the bedroom seemed unusually and remarkably bright. She looked at the clock, it was still quite early, but glancing out of the window she saw the reason why as spread out before her was an unending white carpet.

'A white Christmas, oh brilliant.'

The broad was starting to freeze and she had a quiet chuckle to herself as a couple of mallards tried to land on the ice and ended up skidding halfway across it before they plopped unceremoniously into the water. A pair of coots were gingerly walking across the ice, their huge blue slightly webbed feet giving them a stable platform whilst a grey heron was not as successful as it tried to move along the reed edge. Every so often a foot fell through the ice.

She heard a movement in the corridor. There was a tap at the door, and June and Ginger came in none the worse for their experience.

'Merry Christmas,' said June.

'Isn't it a beautiful day? A white Christmas,' said Ginger.

'Are you three coming?' called a voice from below, 'Or are we going to have to wait all morning to open our presents?'

'That sounded remarkably like Sandra,' said Chris, 'let's go and join them.'

'Come on sis,' said Tim, 'you're keeping us waiting.'

'Sorry,' said Chris, 'Merry Christmas everyone.'

In the lounge all were gathered. The Christmas tree looked great with the fairy lights reflecting off the tinsel. Sandra handed out the presents and quickly delved into hers. The first one she opened was from Mark. She ripped off the paper turned the box round and looked straight at a model of a toy dinosaur.

'Well, you did say you enjoyed Dippy in November,' said Ian wickedly.

Sandra ignored the comment as she looked again at the dinosaur. Hanging from its neck was a small velvet draw-string bag. She opened it and found a lovely silver pendant with her gem stone.

Ian had found the surprise present from Ginger. It was a cassette of Bill Haley and the Comets.

'Well you always say a head-banger goes well in the middle of a music track so I thought I would give you something to aspire to!' said Ginger keeping well out of harms way in case of any retaliatory actions!

Delightful smells wafted through from the kitchen.

The log fire glowed. Tracks from festive LPs like Bing Crosby's *White Christmas*, Jim Reeves *Christmas Portrait* and Andy Williams *Most Wonderful Time of the year*, played softly in the background.

A superb lunch had come and gone so had the Queen's Christmas message. Ian was sitting in one of the armchairs with Ginger on his knee. Sandra in her usual position was sprawled on the floor reading a book. Frank and Sam, exchanging stories, mellowed under the influence of their whiskies. Tony with his arm around Chris was trying his best not to nod off. Meanwhile June, Tim, Matt and Mark were having a heated game of snap!

Jessie and Grace carried in coffee with further snacks and the famed sausage rolls!

'Come on Tim,' said Grace, 'you know what's next.' Tim joined his mother at the piano and the pair of them played a medley of carols with much raucous singing from everyone else.

Tim swivelled around on the piano stool. He and Tony exchanged a silent communication.

Tony extracted himself from Chris and wandered over to the tree. Sandra had missed three small parcels cleverly hidden. He turned to Ginger, June and Sandra and gave them each a small box.

When they opened them nestling inside the cotton wool were tiny silver medallions. Engraved on one side was a triangle with a rainbow outline and a decorative 'S'; on the reverse a heron flying lazily over a bed of reeds.

'They're beautiful,' said June.

Tim simply said: 'Welcome to *Spectrum*.'

SPRINGTIME ON THE BROADS

CHAPTER THIRTEEN

It was the 1st January. All were up early despite seeing the New Year in with Mark and Ian's firework display. One of the rockets, instead of disappearing upwards, tipped as it was lit and shot lengthwise down the Broad but fortunately plopped into the water before it could do any damage. Mark then dropped a jumping jack firework which everyone had fun dodging bar Jessie, who took refuge behind her strapping six foot tall son Matt.

Just after midnight Tony had slipped out of the backway and had proceeded to come in through the front-door, carrying a lump of coal.

'Old Scottish Custom,' he said. 'The first person over the threshold of a house in the New Year must be dark, handsome and with a piece of coal. It's called 'First Footing' you know! It's to ensure good luck prevails in the household for the coming year.'

'First Footing, indeed,' remarked Chris, 'dark you may be, but handsome, you, you know-it-all.'

'Cheek!' He pulled her under the mistletoe.

The Christmas holidays had come to an end, June and Ginger were anxious to return to Kent as their parents were both arriving that evening. Uncle Chas and Aunt Meg, Sandra's parents, had flown in overnight from Botswana and should also be home. An impatient Sandra couldn't wait to see them again after nearly three months. For Tony, when he reached London, it would be unpacking one bag just to fill another. He was due to start his Australian tour at the end of the week.

Tony's car was bulging with their cases. 'At this rate,' he said, as another holdall was handed to him, 'there won't be any room for the driver, let alone passengers!'

Somehow everybody and everything fitted in. Ginger and Sandra were squashed in the back with June sitting in moderate comfort in the front.

An Aston Martin was not normally a car for four.

'Thank you for a super Christmas and New Year and especially for this,' said June touching her medallion. Tim leaned through the window and gave her a peck on the cheek squeezing her hand. 'You deserve it.'

Sandra, excitable as ever called from the back-seat. 'Yippee! It's great. I am at last part of *Spectrum*,' her outstretched hands just short of hitting the Aston Martin's roof and Ginger who managed to dodge the exuberance.

Chris and Tony, deep brown eyes meeting grey blue eyes. The look said everything. 'I'll see you soon,' he said huskily, and tipped up her chin. 'Go on, give me a smile, time will pass in a blink of an eye.'

Chris did, and then reluctantly let him go. She looked at her bracelet, another charm had been added, a heart with an arrow piercing it. Then her fingers travelled to a silver necklace around her neck on which hung a very precious item.

Yesterday afternoon all had been involved in a madcap game of Monopoly. Both she and Tony had been bankrupted after landing on Ian and Ginger's Park Lane which had a hotel. For once Tony, usually so competitive, had seemed quite pleased being knocked out at such an early stage. 'Come on Chris, grab your coat,' he said, 'let's go for a walk.'

Hand in hand the pair of them wandered down to the Broad leaving a trail of footprints in the freshly fallen snow. At the water's edge Chris took her gloves off to pull her hat over her ears. She turned to find Tony on one knee in front of her.

'Chris, I love you lots and it must be difficult for you with so many fans chasing after me and Laurie's comment about keeping our relationship a secret.' He reached into his pocket and took out a tiny velvet blue box and opened the lid. 'With University around the corner I want to make a commitment. I'll always be there for you and ready for marriage when time permits. In other words, Christine Grace Rogers will you marry me?'

Chris's expression of love and delight said it all.

He took hold of Chris's ungloved hand and slipped the beautiful engagement ring onto her finger. Sealing the pledge, he gave her a long, deep and lasting kiss.

1969 was certainly going to be a year to remember.

※ ※ ※

Chris was back on the familiar path to school. She smiled to herself as she recalled Tony's phone call the previous evening. They had just arrived home from Norfolk when he rang. *Spectrum* had knocked him off the top spot, they were number 1! She still couldn't believe they had released records, let alone ones which had been so successful. Chris was still extremely anxious about *Spectrum* being rivals for Tony in what is a very cut-throat industry. If he thought it, he didn't show it. She tenderly fingered the chain around her neck.

Chris tossed back her head as the wind blew strongly in her face tugging at the roots of her hair. The clouds skidded across the sky in one continuous race, each trying to outdo the other, reaching an imaginary finishing line. Her scarf blew across her face. She pulled it back, turned the corner of Rock Avenue and caught sight of Sandra.

'Did your mum and dad get their safari?' asked Chris. She was always interested to hear about the adventures of Aunt Meg and Uncle Chas.

Sandra nodded. 'They actually camped in the bush! Their toilet was a hole in the ground and when it came to showering, there was only enough water for ten of them. They had to draw lots as it was a party of twelve!'

As usual, Sandra was talking nineteen to the dozen in her inimitable way.

'Apparently a pack of hyenas attempted to break into the food trailer overnight. That was exciting but a bit scary. A herd of elephants skirted their camp and at times they could hear lions roaring in the distance. One day they went looking for leopards only to find one had walked through the camp whilst they were out in the 4-wheel drive.'

'That was a bit of bad luck. How about the rest of the Big Five did your mum and dad see those?' asked Chris.

'Oh you mean the rhino, lion, elephant, and buffalo? You bet! They also saw two young male lions, sitting back-to back under a tree, looking like a pair of bookends. The photos are brilliant.'

'What about the Ugly Five?'

'Ugly Five?' queried Sandra

'Hyena, wildebeest, marabou stork, vulture and warthog. All super animals and strangely beautiful in their own way but seem to have that tag,' replied Chris.

Sandra didn't have the chance to answer. The pair of them had reached the school building. June and Ginger had also just arrived so Sandra disappeared off to her class.

'Congratulations!' said Ginger, 'You made it.'

'Congratulations for what?' asked the unmistakable voice of Rachel coming up behind them.

'Oh….. arr…... um…...' stuttered Ginger.

June once more came to the rescue, 'Oh Chris thought that *Spectrum* would make it to Number 1 and she and Ginger had a little wager on it.'

'Oh, is that all. That was cut and dried after its first week of issue. But what about those drug smugglers. It was all over the newspapers that *Spectrum* were involved. I always thought Norfolk was a rather sleepy county stuck out on a limb in the North Sea.

What do you two think about it all ?'

June and Ginger looked at each other, how can they answer without spilling the beans. No one knew they had been in Norfolk over Christmas. Fortunately, Belinda arrived and shooed the Prefects off to Assembly.

Mrs. MacDonald's welcoming message for the new term was a bit different from the normal Assembly.

'Girls, as you know 1969 marks our proud college's twentieth anniversary. To celebrate this momentous occasion each form is to create a presentation homing in on a specific occurrence since 1949. Your form teachers have been given the year you are to commemorate. The presentations will be held at our annual Open Day in the last week of term, just before we break up for the Easter holidays.

Good luck to you all.'

※ ※ ※

Chris was in the library. Her form had been given the Space Race for their presentation, mainly John F. Kennedy's statement that 'the USA would land a man on the moon before the end of the decade.' The moon landing was scheduled for this coming July.

Chris was listing some points…..

1958 President Eisenhower created NASA

1962 The first American, John H Glenn circled the Earth three times.

Project Apollo was under way.

Last month Apollo 8 with a three-man crew had actually orbited the Moon. That was some feat.

She stretched and looked at the clock. Lunch-time. Chris replaced the various reference books and picked up her notes. Suddenly an out of breath Sandra appeared at her side.

She had been looking for Chris.

'Chris, could you do me, well, my form a favour? Our presentation is on the end of food rationing and with the recent release of Lionel Bart's musical *Oliver*, Mrs. Baxter thought it would be a good idea if we performed, you know, *Food, Glorious Food*, from the show.'

Sandra was once more talking at a rate of knots, and rather too loudly for a library.

'Sshh Sandra, remember where you are.'

Now in the corridor, Sandra continued......'Do you think you could accompany us on the guitar? I don't mean your electric Stratocaster but the acoustic one. If you don't, Linda might play the piano and she's absolutely hopeless.'

Chris was now getting a bit *hot under the collar*: 'Just how does Mrs. Baxter know I played?'

Sandra, very sheepishly said: 'Well, I did sort of mention that you.....' but just then her form teacher appeared.

'Ah there you are Chris Sandra has told me that you have some knowledge of playing a guitar?'

'It's been a while, I'm not making excuses, but.......'

'Come, come Chris,' said Mrs. Baxter, 'I'm sure you're being too modest. I'll let you have a copy of the music.' A rather bemused Chris watched her disappear into the Staff Room.

'Played the guitar a bit,' said an indignant Sandra, with arms on hips, tossing her head back, but not quite stamping her foot. 'If only she knew you played it professionally and top the musical charts to boot!'

Chris was now extremely angry. 'Sandra, you know it is imperative that *Spectrum's* secret is kept. You've dug me into a big hole, yes you have, you know I'll have to do it.'

Sandra hung her head in shame. 'I'm sorry Chris. Yes, you are right I was out of order.'

Chris looked at the now, for once, a rather humble Sandra. 'Well *Spectrum's* fate is now in the lap of the Gods. Come on, let's go and find something to eat.'

※ ※ ※

A few days later Chris arrived at school with her Fender. The 6-string acoustic guitar had a highly polished tan top with contrasting darker wood on the sides and underneath. The neck of the guitar was also in mahogany with a rosewood bridge.

Diana, mug in hand said: 'Wow! That's some beast of an instrument.'

June, laying her book to one side, looked concerned visualising a coffee splattered item. 'Careful Diana, coffee and guitars don't go together.'

Belinda was just as impressed. Her collection included artists like Jimi Hendrix, Procol Harum and the Shadows. 'You're not trying to emulate *Spectrum*?'

Ginger and June held their breaths.

Chris laughed. 'What do you think Belinda? Of course I am. We all need someone to aspire to.

Joking aside, Sandra's form needed some music for their presentation and I have been landed with the task.'

Janice, as enthusiastic as the rest: 'Go on play us something.'

'Well I have been trying to learn Fleetwood Mac's latest you know *Albatross*....'

Chris played the opening notes, just enough to whet their appetites, tripping over one of the chords.

'I always have problems with the Country G chord. You have to use all four fingers over the fret, extremely difficult,' she said.

'That was good Chris,' said Belinda. 'It makes me think, if you're willing, we have some music for our presentation. Would you oblige?'

'Great idea Belinda,' cried Rachel. 'It has to be something *spacy* though. You know like the Tornadoes record *Telstar* of a few years ago which celebrated the first communication satellites to orbit the Earth.'

Chris felt cornered. Fortunately the bell went for the start of the days lessons.

'Sorry girls, maths exam coming up. I'll get back to you.'

≈ ≈ ≈

The following weekend Chris and her brothers were in London. It was the big one! After much pressure on the part of Laurie, Tim and Ian had eventually finished the score for *Spectrum's* album. During the run up to the recording they had had some fun trying to sing. Chris had a good ear for music but couldn't transfer that to a song. Tim wasn't much better. However, Mark and Ian harmonised....BINGO. Although their first two hits had been instrumentals Mark and Ian were keen to sing a couple of numbers on the LP. Laurie agreed.

While *Spectrum* was at the recording studios Grace took the opportunity to meet up with her sister Jean. There was a new exhibition at the Victoria and Albert Museum, highlighting the fashion of the Edwardians. The sisters were always interested in such things.

For Tony however, it was not a day for relaxation. Sam was with him for one thing, and one thing only. His tax return was due!

In Tony's London home the dining room table was strewn with paperwork.

'Oh my God what a mess,' said Sam, running his fingers threw his lush if greying hair. 'What am I going to do with you lad. You don't improve.'

197

Tony, hands on hips said: 'No I suppose you are right Sam. I am obviously better at singing than filing.'

‌❧ ❧ ❧

Spectrum spent the majority of Saturday recording. It took a lot out of them. Much of their spare time recently had been studying for their GCEs. Laurie had taken this into account by scheduling the day with plenty of breaks. However, things hadn't gone as well as expected. First off Tim's electric organ refused to tune correctly. Two numbers in a string broke on Ian's guitar. Laurie was doing his best not to show his frustration. Mark's wrists were aching from the drumming and he was massaging them between takes. Laurie noticed this maybe he was pushing them too hard and should not have expected the LP to be completed in one day.

They persevered. An equally weary Laurie eventually called time. The sound engineer had given the thumbs up. The recording was finished.

Tony and Sam appeared as *Spectrum* was discussing the final details with, by then, a reasonably happy Laurie. The nearby desk was cluttered with numerous sheets of paper, a bit like Tony's dining room table.

Tony looked at the various discarded musical scores and picked one up. 'Is this one that you've included? I don't remember seeing it before.' The words were very much akin to his feelings for Chris. It would be a great way to advertise his love for Chris without revealing too much to his fans.

Tim went to take it away from him, 'No we haven't there wasn't room.'

'Do you mind if I use it for my next single? I wanted a ballad and I like the look of *True Love*!'

Ian teasingly said: 'What's in it for us? 70/30?'

Tony joining in the fun. 'How about 60/40!'

'Seriously Tony I don't mind,' said Ian. 'I would be quite chuffed if you did. Between you and me I think Tim had June in mind when he wrote the words.'

'Oh, is it getting serious then?' he said looking at Tim with a twinkle in his eye.

'No of course not,' said Tim and just refrained from once more snatching the sheet from Tony. Yes he did have June in mind when he wrote the words. He was a bit reluctant to relinquish the song. At least with Tony singing it, it would stay in the family so to speak.

❧ ❧ ❧

Chris pondered on Tony's comment about Tim and June on the way to school. Who knew what the future held for them. Tim was studying hard for his GCEs: Maths, Physics and Chemistry. He had a leaning towards science and technology. With the dawn of the digital age and fibre optics it was an exciting time to be into such things. June had an interest in home economics and nutrition. Her thoughts were heading in the direction of teaching.

Chris bumped into a very excitable Rachel at the school's entrance. 'You will never guess. I'm off to the Norfolk Broads at Easter. We've hired a cabin cruiser for a fortnight. I think mum and dad had had enough of me nagging them about the area. Anyway dad loves fishing and I kept on hinting what a great area the Broads is for such a past-time.'

'That'll be fun – looking for *Spectrum* are we?' teased Chris.

Rachel gave a slight smile. They had reached the Prefects Room. She barged open the door nearly knocking Janice flying who was trying to exit. 'Oh sorry Janice, but you'll never guess? I'm off to the Broads for Easter. Isn't it great!' She did a bit of a victory dance.

June and Chris exchanged a silent communication. They were due to be in Norfolk over Easter. They both held their breaths watching Ginger carefully.

Ginger suddenly exclaimed: 'Lucky you Rachel. I would have given anything to go there again, just for the off chance of seeing Tony Dale.'

Panic over….all was good.

'Wouldn't that be great,' said an excitable Rachel doing another twirl.

Chris had a package under her arm. The ever observant Belinda, closing her book, called from across the room. 'What's that you're carrying Chris, anything interesting? It looks like a record to me.'

'Mmm yes it is. Rachel, I know you weren't expecting anything but Ginger, June and I thought it might be rather nice to celebrate your eighteenth birthday with something. If a bit belatedly! Following your comment that you and your parents are off to the Broads it appears to be a rather apt choice. Enjoy.' Chris presented Rachel with the parcel.

'Thanks very much, you shouldn't have.' Rachel ripped off the paper, looked and looked again. 'What…. **WHAT**…I don't believe it!' She exclaimed.

Her comments, as you can imagine, caused a bit of a stir with the other Prefects.

Belinda was the first to find a voice.

'What do you mean?' said Belinda, now at Rachel's side leaning over her shoulder. 'Hey, it's an LP of *Spectrum*.' she cried.

Rachel turned to Chris: 'How the devil did you get hold of this?' she said excitedly.

Before Chris could answer Belinda had noticed something else on the LP cover. 'Rachel, there seems to be some sort of scribble on the sleeve. I've left my glasses on the table and can't quite make it out.'

Rachel looked at where Belinda had pointed.

'It seems to be a name,' said Rachel. 'It can't be. Yes it is. It's Tony Dale's autograph.' She stared in amazement at Chris.

'I was in London at the weekend,' replied Chris. 'I went into HMV in Oxford Street and couldn't believe my eyes. On a stand, just to the side of the counter, was a small number of shortly to be released LPs and nestling in the middle was *Spectrum*. Lucky, eh?

Suddenly behind me I heard screams and there was Tony Dale. He had just walked in, with his entourage, apparently for a publicity stunt for his latest LP, *Dreamtime Plus*. The one you bought last week Rachel.

Well I couldn't miss an opportunity like this. I quickly purchased the LP, and joined the queue. He did look rather startled when I asked him to autograph it. But still, there you have it, *Spectrum's* first LP. Maybe it will beat *Dreamtime Plus* to the top of the Album Charts.'

Rachel laughed. 'An interesting scenario Chris. For once I don't mind who makes it. *Spectrum's A Bolt out of the Blue* is bound to be as good as Tony Dale's *Dreamtime Plus*.'

'Is this a changing of the guard Rachel,' teased Ginger.

Rachel smiled: 'Not really I still think Tony Dale is the business.'

⸙ ⸙ ⸙

The March wind was howling around the school building and any early daffodils were being knocked flat. This saddened Chris a bit. With the dark miserable days of winter behind them, the daffodil always seemed to cast a ray of hope of sunny days to come. Easter wasn't Easter without daffodils in bloom!

Her scarf had blown across her face several times. Her guitar over one shoulder and her satchel over the other it seemed she was battling the wind as much as the flowers were.

The School's Open day was on the morrow. Lessons had been put aside as final tweaks were made to each individual class offering. June was a little bit apprehensive. She and Chris were heading towards the School Hall. Chris had her guitar.

'Chris,' June said, 'are you really okay with doing both forms?'

'Yes I'm fine June, thanks for your concern. At least with Pam playing the piano for her Fifth Form the spotlight should be more on her than me. You know with all those Talent Competitions she enters.'

'The difference there,' said June, 'is that you are the modest one who has achieved, whereas Pam is yet to have any success. I would hate to have such a pushy mother as Pam's, insisting that she enters everything that comes her way.'

⸎ ⸎ ⸎

It had arrived, the School's Open Day. Grace and Aunt Meg, Sandra's mum, had come to support their offspring. They were ushered into the school hall along with the other parents. The red velvet curtains on the stage were shut. A hush descended. Mrs. MacDonald entered. She was wearing a short length black suede jacket over a dark green and blue kilt. The Clan MacDonald originated in the Western Isles and Mrs. MacDonald welcomed the parents in her soft Scottish accent.

'Thank you all for coming. I hope you will be inspired by what is to follow. St. James' College is celebrating its twentieth anniversary and our girls have been working hard this term to trace the historical timeline from 1949 to the present day. Such events as the ending of food rationing, the fashions of the era and the challenge of a Moon landing will be portrayed.'

Mrs. MacDonald left the stage. The curtains fell back. There was a group queueing with ration books. A table covered with scrumptious food now freely available. Gradually members of the Fourth Form crossed the stage holding up storyboards highlighting the journey from famine to feast. Chris could just be seen towards the back of the stage. As the last storyboard appeared so the class came together and sang *Food, Glorious Food,* accompanied by Chris's guitar: a superb ending to a very interesting presentation.

Next the scene was set for a Fashion Show. Members of the Fifth year entered dressed in the clothes of the era. Some from the start of the fifties had been found in Charity shops or raided from parents' attics! The backing music to the display was an interesting medley of the songs of the decades. Pam played exquisitely.

There were straight stovepipe trousers, velvet collar jackets, white shirts, colourful socks full skirts and flared trousers. A-line shift dresses, mini, midi and maxi dresses with varying hemlines as their name implies. The biggest cheer came with the entrance of the Carnaby Street's storyboard, the home of the swinging sixties fashion houses.

The climax was Melanie showing off her *super-scarf*. Oblong in shape, 10 feet long and called an Isadora Duncan. Unfortunately, she nearly ended up with the same fate as poor Isadora. Melanie tripped over the end of the scarf and went flying – at least it didn't get caught around the axle of a car causing strangulation which ended Isadora Duncan's life!

The curtains closed, it was the end of the morning's displays and time for lunch.

Chris and Sandra connected with their mums and headed outside. True it was March but the sun was shining. If they were quick they could get the table under the rose arbour. One of only a couple of places in the school's grounds sheltered from the wind.

Grace produced the picnic. Ham and chicken sandwiches, cheese straws, miniature pork pies and a delightful Victoria sponge filled with homemade strawberry jam. Absolutely delicious! It was very pleasant sitting amongst the spring bulbs and budding roses. House sparrows were swooping low over them hoping to pick up some titbits. A robin sang cheerfully in the oak tree delighting in the warmth of the day.

Lunch over it was time for the Sixth Form's presentation. Again, Chris sat towards the back of the stage. Various satellites and several display boards hung from the rafters. Pride of place was a cardboard cutout of an Apollo rocket.

The display boards portrayed the various milestones which had to be overcome to bring John F. Kennedy's dream to realisation. The landing of a man on the moon and bringing him safely back to Earth before the sixties concluded. Each board was introduced by one of the class.

Halfway through the display a guitar could be heard, softly at first, but gradually gaining in tempo. As Chris finished *Telstar* there was a flash of light and a terrific bang. Everyone jumped. The cardboard rocket shot across the stage at a rate of knots being pulled by the girls in the wings. Apollo 11 was on its way!

The curtains closed. Mrs. MacDonald walked back onto the stage to terrific applause.

'Well I hoped you all enjoyed our Open Day Presentations highlighting some of the very notable events which took place during St. James' College first 20 years. All classes deserve high praise especially our two musicians, Pamela Gibson and Christine Rogers. Such a talented duo, I am sure there is an exciting future in store for them both. Now all that is left for me is to take this opportunity to wish you all a very happy Easter.'

☙ ☙ ☙

The following weekend was the boy's school Sixth form end of term disco. They had invited June and Ginger to accompany them. Sam had rashly said they could borrow his car, so with Tim at the wheel of the family's Ford Zephyr they arrived in style.

The school hall illuminations had been replaced with sound activated strobe lighting creating a fantastic atmosphere. The disco was already underway when they arrived. Tim and Ian found a table in the corner of the room. The boys disappeared to get some coke and 7-ups. In the middle of the ceiling was a large silver ball. As it slowly rotated different shapes reflected off the walls. Several of the teachers were there with their wives all enjoying themselves.

Ian and Tim returned with the drinks just as one of Tony Dale's rock numbers *Bluegrass Blues* was playing quickly followed by, can you believe it, *Running Wild*! All were up twisting and gyrating to a succession of other hits. Eventually the clock reached the bewitching hour and the tempo changed to the inevitable, Engelbert Humperdinck's *Last Waltz*. Arms entwined, Tim and June slowly circled the dance floor. The last notes of the song found the pair of them stationary beneath the glitter ball: an apt place for a goodnight kiss.

Mark and Chris were still up when they returned, Sam and Grace had already gone to bed. Tim knew that his father wouldn't sleep until he heard the car in the driveway. The four of them did try to keep quiet but they were all in pretty high spirits so it wasn't very successful.

They sprawled in the armchairs. Mark, still in the Fifth year couldn't go but had spent the evening with Sandra, Uncle Chas and Aunt Meg. He wanted to hear more about their African safari. Mark was very interested in all things to do with the Natural World and hoped that his future would lay in that direction. However the evening's disco was still fresh in the others minds and it was obvious as far as Ian was concerned the highlight had been dancing to *Running Wild*.

Chris moved towards the kitchen, 'I think coffee is called for.' Tim and Chris had a silent communication. He followed her, carefully closing the door.

'Did Tony come?' he said quietly, so none of the others could hear, 'you know, to talk to dad.'

Chris turned from the kettle her expression said it all. A huge smile making her blue eyes shine. 'He came shortly after you all had left. Yes. All good! I think dad was quite chuffed that Tony had asked permission to marry me.'

Tim gave Chris a quick hug. 'I'm over the moon. I could not have heard better news.'

He picked up the plate of chocolate biscuits and Chris followed with the tray of mugs back to the lounge.

'Oh goody, goody, choccy biscuits,' said Ian, eyes only on the platter completely unaware of a now radiant Chris.

'One at a time Ian or there won't be any left,' said Tim who also had a softer and more contented look.

The ever observant June did notice and wondered what had happened between the twins whilst in the kitchen.

'Sorry, Ginger, June, biscuit?' said Ian though continuing to dunk his biscuit into the coffee – the chocolate began to melt.

'You'll have mocha Ian if you carry on like that,' laughed Ginger, 'coffee mixed with chocolate.'

June and Ginger stayed the night; Chris and Mark were up fairly early, but the party goers didn't make it until lunch-time. In fact for them it was brunch! Sandra joined them in the afternoon.

In the woods the early daffodils had recovered from the winds and spread out under the trees which were just beginning to bud. You could almost start to quote William Wordsworth .... *I wandered lonely as a cloud that floats on high o'er vales and hills, when all at once I saw a crowd, a host of golden daffodils......*

A squirrel scampered off in front of them, in search of one of its winter stores of nuts while a mistle thrush sung from the top of a tree puffing out its brown speckled chest. Its song was easily recognisable with its strong repeating phrases. The bumble bees buzzed around the spring flowers and a blackbird was turning over the leaf litter looking for some small tasty morsels for supper.

In the damper areas the yellow wood anemones were poking their heads out while lesser celandines and primroses looked fresh in the weak March sunshine.

Mark stopped suddenly and pointed. Blending with its surroundings perfectly he had spotted a butterfly. It looked just like a leaf. Its long proboscis was sipping nectar from one of the flowers. It was a fantastic sight. The brimstone then took flight showing off its brilliant yellow wings. It is thought that the brimstone butterfly gave rise to the name Butterfly i.e. butter-coloured fly.

Soon this carpet of yellow would be replaced by a carpet of blue. The green leafy spikes of the bluebells were beginning to surface from the undergrowth.

❧ ❧ ❧

Rachel was full of excitement over her forthcoming trip to the Norfolk Broads. Mary had made the county hockey team and was off to the annual championships in Beckenham. Janice was hoping for good weather as she was spending the holiday in Broadstairs with her brother and family.

'Building sand castles with your niece are you?' said Belinda teasingly.

Janice grinned: 'You bet and probably an Easter egg hunt as well.'

June and Ginger were enjoying the banter. Belinda turned in their direction. 'How about you two, anything planned?'

'Um dad is off abroad again for work so mum and I have a few girly days planned,' answered June. 'We hope to shop in Oxford Street and maybe take in one of the museums. I always love going to the basements of the big Departmental Stores like Selfridges to see what the latest kitchen gadgets are.'

'Grandad is home from hospital after his operation so I'm visiting him for a few days,' said Ginger.

As we all know the vast majority of the holiday will find June and Ginger in Norfolk with *Spectrum*.

And so the Easter break began.

CHAPTER FOURTEEN

The day after they broke up Sam backed the van out of the garage. It was loaded with the musical instruments, holdalls and an overnight bag for him. He was due at Neatishead the next day with Frank for an important meeting. It also enabled him to ferry Tim, Ian, Mark and Chris to Spindle for the school holidays. He and Grace would probably arrive in Norfolk on Good Friday following their return from America. Sam had been invited to a science convention in New York and Grace had been given the opportunity to join him. She had always wanted to visit Central Park!

June, Ginger and Sandra were travelling to Norfolk later in the week.

Chris always liked this time of the year, especially in the Broads. An annual event for her was to walk on her own across the local marshes alongside the dykes just as dawn was breaking in order to catch the sunrise. She had been checking the weather and it all looked good for the next day. The alarm was set for 4.30 a.m. Chris entered the kitchen to see that the ever thoughtful Jessie had left her a flask of hot coffee and a ham roll to take with her.

She pulled on her wellies and grabbed a coat. Letting herself quietly out of the Hall she made her way to the broad then turned into the woods to gain access to the marsh and dykes. The grassy path was muddy in places and in the half-light puddles were not easily avoided. Just as well she was wearing boots!

The night sky was now a mixture of ivory black, cobalt and light blue; on the eastern horizon just a hint of light where the sun would surely rise in a short while. A pair of birds flew across the path in front of her, too chunky to be geese, but grunting, which could point to a couple of bittern.

Chris reached the point in her walk where she sat on a fallen branch by the waterside. The dyke she had been following opened into Teardrop, the sister broad to Spindle cut off from the River Bure. The far bank was edged with reed and in the gathering light tops of isolated bushes could be seen floating like eerie islands in a sea of brown.

Teardrop Broad was the result of an early experiment by her grandfather and Nature Conservancy. They had come up with the idea of isolating a stretch of water from the then polluted river system to see if there would be an improvement in its quality. It had been extremely successful and was now teaming with life. It seemed farfetched at the time but has now become a possible template for other broads to follow.

What clouds there were now gained a pinkish tinge in the diffused light. Slowly but surely a fiery disk began to rear its head above the distant horizon. In front of her, black-headed gulls argued amongst themselves and a lapwing flew around making its fluty call, returning to its mate only to do the same circuit once more.

Then a sound, the epitome of the Norfolk Broads at this time of the year, vibrated around her sounding just like a distant foghorn. The bittern had started to boom hoping to attract a mate.

Suddenly it all happened!

A spectacular red streak stretched across the water in front of her, the sun, climbing fairly rapidly, burst into a glory of deep reds and pale pinks highlighting those clouds with an orangey glow.

Chris was transfixed. The tranquillity was overwhelming. Even the gulls had quietened. Thoughts now filled her mind. The incredible year she and her brothers had had with *Spectrum*; her love for Tony (unconsciously touching her ring). Who knew what the future held.

She shivered slightly in the cold morning air then remembered the flask of coffee, a very welcome item which she enjoyed to the full as the drama of a spring sunrise unfolded.

Returning along the grassy path the dawn chorus was deafening. Nothing could be more awe-inspiring than the arrival of the summer migrants. A sedge warbler with its song of trills and whistles leapt above the reed heads and then parachuted down, hoping that a female might notice his courtship display. Behind her two very different songs from two very similar looking birds; a chiff chaff, singing its name and a willow warbler with a liquid musical rhythm beginning quietly and then descending in strength with a distinctive flourish at the end, just like a toppling plate. Fabulous!

A loud *pitchew* in the tree canopy pointed to one of the many native U.K. birds, the marsh tit. Their call always sounded like a sneeze. *Teacher, teacher, teacher* was another very recognisable sound, this time of the great tit and so the symphony continued.

The sun, now gathering heat, shone on the dried reed which crackled in the warmth. It was as if the grasses were trying to communicate. It was breath-taking! If only a cuckoo had called, that would have been *the cherry on the cake*.

≈ ≈ ≈

Sandra and June were to meet Ginger at Liverpool Street Station. She was coming direct from her grandparents' house in Eltham. June kept on looking at her watch as the train for Norfolk was due to leave in about ten minutes. Where was Ginger?

Reluctantly the girls picked up their cases and headed towards Platform 6. Suddenly a very much out of breath Ginger arrived. A look of relief crossed June's face.

'Sorry all, engineering works on the Circle Line so I had to divert onto the Central Line to get to Liverpool Street.'

The three of them ran down the platform just managing to climb aboard a few minutes before the guard blew the whistle. The train was packed. They walked along the interconnecting carriages and eventually found three seats together. They flopped down. Phew, they had made it!

Who knows what thoughts were passing through their minds. Were they heading towards another adventure or just a few relaxing days on the broads? Time would tell.

Norwich Station was just as crowded. The Yarmouth train was in. They shouldered their way to the exit. There appeared to be no one to meet them. June looked across to the river, ever hopeful she might see a white boat with wavy lines, but no such luck. She was not exactly cross, just a bit anxious.

Ginger, hands on hips, said 'June, Sandra, can you remember what the arrangements were, I thought someone was supposed to be here?'

Sandra turned and saw Matt running towards them. A smile of pure delight crossed her face. This didn't go unnoticed by Matt.

'Hi girls, sorry I'm a bit late, but roadworks held me up. A slight change of plan,' he picked up one of the cases. 'The boats are at Rockland a less busy mooring than Norwich Yacht Station.'

They had reached the car and the bags loaded.

'What do you mean Matt, less busy?' asked June as she climbed into the Capri.

They were now under way and travelling in the direction of Rockland St. Mary.

'Well *Spectrum* is trying to keep a low profile. As you know they are Broads Rangers and in the past the tourists didn't give them a second look. They were usually grateful to have been rescued from their predicaments. However, with the explosion of their musical careers it is a different kettle of fish. The local community who know them respect their privacy but not so the fans. It does not help with the media now linking Tony with *Spectrum*.'

Matt negotiated another set of traffic lights, then continued....

'Chris and her brothers can usually get away with a bit of peace whilst out on the water but somewhere as crowded as Norwich, at this time of the year, is not a good idea. Anyway we all know the writing is on the wall. It won't be too long now before their cover is broken so they are making the most of what's left of the anonymity while they can.'

June had a feeling that this might be the reason. A bit more concerning for her was the effect it might have on Tim and her relationship.

They reached Rockland and there were both *Spectrums One* and *Two,* neatly moored. Chris waved. Tim and Ian jumped ashore and headed straight for them. The usual greeting followed but Ian was a bit more expressive than usual.

'Guess what!' he said with an enormous grin, trying to be modest but not really succeeding. '*A Bolt out of the Blue*, in its first week of release, has topped the charts.'

He punched the air in delight.

'Congratulations,' said Ginger. 'With all the adulation you must now be receiving,.....err, does this mean that I have to make an appointment to speak to you?'

Hands on lapels, an imperious looking Ian answered. 'Of course!' and then grinned.

Ginger couldn't resist it. She reached into her pocket, took out a piece of paper and pen, and offered it to Ian for a supposed autograph.

The others laughed!

Matt returned to his car. Sandra called after him.

'Thanks, Matt for picking us up.' She gave him another very delightful smile.

Matt got into his Capri. He had known Sandra for years as that little girl who was always in Mark's shadow. However, what he saw now was a rather attractive young lady. 'He wouldn't mind being the one who catches her eye!'

Meanwhile Ginger had noticed something unusual about the boats. 'Out of interest what's with the surfboards on top of the cabins? You're not expecting a high tide, are you?' she asked, tongue in cheek.

'No,' laughed Tim, 'we're making a slight detour into Oulton Broad, you know, just by Lowestoft. We're camping there for a few days and hope to do some boardsailing or windsurfing as it is sometimes called.'

'How come two different names?' queried Sandra.

'I don't really know,' said Tim, reaching for one of the cases. 'It could be from the origination of the sport. It all started in Hawaii in the fifties with some surfers hoisting a sail on their boards to save time whilst heading out to the surf. Hence windsurfing or sailing on a board both are apt descriptions of the activity.'

He passed the case to Chris who was still on *Spectrum One*.

'Anyway, it is becoming extremely popular in America and now here in Europe. You never know, it might even make the Olympics,' and offered his hand to June to help her board.

Despite her thirst for adventure, Ginger was looking a bit apprehensive. She was always happy to try something new, but standing on a plank of wood with a sail wasn't at the top of her wish list.

Ian noticed her expression. 'It really is fun to lean back under the sail, speeding along the surface of the water at the mercy of the wind, you know, battling against the elements, taking the odd dip as you capsize!' he added wickedly.

Ginger raised her eyebrows. 'If you say so.' These words did nothing to enthuse her or June if the truth be known.

They cast off. Their route from the River Yare took them along New Cut, a canal excavated over a hundred years ago to connect with the Waveney in order to speed up commercial trade from Norwich to Lowestoft. For over 150 years this river was once a major waterway with shipping actually continuing onto Bungay in Suffolk. Nowadays navigation ends at Geldeston Lock just three miles beyond Beccles.

Plans have been banded to preserve the structure for posterity but not as a working lock. Beyond Geldeston only small craft can travel to Redgrave Fen the source of the River Waveney. An interesting piece of trivia is that this river forms the border between Norfolk and Suffolk. You know the North Folk and the South Folk!

Tim, June and Chris were now on *Spectrum One*, the others on *Spectrum Two*. June had been mulling over Ian's comment about a *Bolt out of the Blue* making number 1. With Tim at the helm, she followed Chris into the cabin to help with the refreshments.

'Chris, I expect you have had the same thought, but what does Tony think about your recording successes? You know, being a very distinct rival in the charts and with a possible dent in his popularity. After all it is a very cut-throat industry. I hope it is not affecting your relationship?'

Chris turned, laying the kettle on the work surface. 'I have tried to say exactly the same as you, but whenever I have raised the issue with Tony, he brushes it off.' Unconsciously she fingered the chain around her neck, and wondered if it was time to reveal the engagement to her best friend. 'As far as our relationship goes, that's still as strong as ever.'

Chris slowly lifted the chain and produced her ring.

'Oh Chris, that's fantastic.' She gently took the ring to have a closer look. 'You kept that pretty quiet.

I must admit I did notice the chain and wondered what it was for.'

'We kept the engagement a secret for obvious reasons. Laurie doesn't know. Tim does, and of course mum and dad, but no one else not even Ian or Mark.'

'My lips are sealed,' said June, handing back the ring and giving her a quick hug. 'Maybe it will happen to Tim and me one day,' she thought.

As the late spring sun was dropping below the horizon the boats reached Oulton Dyke, a narrow reedy channel connecting the Waveney with the Broad. The drought of the boats caused the water level to drop showing numerous holes in the river bank. As they passed, the level would rise again, filling them in. Ginger found this fascinating to watch and hoped a water vole might appear, but there was nobody at home. In a very short while Tim and Ian beached the two boats at the south-western end of the Broad; Mark and Chris jumped ashore and anchored the craft firmly on the bank to avoid any drifting with the tide.

They pitched the tents and while the girls made up the beds the boys collected the wood and Mark built a fire. Soon sausages were sizzling in the frying pan.

'Wow you got that fire going quickly Mark,' said Ginger, 'very impressive indeed!' Mark modestly inclined his head. 'Don't let him kid you,' said Ian, 'he used fire lighters.'

She laughed, 'That's cheating, mm mm but those sausages certainly smell good.'

After they had eaten their fill, night was upon them. Chris pulled out her acoustic guitar and softly strummed Tony's latest followed by some well-known folk songs. Soon all were singing in the growing gloom.

The Jones picked up their cabin cruiser in Beccles. Rachel's dad had miscalculated the distance from Beccles to Oulton Broad so consequently the Yacht Station was full when they arrived. *Tranquil Dreams* was now moored, out on a limb, in Oulton Dyke for the night.

On the distant shore Rachel saw the glow of a fire. Could she hear Tony Dale's latest? Surely not! It was a shame they weren't closer. She would have loved to investigate and maybe join in. It wasn't that she didn't like going on holiday with her mum and dad but at 18 she would have preferred a bit more teenage fun. Rachel had no siblings and felt lonely at times. She sometimes thought how lucky Chris was with a twin and two other brothers.

Her mum joined her in the moonlight. It was so, so peaceful. Joyce knew that her daughter missed having the company of a brother or sister. She and Doug had been lucky to have had Rachel and were advised not to have any further children.

Joyce put her hand gently on Rachel's shoulder. They got on very well and were like-minded on many things. It was a shame that Neil, Rachel's boyfriend, couldn't have joined them for a couple of days. Neil was a Venture Scout leader and the annual camp clashed with their Broads holiday. She did like the lad. He had such a sunny disposition and her daughter blossomed in his company.

※ ※ ※

There was a slight wind the next day as they rigged the sailboards; Ginger, in her borrowed wet suit and bright red buoyancy aid reckoned she looked like the Michelin man!

Chris was enjoying the entertainment. She didn't know which way to look. On dry land Mark and Tim were instructing Sandra and June. Standing each on a board the girls were shown how to raise the sail. June wobbled a bit but Tim was on hand to keep her steady! Of course!

Meanwhile, on the water a precariously balanced Ginger was being put through her paces.

'Ginger,' called Ian, 'at the mast head you'll see a knotted rope.' Ginger nodded. 'This is known as the *apple line*. Now with one foot either side of the mast gently lean out, keeping the knees bent, using the leg muscles. Don't jerk or you'll hurt your back, and the mast should come up and you can grab the boom, the bar across the sail face.'

Ginger did as she was told, but the mast and sail came up too quickly and with a quick somersault and a yell, she disappeared into the depths. Ginger surfaced, spluttering, and laughing. She heaved herself back on to the board looking a bit like a stranded whale in the process! Despite her earlier misgivings, she was enjoying herself!

Ian sailed up to her he was also grinning but thought it best not to comment. He checked that she was okay, and once more Ginger tried. After several more abortive attempts she eventually shot off down the Broad with Ian in hot pursuit.

'Lean out Ginger, use the boom as a support,' he called: 'don't stand so straight or you'll.....'

Too late, there was a loud splash and Ginger once more went to inspect the bottom of the Broad.

In the afternoon Sandra and June both had attempts. June, like Ginger, eventually got it going and sailed so far down the Broad that she had to be towed back!

The next day the wind gained in strength with the occasional white horses on the surface of the water. Tim gave them a display of trick windsurfing. He attempted to railroad. That is sailing the board along on its edge, but he had just manoeuvred it into the right position when a terrific gust of wind literally catapulted him from the rig. It didn't help matters that at the same moment an outboard roared passed him at a rate of knots quickly followed by a second.

'Go on Tim,' called Ian. 'Do it again.'

'You must be joking,' he said, as he clambered back onto the board.

Ginger was puzzled. Her eyes had followed the fast-moving craft. 'Ian I thought there were speed limits on the Broads?'

'Yes there are,' he said. 'Oh you mean those boats. They are probably from the Oulton Broad Motor Boat Club practising for the coming season.'

Ginger still looked a bit bemused.

'Okay, let me explain,' said Ian. 'Speedboat racing is regularly held on Oulton Broad, the oldest motorboat sporting venue. The inaugural event in 1903 was won, would you believe, by a steam launch!'

'Wow! Do they race around buoys like the dinghies do?' she asked.

'You could say that. The circuit is about half a mile long, and an average lap takes about 36 seconds. A major milestone for the Club happened a couple of years ago with a visit from the Queen and Prince Philip. Their Royal Highnesses were treated to a drive-past of some of the racing craft. On competition day it's a good idea to keep away from Oulton Broad.'

Very soon the wind once more increased in strength and Tim called a halt to the proceedings.

After lunch Matt radioed through from Spindle Hall. Bob Cowen of the sea cadets wanted a favour from Tim and wondered if he would meet him in Yarmouth.

The following morning the tents were dismantled and the boats loaded. Tim and June headed in the direction of Yarmouth and the others to Spindle.

While they were motoring across Breydon, an hour before slack water, Tim at the helm noticed a boat stuck on the mud. He reached for the binoculars. 'Why people get stuck is beyond me,' he muttered, 'all they have to do is stay between the posts. Wait a minute…. June!' he called, 'I might be hallucinating but did you say Rachel was coming to the Broads?'

June came on deck drying her hands. She had been sorting out lunch. She looked across to the far bank and grabbed the binoculars. Focussing, there was no doubt about it…'Yep Tim that is Rachel!' she said, but started to giggle. 'Oh Tim, we must do something, and quickly or I can see Rachel or her dad taking a nose dive into the quagmire!'

Rachel was laying flat on the deck towards the bows with a pole in her hand, her mother hanging on to her feet. Meanwhile her dad was standing in the stern, he too had a pole. They appeared to be trying to push the boat free.

As you can imagine poles just sink into the mud without gaining any traction!

The laughter continued, June couldn't help it. To add to his dark glasses Tim now donned a Captain's cap set at a rakish angle. Not only that the braided peak was denoting the rank of an Admiral!

'Do I have to salute you now?'

Tim grinned. 'Of course!' With a bow, June then went below to keep out of sight.

On *Tranquil Dreams* Rachel looked up. There appeared to be a boat heading in their direction. As it neared it turned broadside on revealing colourful rainbow lines.

'No it can't be! Yes it is!' she couldn't believe it, it was a member of *Spectrum*. She dropped her pole and would have followed it if her mum hadn't been hanging on to her feet.

Her father had also seen the craft he wiped his brow. 'Thank Heavens.'

'Ahoy there, do you require some assistance?' called Tim.

Doug nodded with relief.

Tim moved *Spectrum One* as near as he dare and threw a rope. Rachel's dad caught it and tied it to the bows. Tim eased the throttle and *Spectrum One* slowly pulled *Tranquil Dreams* into deeper water.

Meanwhile Rachel dashed below ever hopeful for another treasured autograph. She searched quickly but could not find a piece of paper or a pen. She heard the engine start. Her camera was on the table, Rachel grabbed it. 'At least I might get a photo,' she muttered.

Back on deck she saw the two boats were now drifting apart. 'I can't thank you enough for helping us,' her father was saying to their rescuer. 'Do you have to do this often or are we a one-off?' asked Doug.

'Mm, well you are not the first person to get stuck here. That's what we are here for! Just remember to stay between the posts, when you cross Breydon Water.'

'I will, and thanks.'

'Enjoy your holiday,' said Tim and *Spectrum One* continued its journey.

Rachel clicked the camera. If she wasn't able to get the autograph, at least she will have a photo.

'Oh dad, I wish I could have got an autograph as well. It would have been great to show the girls at school, especially to Chris. She was trying to be *Spectrum* at our Open Day presentation when she played *Telstar* on her guitar.'

'Never mind lass, with the photo I think that will be enough to convince them about our rescue,' said her dad, even though he was a bit embarrassed by it all.

❦ ❦ ❦

After seeing Bob, Tim and June headed up the River Bure to return to Spindle. The river twisted and turned in these lower stretches with many shoals of shelving mud, especially at the sharp bends. June kept silent for a while. She looked around her at the marshy landscape and the many wind pumps which lined the route. Behind her you could see Great Yarmouth with the North Sea glinting in the sunlight. As they neared the Stracey Arms she asked, 'Tim, are the Broads natural formations?'

'Some are and some are not' he replied. 'To make it easier let's split them into two sections. The Southern waters consist of long-standing navigable rivers with very few Broads as such. What Broads there are were caused by gradual reclamation of land as the sea retreated. The Northern Broads and waterways were originally flood lakes when river estuaries became blocked by silt. During the Middle Ages, turf-cutting for fuel linked the lakes into a network of waterways and thus we have the Norfolk Broads. A wildlife paradise. Well, it was once.'

'What do you mean Tim, once?'

'When the holiday trade took off pollution from hire cruisers, not to mention adjoining industrial sites and farmland, caused massive contamination of the rivers and bankside vegetation.'

June looked around her, it was so peaceful. The reeds were swaying in the breeze. A pair of swans swam by with their two youngsters straining to keep up. 'To my uneducated eyes it seems okay to me.'

'Mmm... it's much improved now mainly thanks to various experiments. A prime example is sealing privately owned Broads from the river system and clearing the contaminated mud. Grandfather did this with Teardrop. The RSPB have followed suit and their Broad is now abundant with a massive selection of once rare insects and plants like the water soldier. The water is so clear you can almost see the bottom.'

By now they had reached Spindle. Of the others there was no sign, just three boats neatly moored at the jetty. They looked around them and then a slight splashing could be heard in the distance.

'They can only be in one place June the pool must have been filled. Come on, let's go and join them.'

The pair headed to a long low thatched building to the right-hand side of the Hall. The pool was a new addition. Sam had designed a gizmo for one of the James Bond films and had received a rather substantial one-off payment. He decided to use the money to convert the old hay barn into an indoor heated swimming pool. The local primary school had a free use of the pool during term time as swimming lessons were now on the curriculum. An important skill when living in a place surrounded by water!

Tim pushed open the door, and sure enough there they were. 'Hi you two,' called Mark 'come and join us the water is lovely.'

'Did Bob want you about the raft race?' asked Matt.

'Yes, I have agreed that we would do the marshalling as before, and ....,' but he wasn't allowed to finish as a pair of arms sneaked out of the water and grabbed his feet, and with a yell Tim fell in, fully clothed! Splash!

June did her best to escape but Chris and Sandra had crept up behind her and she too followed him into the depths. They both surfaced spluttering and laughing.

The next morning they walked to the Broadland Conservation Centre at Ranworth. On their way they passed St. Helens Church known as the 'Cathedral of the Broads'. From the tower the view was tremendous. You could see over Malthouse Broad, across the Bure Valley to St. Benet's Abbey. On a clear day even Norwich Cathedral with a spire of 315 or 316 feet, depending on which book you're reading at the time; the second highest spire in the country, the tallest being that of Salisbury Cathedral.

The church was open giving Ian the chance to extol the virtues of St. Helens.

Just inside the entrance was the Antiphoner illuminated manuscript in a glass-topped steel box.

'This service book dates from the fifteenth century and has over 285 sheepskin pages,' Ian explained. 'Look at the stunning representation of Jonah and the Whale!

Ultramarine blue, agate and gold leaf were used which is proof of great wealth in this parish.'

'Fascinating!' June said, 'however, impossible to read unless you are a scholar of Latin script!'

Ian led them to the end of the aisle where the medieval rood screen was separating the chancel from the main part of the church.

'You wouldn't believe it,' he continued, 'the finest in England! Extra special because so many rood screens were destroyed during the Reformation; the twelve apostles are particularly well painted, carrying their emblems by which illiterate worshippers could recognize them.'

'Don't you find it peculiar?' Ginger asked. 'The apostles all wear rich clothes but they are bare-footed.'

'Ah!' Ian replied, 'this is to show humility, I think.'

'Are you ready for another ghost story!' He added, 'a peaceful haunting this time!'

They all sat in the choir stalls.

'In 1538 Brother Pacificus, on loan from the Abbot of St. Benet, spent months restoring and redecorating the rood screens of the church. He would row across the broad accompanied by his little dog Caesar. One summer evening Brother Pacificus returned to his Abbey to find it had been sacked by King Henry VIII's soldiers and put to the torch. Totally distraught, he roamed the burnt-out ruins of the Abbey until he died. His body was then laid to rest in the shadow of the church. Occasionally, the ghost of what looks like a monk can be seen, at dawn, rowing a small boat across the water with a little dog standing in the bow. What do you think? Could this be Brother Pacificus!?'

Ian had excelled in his presentation of Ranworth Church. Ginger was so impressed by his talent in recounting historical facts, and was falling head over heels in love.

Exiting the church they strolled along duckboards, across bog and marsh. The trail was an example of *succession*. How oak forest emerged from open water. The route passed the vegetation change of woodland to alder carr, onto tall herb fen and finally reaching the broad. They arrived at the reed roofed Information Centre which was originally refused planning permission. To get around the problem the Norfolk Naturalist Trust built the Centre on a floating pontoon accessing it by a drawbridge.

The area is also one of the few places where milk parsley can be found, the food plant of the caterpillar of Britain's largest resident breeding butterfly the swallowtail. It was once found throughout Southern England but now restricted to the Broads. This pale yellow butterfly with prominent black veins and blue margins to the wings cannot be mistaken as it flies powerfully over the foliage seeking somewhere suitable to lay its eggs.

They spent a good while looking around the various displays in the Centre, similar to the ones which they had experienced in Norwich Castle back in November. The girls went up the twisty stairs to the balcony and looked through the binoculars over the Broad. A grey heron was fairly conspicuous and June had the surprise of her life as the dark-brown small duck she was focused on, suddenly dived beneath the water. It was a dabchick the smallest member of the grebe family, (or to a Norfolkian a didopper).

A pair of great crested grebes swam close, unmistakable with their piercing red eyes and blackish ear-tufts. These elegant birds sport prominent chestnut and black frills on the sides of their heads in the breeding season. It was hunted to near extinction in the late Nineteenth Century for its feathers.

A formidable band of women lobbied for the end of using wild bird plumage and their skin to adorn ladies' hats and in 1889 started The Society for the Protection of Birds. Five years later Queen Victoria joined the campaign. The Society from then on became known as the *Royal* Society for the Protection of Birds, the RSPB.

As they left the building Mark was let loose on his favourite subject, explaining about the different flora and fauna as they retraced their steps along the walkway. A habitat which at first sight gives a view of acres of desolate grassland, rippling in the breeze, but in fact houses one of Britain's richest. A myriad of insects take up residents within the reeds hollow stems and plants like the marsh pea, valerian and helleborine jostle for position offering a feast of nectar for the hungry invertebrates.

Standing still the bird song was fascinating with the shy water rail's pig squeal and laughter from a female mallard duck. Then there was the short sharp shrill of a cetti's warbler, the machine-gun rattle of a cheeky Jenny wren and the *pinging* call of the very attractive bearded tits. It was all so incredibly amazing.

In spring the boom of bittern can sound eerie, the riotous call of the warblers and the fluting flight of the lapwing add to the mysteries of the secret world of a reed bed. Suddenly a bird with a black head and white collar popped up on the top of a reed stem. '*tseek, tseek, tseeeeek*' it went. As if counting, but not quite making four!

Ginger pointed, 'Mark, what is that bird?'

'A reed bunting,' he answered. 'A fairly common resident but as you can hear, has a problem with his arithmetic!'

That afternoon the sun glinting over Spindle Broad was a very tempting sight especially with the sun loungers on the grassy bank by its side. Jessie, donning her coat, was off to Wroxham to visit her sister Liz who worked in the sail loft at one of the traditional boat builders.

'You know your fan mail has arrived from Laurie,' she called after them.

Spectrum stopped in their tracks. Chris looked directly at Tim and Ian, 'I believe it's your turn, isn't it?'

With a shrug of the shoulders and a last look at the appealing scene by the jetty, Ian and Tim reluctantly turned and headed in the direction of the library.

Ginger, June and Chris took up residence on the loungers.

It wasn't long before Ginger and June were dozing. Chris watched with amusement at the antics of Mark and Sandra, each in single-seater canoes, racing around an old marker buoy.

It was very relaxing in the warmth of the spring sunshine and she reflected on the extraordinary happenings of their lives over the last year; she still couldn't believe that they had such a fan following. It was also good that she could share their fortune with her two friends.

She began to feel a bit restless, the sun reflecting off the water made it look very inviting. Mark and Sandra were now on the far side of the broad. Over to her right she could see Ian and Tim in the double canoe. Obviously, the pair of them had had enough of scribing. Slowly but surely, they were creeping up behind Mark and Sandra, a water fight followed. She chuckled.

Chris removed her shorts and T-shirt revealing a swimsuit. She dived into the Broad, and gasped, it was colder than expected. However undeterred she swam strongly over to them and tried to capsize the double canoe; her brothers retaliated by half drowning her. She gave in.

'Hey Tim,' said Ian, 'June and Ginger look rather too peaceful, shall we go and disturb them?'

So with Chris hanging on to the back of the canoe, the *Spectrum* Armada of two single and one double canoe converged for the attack. With paddles at the ready, hails of water sprayed over the girls.

'You rotten lot!' cried Ginger, 'Wait till I get hold of you Ian!' She and June then swiftly jumped into the broad and with the help of Chris, Sandra and Mark they managed at last to capsize the double canoe and turn Ian and Tim into the broad.

It started to turn chilly as the sun disappeared behind a cloud. 'I don't know about you lot,' said Chris, 'but I'm for a hot shower and buttered crumpets.'

'You bet!' was the universal call.

Jessie had laid a fire in the lounge. They pulled up the armchairs and beanbags into a semi-circle around the warmth; Chris kneeled on the floor in front of the burning logs, and toasted the crumpets on a three-pronged fork. Tim placed a Beatles LP on to the record deck. Ian by now was digging into the crumpets with butter dribbling down his chin.

'Honestly Ian,' said Ginger, 'can't you do better than that?' She handed him one of the napkins to mop himself up.

Ian took it. 'Sorry…. mummy!' They laughed.

The crumpets were soon polished off. Straws were drawn to see who would wash up. Ian and Mark were the losers. Ian donned one of Jessie's frilly aprons much to the amusement of the others.

Ginger wandered into the library. On the walls were several water colours of the area. She stood in front of a delightful depiction of Spindle Hall. She turned as Chris joined her.

'I love the pictures,' commented Ginger, 'especially this one of the Hall. It seems to capture the moment. Are they from a local artist?'

Chris smiled: 'No they're mum's. She turned to art as a form of relaxation. As much as she loves her music mum finds another level of solace whilst painting her landscapes. She does do the odd commission and I believe there is one of Barton Broad hanging in the old operations room at RAF Neatishead.'

CHAPTER FIFTEEN

The next morning June and Chris decided to go into Norwich. Matt dropped them off by the cathedral on his way to Pterodactyl Engineering to pick up a couple of spare parts for the Spectrum engines. The others stayed at Spindle. Ginger was determined to conquer windsurfing and Ian was only too pleased to assist.

June and Chris were having a girly day. They were enjoying themselves wandering from store to store looking at the spring collections and donning the odd outfit. A couple of shops displayed the latest innovation, hot pants. Of course, the girls had to try those.

'June, what do you think the girls would say if I suddenly walked into the Prefects Room wearing a pair of these?' Chris did a spin showing off her deep blue satin attire with a bib front.

'I supposed there is a bit more modesty attached to this outfit compared to the *micro* mini-skirts on the market last year.'

June laughed: 'Not only them but what about Mrs. Mac!' She did a twirl, in her choice of burgundy red velvet ones.

'I am sure there have been hot pants wedding outfits designed, probably by Mary Quant.'

Chris chuckled.

'I believe heads would turn if I walked down the aisle in a pair of white lacey ones!'

In the end June bought a small patterned leather shoulder bag, navy slacks and matching sandals whilst Chris a short-sleeved cotton blouse and a flame red trouser suit. They both decided to give the hot pants a miss.

June checked her watch. 'I could do with some coffee. What about you Chris?'

'Good idea. Let's go to one of the waterside cafés.'

They headed to the river. Several brave souls were making the most of the spring sunshine and drinking outside.

June suddenly stopped, grabbing Chris by the arm and pulling her into the shadow of a nearby horse chestnut tree. 'Oh my God Chris, there's Rachel!'

They looked at each other. 'Oops, she doesn't know we are in Norfolk.'

Rachel was sitting at one of the tables just to the left of the tree. She and her companion were having an animated conversation. A slight wind was blowing Rachel's dark hair across her face. She pushed it behind her ears. They suddenly stood up and with a hug the girls parted company.

Rachel was now walking towards them across the brick-weaved roadway. June and Chris waited for a bit and were just about to reveal themselves when a white transit stopped in front of them. The door of the van opened and to the girls surprise Rachel was pushed into the back. The vehicle then swiftly drove away towards the ring road.

Chris and June looked at each other, mouths agape. Had they just seen Rachel abducted! The pair were in shock. June was shaking. Chris wasn't faring much better but it was such a slick operation there was no reaction from anyone else. They were oblivious. The café continued serving and people carried on going about their day-to-day business.

Where was a bobby when you needed one!

'Come on June!' Chris turned and ran off down the road closely followed by her friend. They reached Bethnal Street and headed to the Police Station.

The duty officer, Sergeant Gerry Duffield, was working on the roster for Easter. The holiday coincided with Norwich City's home game. At least it wasn't against Ipswich Town which had caused problems with crowd control in the past. He yawned, and took another sip of his coffee.

Suddenly the door burst open, startling him. His cup went flying as did the umbrella stand behind the door!

'Oh it's Chris, isn't it? What's wrong?'

Out of breath she said, 'Sgt. We...we have just witnessed an abduction.'

Hearing the commotion Inspector Devenport came out of his office. 'Chris?'

'Oh Inspector, we've just seen one of our school friends kidnapped.'

'Can't believe it,' said June.

'Whoa girls, slow down.'

His voice did much to calm them.

He looked at his Sgt.

'Two cups of tea please Gerry.'

He took June and Chris into his office.

'What is this all about? You say someone has been kidnapped, someone you know?'

'Rachel, one of our school friends,' said Chris.

June was too upset to say anything.

The Inspector picked up his pen and started writing:

'Okay. I need you to give me as much information as you can. To begin with, what is the colour of your friend's hair? Was she wearing, jeans, skirt? How tall is she?'

The Inspector looked up.

'Rachel Jones is one of your school friends from Kent you say. I assume of the same age. What is she doing in Norfolk?'

'Holidaying with her parents in a cabin cruiser,' replied Chris. 'I think they might have picked it up from Beccles.'

'Actually, I was with Tim when there was a little incident on the river. He pulled them off the mud in Breydon Water,' said June. 'The craft was called *Tranquil* something or other.'

'Now do you know of any reason why Rachel could have been kidnapped? Are her parents wealthy or do they have important jobs?'

They shook their heads. 'I don't think so,' replied Chris.

'Have you any idea who her companion is?'

'No, but come to think of it they were very similar in appearance,' said June.

'Now were there any distinguishing marks on the van?'

Despite everything, Chris did raise a wry smile for this question. 'There seemed to be something pink on the back, it could have been a crab or something similar. You know, like, *Norfolk the home of the Cromer Crab*.'

The Inspector considered his notes. He was still concerned about the girls. 'I have enough information for the time being. Are the pair of you alright to get home or shall I arrange for a squad car to take you?'

'No, we'll be fine. Thank you, Inspector.'

Brian Devenport closed the door behind them, picked up his now cold coffee, and pondered on the situation. A short while later his sergeant knocked.

'Sir, I have Josh Shaw from *Elephonnics* on the line he would like to speak to you urgently.'

'What now,' he sighed.

'Put him through Sgt.' The coffee cup returned to the desk top.

Elephonnics, was a local company which was leading the digital age, or the Third Industrial Revolution as some people called it. The Inspector knew its founder Kenneth Shaw, Josh's father, quite well.

'Inspector thank you for your time. I am extremely puzzled by a phone call I have just received. The caller said they were holding my daughter and demanded a £10,000 ransom for her return. Further details of where to send the money would follow, they said. Before I could ask any questions the mystery caller hung up. You're not going to believe it, but as I am speaking with you my daughter Louise is sitting across the room from me.'

'Umm.... Josh, can I have a quick word with Louise please?'

Josh passed the phone to his daughter.

'Louise, have you noticed anything unusual over the last few days?' asked Inspector Devenport. 'Could someone have been following you?'

'Not really though I did see a van careering up Riverside this morning after I left my cousin. Rachel and I were having a coffee at *Coquilles* by the river.'

'Rachel, would that be Rachel Jones from Kent?'

'Yes, that's right,' answered Louise.

'Thank you Louise. Can you quickly put your father back on the line please?'

'Josh, bad news, I think it's actually Rachel Jones they are holding. I've just had a couple of her school friends in the office who happen to have seen the abduction. I think it would be wise to keep Louise out of sight for the time being.

When they contact you again, keep up the pretense that they have your daughter. Don't mention either Louise's or Rachel's name. I will get a trace on your phone so when they ring again we might be able to track the call.'

'That's terrible,' replied Josh. 'I can't imagine what Doug and Joyce will be going through. That's Rachel's parents by the way. Inspector you must tell Doug and Joyce they are welcome to stay here until Rachel is found.'

The Inspector then made several phone calls to set the wheels in motion. Obviously a low profile search had to be carried out, especially as they will be holding the wrong girl. He spread out a local map on his desk. The kidnappers couldn't be far away taking into account the time difference between Chris witnessing the event and Josh's phone call.

※ ※ ※

That evening everyone was trying to relax in the lounge after their dinner. The gammon steak with fresh vegetables followed by jam roly-poly and custard was extremely tasty. June and Chris didn't have much appetite after what they had witnessed that morning. A coffee percolator was bubbling away in the corner of the room alongside a plate of Jessie's delightful home-made shortbread. The Inspector had rung just before they ate saying he had nothing to report.

They all had been stunned on hearing about Rachel. However, to take their minds off the situation Mark, Sandra, Ian and Ginger were now playing a game of Cluedo. June and Chris had been encouraged to join in but had declined.

Tim was extremely concerned for his twin and June. Should *Spectrum* help the Inspector? They could be unobtrusive. They would search some of the rivers surrounding Norwich. However, he was a bit anxious especially regarding Mark and Sandra being younger than the rest of them. He knew Mark would not want to be left behind but kidnapping was a serious crime. Tim was still very mindful about the dramatic events last summer and the drug smuggling incident at Christmas.

'I've got an idea,' he said, shutting his book with a loud bang.

All conversation stopped – Ian was a bit put out as he was just about to reveal the murderer and so win the game.

'How about if we lend a discreet hand to the police and start a search for Rachel ourselves? We were contemplating a tour of the Broads over the next few days and this would give us a reason and a target. However, I have a duty to warn you that it won't be a walk in the park and might well be dangerous.'

'I'm definitely up for it,' said Ginger, 'You made me an honorary member of *Spectrum* so I'm going to fulfill my obligation.'

Ginger was not going to miss out helping to find Rachel.

Hazardous or not June thought doing something like this might benefit her in coming to terms with what she had witnessed. She felt more confident now and like Ginger didn't want to be left behind and sought to do the utmost to help their school friend.

'You can absolutely count on me as well,' she said.

Sandra didn't exactly say anything, but from her expression she was in as well.

Despite what Tim had said he still had slight misgivings about the task in hand. 'You might not like this Mark but I want you and Sandra to work closely with Ian and Ginger and obey their instructions. Otherwise, we will have to leave the pair of you behind.'

Mark reluctantly agreed and Sandra wasn't exactly pleased with the situation either.

Tim spread out a map. 'Now if you four head towards Yarmouth you can then search as much of the Broads network around Norwich as is possible, and keep in radio contact with each other. June and I will travel towards Barton and Hickling.

Chris, knowing Tony, he will not want to miss out so when he arrives, search locally taking in South Walsham and Wroxham Broads.'

🐝 🐝 🐝

Breakfast the next morning was a bit ad hoc but Jessie coped. Every time somebody came a cooked breakfast of bacon, egg, baked beans, mushrooms, tomatoes and sausages miraculously materialised in front of them. Ginger was keyed up and for once appeared before anyone else. She had finished her toast and drinking her second cup of coffee when the boys arrived with Chris. June and Sandra were the last at the table but, as mentioned, cooked breakfasts were always available!

Jessie topped-up the boats supplies with pre-prepared cottage pies and chicken casseroles that only required re-heating. Each boat was also presented with a cake tin full of fruit buns and flapjacks. The Rogers household relied a lot on Jessie and hoped she knew how much they appreciated what she did for them.

Jessie loved keeping Spindle running. She knew that both her husband Frank and son Matt would have a large hole in their lives if they weren't involved with Grace, Sam and of course, *Spectrum*.

They left Chris on the quayside. The boats were soon out of sight. She turned back to the garage and took out her bike. She couldn't settle and had to do something. She cycled down the drive and onto Wroxham. It was busy. Walking with her bike on the pedestrian crossing alongside the humpback road bridge, she looked down onto the river. Day boats were coming and going and the steam launch *Falcon* was taking on passengers for a trip. Chris loved seeing these historical vessels. They always seem to have interesting names. One which always amused her was called *Bubbles*.

Chris then cycled onto Coltishall where the ice cream van was doing brisk business on the common.

❧ ❧ ❧

Meanwhile the three boats were making their way down the River Bure; Tim and June with *Spectrum One* left the others at Ant Mouth and headed towards Barton Broad, along a twisty, foreboding stretch of water.

In a very short while they reached Ludham and Tim was sounding the horn of *Spectrum One* as they motored under the bridge and moored just near to the caravan park.

'You stay here June. I'm just going for a wander up to the site.'

Soon Tim was out of view. June looked around her at the fairly busy scene. Every time a cruiser passed, *Spectrum* rocked gently from the wash. She watched in amusement at a pair of coot making a terrific din, trying to defend their territory. While June waited she gradually felt a bit of a fraud. As boats passed she could hear the words. 'That's *Spectrum* isn't it?' and then the click of a camera.

Tim jumped back on board. 'There's nothing unusual there; are you feeling a bit like a goldfish in a bowl?'

'A bit.'

'Well, we'll soon be lost in the wide expanse of Barton Broad.' He started the engine, slipped the moorings and drove on up towards Irstead Shoals where the river narrowed considerably on its gravelly bed.

As they entered Barton Broad the first thing they saw was Pleasure Island which was gradually sinking. It was incredible to think that at one time there was a bandstand on the island when dancing and picnics were the norm. Fortuitously there were plans in the pipeline for it to be restored, and possibly turned into an island nature reserve. It was also reputed that Nelson learnt to sail here.

Spectrum One passed the island to the east along Dead Man's Hole, a rather narrow channel allegedly named after a prehistoric burial ground. Their destination was the north western arm of the Broad by Barton Turf.

Barton Turf, a quiet Broadland Village had several possible hiding places. Tim thought a good starting point for any possible clues for finding Rachel would be the row of quirky cottages built for the Queen's Coronation. From there their route would take them through the village to St Michael's All Angels church about a mile from the quayside. This had an impressive rood screen which, he thought, might interest June after seeing the one at Ranworth.

June was getting the hang of mooring a *Spectrum* and was ready with the rope as Tim maneuvered the boat alongside the staithe. She jumped ashore and with a couple of half-hitches had the boat secure. June's interest was sparked by a black shed just behind her with a couple of benches attached to it.

'What's that for?' she asked, pointing at the shack.

Tim looked. 'That was a beer house once known as the *Hole in the Wall*. It was actually an off-licence but to get around the licencing laws they used to sell beer through a *Wicket*. The clientele sat on the benches to drink. I think it might have been the last beer house. It shut down about three years ago.'

'*Wicket* …. what do you mean by a *Wicket*?'

'Just another name for a window:' Tim joined her on the quay. 'Come on June let's go and do some investigating, we could both do with a bit of a walk.'

Hand in hand the pair of them wandered passed the cottages and on up to the church.

☙ ☙ ☙

Down towards Yarmouth, Ian and Mark had a mini race across Breydon Water which was surprisingly empty. The two boats then turned down the River Waveney to St. Olaves.

The *Spectrums* were moored securely at St. Olaves. The tide was running fast causing the river level to fluctuate between two and three feet.

Mark was still smarting at Tim's instruction of taking orders from Ian. However, he was quite pleased when Ian suggested that he and Sandra search the river path to Fritton Decoy. Mark guessed that Ian wanted them out of the way so he and Ginger could have some quiet time together whilst they checked the St. Olaves area!

Like the majority of the Broads the lake had been dug in medieval times for peat. The name Decoy referred to the hunting of waterfowl. Channels were constructed and netted. Dogs chased the ducks along the channels trapping them for the pot. Mark was once more in his element as he went about identifying the different birds for Sandra. She was always a good listener, even when not interested!

The gadwalls were very noticeable with their grey speckled bodies and black rears. A bit more colour surrounded the pochard showing off its chestnut head and black chest. However, the shoveler had a very distinctive spoon-like bill and dark reddish flanks.

In World War Two the Decoy was a secret facility to train tank crews. Now there were plans in the pipeline to turn the area into an exclusive holiday destination. At present a few of the traditionally built cottages with walls of flint and roofs of pantiles were available to rent.

Meanwhile Ian and Ginger not only checked the village but walked around the ruins of the thirteenth century St. Olaves Priory. There were still parts remaining of the cloisters, church and the refectory whose vaulted ceiling was a striking sight for all to see.

Ginger had been very impressed with Ian's explanation of the rood screens at St. Helens, and hoped that he had a similar account for this site. Ian didn't disappoint.

'The priory became a victim of Henry VIII's dissolution of monasteries,' he said. 'However in 1547 Henry Jerringham decided to construct a new manor incorporating the remains of the monastic building into his house. By 1784 there wasn't much left of the brickwork. Somehow people still found use of the residual and in the 1820s the parish church at Herringfleet was refurbished using the stone.'

Ginger was about to comment. Ian held up his hand.

'It doesn't stop there, Ginger. Would you believe that the undercroft was converted into a cottage and lived in until the beginning of the twentieth century?'

Ginger was once more amazed at Ian's knowledge and decided that maybe it was time for her to learn more about these ancient monuments!

By now they were sitting on the old low wall waiting for Mark and Sandra to return.

Ginger gently placed her hand on Ian's arm…'Any ghosts this time?'

'Now it's funny you should say that,' he said.

'Allegedly there is a tunnel under the floor of the former entrance hall which is reputed to lead to Burgh Castle. One day in the distant past, a fiddler, playing his music, entered the passageway. As he disappeared from view so his music gradually faded and he was never seen again.'

Despite the warmth of the afternoon, Ginger shivered!

☙ ☙ ☙

Spectrums Two and *Four* continued their search elsewhere. They cruised along New Cut to join the River Yare and thence to Reedham. They moored at the jetty in between the two river crossings. To the east was the swing bridge which carried the railway to Yarmouth. To the west was the vehicle chain ferry that had been in operation since the seventeenth century. In those days horse and carts made the crossing. Now there was only room for three cars on the ferry!

Reedham used to be full of boat builders. Wherries like the *Wonder*, the largest and the *Fawn* the fastest were built there. Now very few companies were involved in the industry, it was more to the tourist market they were heading.

This did not deter *Spectrum*. They had a job to do. But like St. Olaves and Fritton they could not find anything unusual in the area.

☙ ☙ ☙

It was quiet in Spindle that evening. Jessie had returned to her cottage in the grounds. Matt, however, stayed so Chris would have some company in the Hall overnight. Tim had been on the radio. All their searches had drawn a blank, so the boats were returning to Spindle.

The next day the cycle was in use once more as Chris decided to go in the opposite direction from Wroxham.

'Jessie, I'm aiming to do a bit of snooping around the South Walsham area. I should be back in time for Tony's arrival.'

Jessie came into the driveway, 'Right-oh Chris, lunch will be ready about one. Now you be careful.'

With a jaunty salute, Chris cycled off. At Malthouse Broad she waved a cheery greeting to the owners of the café on the quayside preparing for another busy weekend and then cycled on across Ranworth Marsh.

By the farm, a vibrant scene unfolded. Shading her eyes from the glare of the sun she saw a marsh harrier, high above the reed bed gliding effortlessly on the thermals, waiting for the right moment. Suddenly, with wings swept back in an arrow formation, it dived to the ground.

'I wonder what small mammal is its breakfast?' she muttered to herself. Chris turned her back on the marsh and looked at the old barn behind her. 'Not long now and that'll be full of squealing chicks, when the swallows and house martins return for the summer.'

As she remounted her bike she noticed a barn owl surveying her from the fence post. Its pale face, black eyes and glorious speckled tanned feathers, looked fabulous in the sunlight. It almost made you want to cuddle it! The owl just stared, and then silently flew off across the fields to the distant woods. A slight shiver of wonder followed the encounter.

Chris cycled on, if unsteadily, due to the cart track. Soon blue glinted beneath the trees as South Walsham Broad came into sight. Well, the posh end of the Broad, as that was what she and her brothers called it when they were young.

Chris paused by the wrought iron gates of the manor. There were a couple of cars in the driveway. 'That's strange,' she said to herself. She thought the Coopers were away until July. 'Maybe the house had been rented for a few weeks.'

She was about to leave when a white transit turned up. Chris trained her binoculars on the vehicle and became curious yet again.

The driver got out and opened the back door of the van. A second man jumped down followed by, it seemed, a reluctant young lady.

Chris heart missed a beat. 'A long shot. Could this be Rachel?' The colouring and stature seemed about right.

Although they were some distance away, Chris quickly took out her birthday present from Tony, a Polaroid camera, and snapped a photo. Hurrying the process it was fuzzy!

Suddenly she was startled by a Rottweiler snarling at her from behind the gates. A balding man in his late fifties appeared. 'Move on,' he said in a harsh voice. 'This is private property,' and grabbed the dog by its collar.

'Why should there be a guard dog? A Rottweiler at that! What are they hiding?'

This is what Chris was thinking.

With one last look into the grounds she carried on down the track now lined with houses. The not so posh end, where you would find holiday cruisers moored.

The sun was high in the sky. Chris cycled into the boatyard and waved to her friend, Kevin Appleton, who helped his father run the Yard and hire fleet. He was just seeing to some customers. She stood in the shade of the trees impatiently waiting for him to finish. She looked at her watch. If she didn't leave soon she would be late for Tony!

Kevin eventually wandered across the yard in her direction.

'Well hello Chris, what brings you to this neck of the woods and on two wheels instead of the usual conveyance?'

'Hi Kevin, it's great to see you again, but yes I do have an ulterior motive. I'm actually on official business. I can't explain it all in detail but have there been any strangers around lately or anything out of the ordinary?'

He thought for a moment, 'There have been a couple of city types in the Ship up in the village, but that's all I can think of at present.'

'Thanks' said Chris. 'Er Kevin, aren't the Coopers away until July?'

'Yes they are but wait a moment,' he said, 'It's funny you should mention that. Andy along the Broad, muttered something the other day about trespassers on his land looking for the Cooper's place. Does that help you at all?'

She nodded but all further conversation had to stop as more hire craft arrived at the staithe. It was change-over day so extremely busy. Kevin turned back to the quayside, 'I've got to go,' he said.

Chris remounted her bike and headed back to Spindle deep in thought over the events she had just witnessed at the manor.

CHAPTER SIXTEEN

Chris freewheeled down the drive of the Hall just as Tony was getting out of his car. Her tyres skidded on the gravel as she came to a halt in front of him.

'What's this then, one horsepower transport or something?' he laughingly said.

'Hi darling! Well it was such a super day that I thought I would go for a bike ride.'

Tony gave her a passionate kiss, grabbed his holdall and arm in arm the pair of them walked into the Hall. Chris then explained the real reason for the sudden burst of energy.

'Not THE Rachel whom I met at the Christmas Disco?'

'Yes, that's right. Tim and June have been in the Barton Broad area, whilst Ian and Mark have covered the southern network. They are all on their way back now, having unfortunately drawn a blank.'

She showed him the fuzzy photo.

'The camera came in useful then,' he said, handing it back to her.

'It was decided that I would stay local which brings me back to why I was on my bike. I cycled over the marsh to South Walsham Broad to have a look around from the landside.' She paused as Jessie came in with the lunch.

'Jessie, you have a shrewd idea of what is going on in the villages around here. Aren't the Coopers abroad?'

'Yes. My cousin keeps house for Sadie Cooper and her family when they are in Norfolk: she said they were not due back until the end of June.'

'Does she look in at all when they are away?'

'She usually does. However, it's funny you should say that,' said Jessie as she sat down to join them. 'But she's been laid up and hasn't had a chance.'

Jessie paused: 'Why do you ask?'

Chris looked up from her pizza. She had noticed the slight hesitation from Jessie. 'I have a feeling someone is in there at present,' said Chris. 'I had a close encounter with a dog this morning which makes me think something funny is going on around the property.'

Jessie laid down her knife and fork and then seemed to choose her words! 'Betty mentioned that she had lent the keys to one of her neighbours who had offered to help with her duties at the manor whilst she was laid up. I didn't say anything at the time as Betty was rather stressed. You see that lady's husband is in prison. Not her fault, she is a very nice, honest person but there is more trouble in the family. Her son Jack hasn't taken too well to his father being away and has since crossed the law on a couple of occasions.'

'Oh,' said Chris.

'Are you sure it's Rachel?' asked Tony. He was getting a bit worried about Chris. She could be impetuous at times and he didn't want to have last summer's experience again.

Jessie was also a bit concerned, with Sam and Grace presently out of the country parenting duties for the young Rogers were her responsibility.

'99%,' replied Chris. 'But I have an idea of how to check.'

By now they had reached apple crumble and ice cream – delicious!

Between two mouthfuls Chris went through her plan and it was agreed that she should phone Inspector Devenport immediately.

With the phone on loud speaker so Jessie and Tony could join in, Chris – with some trepidation – rang.

'Chris?'

He paused for a second.

He sighed.

'We could do with some news from your side. Any kind of news would be very good indeed. I know I told *Spectrum* not to get TOO involved, but then we have known each other for too long, right?'

'You are right!' Chris exclaimed. '*Spectrum* has actually been on the broads for the last couple of days doing a discreet sort of search. Tim, Ian and Mark have drawn a blank, but I might have found something of interest.'

On hearing her story, he asked: 'We must exercise caution, you understand. Are you truly convinced that it is Rachel?'

'Convinced as possibly I can be. The transit looked similar to the one we saw abduct Rachel. The photo is of poor quality, I admit. I do so want it to be her that maybe my judgement is clouded. But I have an idea which might confirm the situation.

I know the layout of the manor well and of a backway into the grounds. We thought that Tony could wander around the gardens, and if challenged he would say that he was checking the site as the Coopers had asked him to perform at a family celebration.

Meanwhile Tony's distraction would enable me to check for anything out of the ordinary.'

'If you confirm that it is Rachel,' said the Inspector, 'it would be difficult to rescue her with any degree of safety, especially as the kidnappers will probably be armed!'

Not to be put off Chris continued. 'That is why I have a second thought.'

Inspector Devenport listened. The proposal put forward would place both Chris and Tony in some degree of danger. Following their engagement he could understand why Tony wanted to be with Chris for something like this. But with Tony, so well known, the tabloids would have a field day if things went wrong. He dreaded to think how his Chief Constable would react. Especially following the unwelcome headlines experienced by the Police last year with the escaped convicts.

'Tony, is your Manager aware of what you are intending to do?'

'Laurie is away at present attending a Retreat in India,' answered Tony. 'I have no means of contacting him. So, to answer your question, no, he will not know.'

'Hmm…..But I want a police presence with you and they will take the lead.'

A short while later Sgt Duffield and Neville Skinner, his constable, arrived. *Spectrum Three* slipped her moorings and with Tony at the wheel they made their way down Ranworth Dyke to the main river. High clouds drifted over the spring sunshine and a slight breeze ruffled the surface of the otherwise still waters of the River Bure. A pair of mallards scuttled out of the way of the boat, a moorhen complained at being disturbed, flicking its white tail coverts in the process. A grey heron flew lazily overhead making its way to a roosting place for the night.

Tony breathed in the clear crisp air, 'Mmm that smells good, farewell to the clogged air of London and hello to the Norfolk ozone.'

The sparkling weather would not deter Tony from the possible danger they might well face later.

Soon they reached Fleet Dyke and the 'Outer Broad', the public sector of South Walsham Broad. Tony handed the controls to Chris and she took the boat across the stretch of water to the so-called posh bit! Tony heaved the plumb weight over the side, a hefty stone on the end of a rope. It was the way of anchoring a cruiser in open water.

Chris scanned the banks until she came across the Coopers' place and handed the binoculars to the others.

'Can you see the third house from the left, the one in its own grounds?'

'Is that the manor, where you think Rachel is being held?'

'Well it's the possibility.'

Chris then radioed the Police H.Q. to say they were in position.

With the sun now hidden behind a cloud the four of them left the boat and stealthily made their way through the reeds and bushes on the Broad's edge. They reached the single gate at the back of the house only to find it well and truly locked.

'If my memory serves me correctly,' she whispered, 'there should be a hole in the wall just to the right.' She felt her way along the border, stopped herself crying out as her fingers touched a rusty piece of metal, and finally found the loose bricks. With Gerry's help she worked them free. Constable Skinner stayed behind while the others squeezed through the gap. Chris stood in the shadows with Gerry at her side. Tony wandered across the lawns. It wasn't long before someone appeared.

'This is private property, you are trespassing,' the newcomer said, gesticulating with his rifle.

'Oh sorry,' said Tony, 'but Mrs. Cooper told me I could drop in any time. I'm due to sing at their Golden Wedding Anniversary next month. I'm Tony Dale you know. Is Sadie available?'

'Pop star or not you are still trespassing.'

By now another older but beefier man joined them – you wouldn't want to meet him in a dark alley! He too had a rifle.

'Many apologies,' said Tony, eyeing the hardware and holding up his hands. 'I must have come to the wrong address.' He turned and the two villains encouraged him to the exit gate with the odd prod from a gun barrel!

Meanwhile Chris and Gerry had been scanning the manor and as Chris's looked towards the gable end a face briefly appeared at the window before it was pulled out of sight. There was no doubt in Chris's mind that it was Rachel. She gave a thumbs up to Gerry and checking all was well with Tony, they slipped back through the gap in the wall. On board *Spectrum Three* Chris radioed the Inspector to confirm the sighting.

As dusk fell Chris, Gerry and Neville made their way to the manor. They once more squeezed through the hole in the wall. Standing behind the hedge she visualised the layout of a garden of which she used to know every nook and cranny when she played with the children of the Big House, as it was known way back in her childhood.

Leaving the others Chris picked her way through the tangled undergrowth until her feet scraped on the gravelled path. She moved along the edge of the driveway keeping as much to the shadows as possible. She eventually hit the open ground which led up to the front of the house. Chris was just about to cross the grass when she saw two men, their cigarettes casting a weird glow in the dark. They stopped by her hiding place, mumbled a few words to each other and then went on their way.

The moon shone briefly as Chris dashed across the lawn and into the safety of shelter once more. She had now reached the corner of the manor. The kitchen window appeared to be open. Chris quietly climbed into the room and hid as she heard footsteps and voices.

A grey-haired woman in her early sixties entered followed by a young lad probably in his late teens. The woman obviously wasn't happy as their conversation continued in Chris's hearing.

'How could you possibly get caught up in such a thing Jack, I've done my best to keep you on the straight and narrow after your father's demise. Oh, by golly yes, I have and this is how you repay me by getting yourself, and ME, involved in a kidnapping!' A mug and plate were slammed down onto a tray. The woman turned towards the boiling kettle.

'Come-on maw, it's not that bad. It's only a tiny job and think of the dosh. Our share should solve a lot of our problems.'

This did nothing to mollify the woman who picked up the tray and key lying on the table. 'Humph!' she said, leaving the kitchen with the young lad trailing miserably behind her.

Chris moved across the room and opened the door a crack. The hall appeared empty. Keeping to the cover of the floor to ceiling velvet curtains, the pride and joy of Grandma Cooper, she quietly followed her quarry up the stairs.

At the last room on the left the woman took out the key, unlocked the door and carried the tray through. Chris disappeared deeper into the curtains as the shouting which followed was enough to wake the whole house. There was no mistaking that voice, it was Rachel!

The women beat a hasty retreat leaving the key in the lock.

When the coast was clear Chris tiptoed along the corridor and quietly unlocked the door.

Rachel spun round, missile in hand, which she promptly dropped!

'Chris! Chris, what are you doing here?'

'Shush, no time for questions, we've got to get out of here.'

They crept along the landing and ducked out of sight as a man walked across the hallway. A few seconds later all was clear. Chris slid back the bolts to the front door a rush of cool air hit their flushed faces.

The two friends tore across the lawn and into the shrubbery just as the first shouts were heard from the house. The escape had been discovered! Chris and Rachel had reached Gerry and Neville and with their assistance climbed through the hole in the wall. Crashing feet and excited dogs were nearing.

Tony hearing the commotion had moved the boat nearer and kept the engine running. The friends reached the Broad as the first shots echoed behind them. They waded into the water and with Gerry and Neville's assistance Tony pulled Rachel on board, quickly followed by Chris.

Tony opened the throttle and the boat accelerated with a tremendous bow wash. Soon all sounds of pursuit for them faded.

Meanwhile Sgt. Duffield and Constable Skinner, now on dry land, skirted the manor and joined a very relieved Inspector in the lane. With Rachel safely out of the way the police entered the grounds and gradually the kidnappers were rounded up and taken into custody.

※ ※ ※

'I'd better radio in,' said Chris, and turned to a rather befuddled Rachel. 'Are you all right Rachel?'

Rachel just nodded and looked around her in amazement. 'How did you find me, and what is all this?'

'Ah, yes, I think some explaining will have to be done, but meanwhile go and say hello to, er…… Cliff properly, I think you're going to have a bit of a surprise there.'

Rachel wandered over to Tony, 'Okay Rachel?'

'Yes thanks, but how did you two find me?' and at that moment Tony turned full face to her, 'B….but you're Tony Dale!'

'Yes, that's right Rachel, as Chris said she's a whole lot of explaining to do.'

Rachel was still looking bewildered as Chris came and joined them with mugs of steaming coffee.

'I see you've found out who Cliff is.' Rachel nodded, 'But where does all this fit in?'

Just then the radio crackled, '*Spindle* calling *Spectrum Three* come in please,' Chris once more went below to answer it.

'Is this *Spectrum*, is Chris *Spectrum* then?'

'Yes, well not just Chris but of course her brothers as well.'

'Are they really *Spectrum*, *Spectrum*, you're not kidding me, are you?'

Tony shook his head. Rachel just sat there, sipping her coffee trying to take it all in. Chris rejoined them in the cockpit and took the controls from Tony as they neared Malthouse Broad.

'Chris are you really *Spectrum*, and is Cliff, I mean Tony, really Tony Dale or am I dreaming?'

'No, you're not dreaming Rachel, and you've a few more surprises yet.'

They reached Spindle Broad and Mark was at the quayside. Tony threw him the mooring rope.

Mark tied *Spectrum Three* securely and took Rachel up to the Hall.

The first people she saw were Ginger and June.

'Ginger! June! What are you doing here?' Once more Rachel was a bit perplexed to say the least.

Mark left the three friends.

'Yes I suppose it is a bit confusing at present, and I believe you've now realised who Chris and her brothers are,' said Ginger.

'But how do you all fit in, and how come you knew about Chris, you kept that pretty quiet.'

'Well, we obviously haven't had to keep Chris's secret as long as she has,' said June. 'But if you think back a bit to last summer and the to do over me and Chris during the holidays, you'll begin to see daylight.'

'I remember that, because at the time I thought it strange that one minute we were all hostile with Chris over you being so ill, and then next thing we knew you three were the best of friends. How come?'

'Well it was Sandra who overheard us talking about the incident and with a bit of persuasion she told us everything, and you know the rest from there.'

'So in their last escapade over Christmas you were involved in that?'

They nodded.

'Other things are beginning to fall into place,' said Rachel, as she flopped down into the armchair.

'Chris getting the *Spectrum* album autographed.

Going to Tony's concert and meeting him backstage.

How could I have been so dumb in not recognising him when he was with Chris. No wonder his face was so familiar.'

'Do you remember being pulled off the mud in Breydon Water?' asked June.

Rachel nodded, 'You weren't there as well were you?'

'Yes. Tim recognised you and I kept out of sight until all was clear.'

'Where is everyone now?'

'Well I think they're sorting the boats, we were all out looking for you,' said Ginger. 'I was with Ian, Sandra and Mark. June with Tim and of course, as you know, Tony was with Chris.'

If on cue the latter two joined them, 'How's the patient then, feeling better?' asked Tony.

Rachel had a sudden attack of shyness, to be in the presence of her idol, of someone so famous. The door opened and there were her parents. Rachel ran into their welcoming outstretched arms.

※ ※ ※

As Chris saw Rachel being reunited with her mum and dad she now knew that *Spectrum's* anonymity as that mysterious Group was at an end. She was ready for it. She was ready to be a supposed star of the pop world, if only for a short time. Being in the spotlight will probably not last much longer. The entertainment world is pretty fickle. New prodigies are being discovered all the time.

Her engagement to Tony will also no longer be a secret. She hoped his fans would still support him and that he will continue to be admired as an icon at the top of his chosen profession. She was quietly confident that he would.

FOURTEEN YEARS LATER

CHAPTER SEVENTEEN

Chris stirred, rolled over and looked straight into those crinkly brown eyes she knew and loved so well.

'Come on', said Tony, 'Wake up! Our peace should be shattered any minute now!'

They smiled and if on cue, two pairs of feet could be heard pattering down the corridor in the direction of their room. The door opened. In burst their twins full of energy. The Easter Holidays had started and they were keen to feel the freedom of days spent out of doors. They sprang onto their parents' bed.

'Can we go out in the boats today mum?' asked Simon.

Simon was the spitting image of Tony with his dark hair and brown eyes, whereas in contrast his twin Lucy had taken after Chris, with fair hair and blue eyes.

Chris looked across at Tony. There was nothing unexpected in their son's request. Simon was a natural in boats which wasn't surprising considering his parents' history, especially Chris's involvement with *Spectrum*.

Now, some fourteen years on after their last adventure Tony's career had turned from international pop star to producing. He had become very successful in that field as well. Although living in Norfolk they still kept a small flat in Chelsea for when they were in London.

With Chris's brothers scattered around the country Sam was so pleased that Chris and Tony had agreed to take on Spindle Hall. He was keen to keep the property in the family and anyway, it was a great place to bring up children!

Tony lost his parents at the age of two and had spent his childhood in orphanages and temporary foster homes. He always yearned for a family life. Meeting the Rogers family in his early twenties had become a revelation. Grace Rogers immediately treated him as part of her brood. Tony, at long last, was a happy young man especially, as with the Rogers' only daughter Chris, it was that old adage: love at first sight. They had married soon after Chris had graduated with a Bachelor of Music degree from Cambridge University. And then, the cherry on the cake, not only had he become a daddy, but a double daddy at that! The twins arrival – Lucy and Simon – had put a permanent smile on his face.

Every so often he was asked to perform on stage and quite enjoyed the occasions, even more so when Chris and her brothers got together and accompanied him as *Spectrum*.

He looked down at his son who was patiently waiting for his reply, whilst Lucy climbed under the covers and snuggled up to her mother with teddy bear under her arm.

'Umm let me see,' he said, with a thoughtful expression, hand under his chin. 'I do have paperwork to do before my next meeting and that would take a couple of days. Your mother has promised to give some swimming lessons in the pool.....'

Simon's expression was visually drooping and his sister wasn't fairing much better.

'Stop teasing, darling,' said Chris.

Simon looked up, 'was his dad *pulling his leg*?'

'Mmmm.....okay Simon, Lucy, all good. We're off in *Spectrum Three* for a few days.'

'Yippee!' cried a boisterous Simon, who started to leap up and down on his parents' bed. Lucy's teddy bear went flying as she threw up her arms in delight.

'That's enough of those high spirits young man otherwise your mum and I will have nowhere to sleep,' and grabbed Simon as he came down for his next bounce.

'Now, the pair of you, go and get washed and dressed, and don't forget to clean your teeth!' Tony called after them as they ran off in great excitement.

He looked across at Chris and winked. What they didn't add was that he and Chris were going to try the twins in an Optimist on Wroxham Broad later that day. Many 5 and 6 year olds learnt to sail in these single-sail fibre-glass crafts.

After breakfast *Spectrum Three* was packed with stores and warm bedding. The twins were wearing their brand new bright red buoyancy aids, an early birthday present from their grandparents. Chris cast off and Tony took the helm.

They motored down the dyke from Spindle to join the River Bure just above Ranworth Broad. Chris never tired of the scenery around her, especially in those areas where the sky seemed to stretch endlessly into the distance with seemingly no barriers. It was not surprising that Norfolk had had such a reputation for big skies. She recalled that in 1976 water levels were extremely low. It was the second hottest summer on record. In places you could make out the remains of wherries which had been sunk during the Second World War to prevent Germany landing their sea planes.

On reaching the Bure they turned in the direction of Wroxham. The April sun shone brightly and a grey heron flew lazily by. A couple of mute swans swam out of their way, hissing at being disturbed. To break the journey to Wroxham, Tony steered the boat into Salhouse Broad and headed towards the shallow end close to the sandy beach. Chris, now standing in the bows, dropped the anchoring mud weight into the water to stop them drifting.

While Chris was preparing lunch, Tony slipped the rubber dinghy over the side, hopped in and then with the twins on board, paddled off to the shore to give the children a chance to let off some steam.

In the afternoon they reached Wroxham Broad. Chris looked across at the clubhouse where standing on the quayside was Kevin, a friend of long standing. Up until recently Kevin had been helping to run his father's boat hire business on South Walsham Broad but now ran a sailing school.

Once more the rubber dinghy was launched and they rowed the short distance to the quayside.

'Hi Chris, Tony, are these my two new pupils?' asked Kevin eyeing the twins.

Simon glanced up in surprise and then noticed moored nearby an Optimist with its white sail gently wafting in the breeze!

'Do you mean we are actually going to sail?' an excited Simon asked. Beaming, he turned to his sister who seemed to catch her brother's exuberance. A big grin crossed her face.

'Yes you are. Only if you want to,' answered Chris.

'Wee!' cried Simon. 'You bet!'

Kevin took out a penny. 'Who is going first?' He looked at the twins and tossed the coin.

'Heads' called Simon before Lucy could react. He was unlucky – it was tails.

Helped by Kevin, Lucy eagerly climbed aboard the Optimist and with Kevin at the helm the pair sailed around the Broad.

Chris was feeling a bit emotional. She brushed a tear out of the corner of her eye as she saw her daughter take her first sailing lesson. Tony helpfully offered her a tissue!

Meanwhile, Simon, hopping from one foot to the other, was trying to be patient. The dinghy duly returned and the twins swopped places. Simon launched himself into the craft. No finesse in his boarding! This action proved how stable an Optimist was; any other boat would have capsized!

❧ ❧ ❧

Approximately fifteen years ago *Spectrum* had helped the Police catch two convicts who had absconded from the Barracks, the nickname for the local prison. Jacob Wright had been sentenced to twelve years whilst his accomplice Michael Henderson, seven years. In actual fact Michael Henderson mended his ways and became a model prisoner, resulting in him being released three years early.

It was a different kettle of fish with Jacob Wright. On several occasions he had been extremely violent thus ending up in segregation. During the extra years added to his sentence he seemed to have calmed. No longer was he ranting to get even with *Spectrum* for putting him behind bars.

He may have pulled the wool over the majority of the wardens' eyes but not so the Prison Governor. Ted had many years experience in the job and felt there was more to come from this clever and evil man.

On the day of Jacob Wright's release, Ted, after much sole searching, made a phone call.

※ ※ ※

The next day the twins had a further session with Kevin. Chris and Tony could see that even after such a short time Lucy and Simon were gaining in confidence as they took turns at the tiller. With careful instruction they each managed a figure of eight course on the broad. Very impressive!

Their lessons duly came to an end and the twins, reluctantly, had to say goodbye to their instructor.

Safely back on-board *Spectrum Three*, the family motored out of Wroxham Broad and onto Wroxham itself. Through this part of the river, surrounded by hire companies, it took a lot of concentration on Chris's part to negotiate the waterway safely. The tide was low so they easily cleared Wroxham Bridge and then headed towards Coltishall to moor by the Rising Sun for the night.

The children were still full of their sailing experience.

'Mummy,' said Lucy, 'Can we do that again please?'

Chris and Tony were getting exactly the reaction they were hoping for because nestling back at Spindle, and kept under wraps until their return, was the twins' birthday present: a spanking new Optimist.

'Of course,' replied Chris.

'Yippee!' cried both children in harmony.

By now they had reached the Green at Coltishall, and this time it was Tony's turn to safely moor *Spectrum Three*, by jumping ashore with the rope and tying it to a convenient bollard with a couple of half-hitches.

Later that evening, with the twins tucked up in their bunks, Chris and Tony sat in the cockpit in the gathering gloom of the night which was lit up by the most spectacular sky. The absence of the moon gave prominence to the twinkling of the tiny specks of light. Even Mars glowed, its vibrant colour endorsing its name as the Red Planet!

'Look!' pointed Tony, as a shooting star appeared very briefly. 'Go on, make a wish', he said.

Chris obliged.

'What did you wish for?' he asked.

Chris snuggled up to him. 'Can't say,' she said, 'or it won't come true.'

Tony put his arm around her. 'Yes you're probably right,' and took a sip of wine.

If you had been looking up into the Heavens in 1915, it wouldn't have been shooting stars. You would be seeing a German zeppelin which had mistaken the River Bure for the River Thames!

The next morning the twins eagerly bounded out of their bunks, their seventh birthday had arrived. *Spectrum Three* was already under way with Tony at the wheel.

'Come on you two,' said Chris, 'breakfast.'

Simon and Lucy looked at each other. Hadn't their mother realised it was their birthday! They reluctantly took their places around the table. Simon reached for the cereal. Lucy took a piece of toast. The pair of them exchanged a silent communication.

'It is our birthday,' Lucy whispered. 'I know it is.' Simon nodded.

Chris was quietly smiling. She dished up their scrambled eggs and poured out the orange juice. As they finished their meal Simon couldn't wait any longer.

'Mum, you do know what today is?'

'Mmm, Saturday I believe,' and turned away once more.

'But…. but it's our birthday,' he started to say as his mum turned round once more, this time with two bags of goodies.

'Happy birthday you two.' They hugged her in delight.

'Thanks mum,' they said in unison. 'You're the biscuit!'

For a few silent minutes all that could be heard was the ripping of paper and their cries of 'oohs' and 'ahs'! Amongst the gifts were a couple of project books, for Simon it was on all things mechanical, whilst Lucy's was on all things to do with the natural world. She had taken after her Uncle Mark in that respect. Chris was not unduly surprised at her son's next request.

'Can I go and drive the boat with daddy please?'

Chris, with a throw away comment to Tony. 'Your co-pilot is on his way darling.'

Lucy, pencil in hand with Chris's help was doing some little drawings on one of the pages of her project book.

Simon, now sitting on his father's lap, was steering. Well so he thought, but Tony was keeping a firm hand on the wheel to ensure that nothing untoward could happen, especially through Wroxham. As mentioned before, this part of the journey was always chaotic. It didn't help matters as it was change-over day. New hirers of the holiday craft were all over the place trying to get use to their different mode of transport.

By mid-afternoon *Spectrum Three* arrived at Spindle. They were just tying up when Tim and his young son Jamie appeared on the quay.

'Uncle Tim, Uncle Tim,' cried the twins as they jumped out of the boat, helped by Tony, and ran to greet him.

'Happy birthday you two', and swung each of them around in celebration.

'June is up in the house,' said Tim to Chris. Jessie's making her usual fuss of our Jenny. You know cupcakes topped with hundreds and thousands, amongst other things.'

Chris smiled. It was great that her twin and best friend's relationship had lasted. They married a few years after Tim had graduated from university and now lived a few miles out of Cambridge where Tim worked in the Science Park. Jamie was a couple of years younger than the twins whilst Jenny was the baby of the family at 3 but don't ever say that in her hearing! Being 3 going on 4, meant she was into everything, especially her brother's toys which didn't go down very well with Jamie!

June had followed her dream and had left Teaching College with a magnificent First. Now, with a young family, she was teaching part-time in a special needs school within walking distance of their home at St. Neots.

Chris's thoughts then wandered to her other brothers. Ian to begin with couldn't make up his mind what he wanted to do when he left school. He had reasonable A level grades but didn't fancy university. He floated from job to job then suddenly something happened that changed his life.

Uncle Nick had a fall at *Marygold* whilst picking the annual fruit crop. At the time, Ian was between jobs, so ended up at the family farm helping with the harvest. He enjoyed himself so much that he now knew what he wanted to do. Nick couldn't be happier. He had always hoped that one of his nieces or nephews would take on the business. Ian was just finishing his last year at Agricultural College in Tonbridge and to top it all, he and Ginger had just got engaged!

Mark and cousin Sandra were still best of mates. Mark did attend university and left with an Honours Degree in Zoology, but he decided to tour for a few years. Sandra was only too pleased to accompany him. The last they had heard of them was from New Zealand where they had been for the last 3 months. Both Sandra and Mark recognised the fact that their travels wouldn't go on forever but, even if one of them did ultimately meet a partner, they knew their friendship would last.

'I've just seen what's hidden around the corner,' commented Tim. Chris noted that her nephew was trying his best not to spill the beans.

The twins glanced at their parents, 'Come on you two,' said Tony, 'let's see what else has appeared for your birthdays.' The children ran round to the side of the boathouse. There, snuggled in the reeds and securely anchored to the shore was their very own Optimist!

'Is, is that for us.' Simon stared in amazement and then let out a loud whoop. Turning to his parents: 'Can we go out in it please?'

Lucy gently tugged at her mother's jumper. 'Thank you!' she quietly said.

Chris helped them board. They cast off. Tony paddled alongside them in the single-seater canoe. The twins took turns at the tiller as they went for a short trip around the Broad.

Jamie with a wistful look turned to Tim. 'Daddy can I have a go please?'

Tim gazed at Chris who nodded. 'Okay son,' said Tim, 'We'll ask Simon and Lucy if you can have a sail when they return.' A smile of pure delight crossed his son's face.

❧ ❧ ❧

The next morning with four youngsters in the house nobody had a lie-in, which was just as well as Tony was due in London for a couple of important meetings and had to leave early; he was not returning until the weekend.

After the twins had said their goodbyes to their dad, it was obvious there was only one thing on their minds. 'Right oh you two,' said Chris, 'time for some more sailing.' With delight they ran to the shore to their brand-new Optimist which had now been named *Bishy-barney-bee*. Norfolk dialect for ladybird, as the craft had a bright red sail.

Tim in the double canoe - with Jamie in the front seat paddled alongside Chris who was in the single canoe. The twins once more took turns at the helm as they cruised over the still waters. Meanwhile June and Jenny went for a swim in Spindle's pool.

About half-an-hour later June and Jenny left the barn. Much to June's amazement she noticed a car on the driveway. She couldn't believe her eyes. 'Is that you Inspector, or should I say Superintendent?'

'June, what a pleasant surprise: are you staying long?'

'Just for a couple of days. Oh, and congratulations on your promotion by the way. It is high time your flare and excellence are rewarded.'

'Many thanks,' he replied modestly. They walked back to the Hall and into the lounge.

'Are Chris and Tony around?' He asked.

'Well Tony is on his way to London as we speak. Chris has taken the twins out in their new sailing dinghy and Tim with Jamie are canoeing.'

A minor commotion from the back of the house announced the return of the intrepid sailors. Simon and Jamie burst into the lounge full of high spirits and skidded to a halt as they saw Brian Devenport.

'Oops – sorry Superintendent, I didn't know you were here,' said Simon.

The others followed the boys more sedately into the room. 'Superintendent,' exclaimed Chris. 'It's great to see you.'

'Morning Chris,' he said and acknowledged Tim. 'Is there somewhere we can talk?'

Tim raised his eyebrows, this seemed a bit ominous. Chris also recognised the signs.

'Can you go on into the snuggery?' said Chris to the children

Jenny was holding June's hand. She looked up at her mum. 'Go on sweetie,' she said to her daughter. 'Go with Jamie.'

Simon and Lucy took their cousins into the playroom. The four adults sat down.

'What's this all about Superintendent?' asked Tim.

Brian Devenport began his story. 'Not good news. Chris, Tim. You remember that incident which involved Jacob Wright and Michael Henderson.'

Chris pulled a face and instinctively rubbed her arm, flexing it in the process. 'I don't think that's something I'll ever forget,' she said. 'I still get twinges, especially in damp weather, why?'

'Well,' continued the Superintendent, 'Michael Henderson was released early, a reformed character, and there is no problem there. As far as I am aware he is now a groundsman at Blickling Hall and doing a great job from all accounts. He seems to have integrated well back into society.

But what is causing the problem is Jacob Wright. He was pretty violent at times and on one occasion held a warden hostage at knife point. But, having served his term, an extended one at that, the Law being the Law had to release him. He is now on probation in the Norwich area.

However Ted, the Prison Governor, is of the opinion he still carries a threat to get even with *Spectrum*. Maybe Chris, as you are the only member of *Spectrum* living in Norfolk, you should go somewhere, possibly to your parents in Kent, until things blow over.'

'I trust you are joking,' she said. 'I am not belittling your advice, but we can't hide for the rest of our lives.'

Chris, jumped up, impetuous as usual. 'If he comes close to me and my children I'll give him what for....'

'Steady Chris,' said Tim trying to calm her and continued......

'Superintendent, have you any thoughts on what Jacob Wright might do?'

'We obviously have no idea what he could be planning, but just be aware.'

Brian rose to go. 'I'd like to position one of my men here but unfortunately I'm short staffed.'

'That's alright Sir', said Tim, also rising. 'Thanks for the warning and we'll now be on our guard.'

Brian drove off down the drive, he sighed. He always had a soft spot for Chris and her family.

'Why are things no longer straight forward,' he thought. 'Maybe it's time for retirement.'

June looked questioning at Tim, she was obviously aware of her father-in-law's dealings with RAF Neatishead.

'Tim, do you think you should have a word with Sam?' asked June.

Jacob Wright and Michael Henderson had been sent down for the arson attack at RAF Neatishead. The whole affair was thought to be a diversion so the blueprints of *Aquillus*, a radio-controlled *Spy in the Sky*, could be stolen. Sam Rogers and his partner Frank Morris had been working on the highly secret innovation which enabled information to be obtained remotely.

However, before they could discuss the situation further, raised voices from the snuggery followed by a few cries meant some supervision of the cousins was now required.

That evening Chris managed to track Tony down and told him about the Superintendent's warning. Tony was all for dropping everything and coming back to Spindle but Chris pacified him, reminded him how important his meetings were, and that she would see him, as planned, at the weekend.

'Okay,' Tony reluctantly agreed, 'but you must tell Jessie, Frank and Matt about the threat. I want as many people aware of the situation as possible.'

Before Tim could speak to his dad, Sam was on the phone. He too had been informed of the release of Jacob P Wright, and was just as concerned about his children's safety as the Superintendent. Although time had marched on and *Aquillus* had been replaced by updated technology, the original templates of the design were still worth something on the black market. He was mindful of possible pressure placed on the Rogers family to obtain the necessary information.

※ ※ ※

The next morning Tim and June had to return to Cambridge. They were very reluctant to go. 'Now you be careful sis.'

'I'll be all right,' assured Chris, 'as we said to the Superintendent, forewarned is a good defence.'

June hugged Chris and as her brother's Vauxhall disappeared down the driveway Chris called the twins. The three of them then went on to the Broad so Lucy and Simon could have more fun with *Bishy-barney-bee*. The twins were now reasonably proficient at sailing their little craft.

Unbeknown to the family someone was watching them through a pair of binoculars. Head shaven with a scar across the left cheek from a knife attack when he tried to defend his grandfather's name whilst inside,

Jacob Wright had appeared! He grunted with satisfaction and returned to his beat up old Ford Consul. His plan was forming. He had every intention to get even with *Spectrum*!

Revenge is a dish best served cold!

Jacob Wright had had a very troubled childhood. He was maltreated by his mother, a teenager, who was more interested in having a good time than looking after a baby. It wasn't until his grandfather took him in hand that he began to settle. But this didn't last. His grandfather died when Jacob was a mere seven years old, the age of Simon and Lucy now. No one had any time for the young Jacob Wright and it wasn't too long before he ended up on the wrong side of the Law.

CHAPTER EIGHTEEN

The Easter holidays had finished and the twins were back at school. Tony had returned from London, his meetings had been a great success and the threat from Jacob Wright gradually faded into the background.

Chris stretched and stood up from the piano. Her neck ached from bending over the musical score on which she had been working for the past hour. Historically, her twin Tim and brother Ian used to do all the writing when they were performing. Chris had composed several short pieces whilst at university, and in her final year had sketched out an idea for a musical. However, marriage to Tony, and then the twins arriving, had pushed the concept into the background. Now after nearly ten years Tony was encouraging her to complete it.

The Wind and the Willows by Kenneth Grahame was a favourite book since childhood. She loved reading it to the twins when they were younger, and took them to see the *Wind and the Willows* fountain on Hay Hill in Norwich. The interaction between Ratty, Moley and Badger was great to express to music. She was now concentrating on the weasels and stoats occupation of Toad Hall.

Chris didn't have any real intention of publishing her score, but it was fun to do and she would feel a sense of achievement when it was finished.

She walked over to the window and gazed down at Lucy who, with net in hand, was busy pond dipping from the jetty. The sun was out and it seemed so pleasant and inviting around the broad.

'I've done enough for today,' she muttered to herself, as if to justify that she was now going to join her daughter rather than continue her writing.

Lucy saw her mum. 'Look,' she said excitedly, 'I've just caught a water stick insect,' and there crawling around the bottom of her dish, trying to find some shade, was a huge thin stick with four skinny legs, two very long antennas and a spikey tail. Chris then eyed her daughter's other catches. There were water boatmen, back-swimmers, phantom midge larvae, red mites and a diving beetle nymph which was happily munching on something. Lucy continued her list. 'And also I have a water scorpion. No! It's disappeared!' She exclaimed.

Chris smiled. 'That's because it has just been eaten.' Her mother pointed out.

'Oh, bad luck,' said Lucy.

Chris carried on. 'You see that one over there in the corner of the dish, that's a great diving beetle larvae and it will eat anything it can get close to. Your little red mites have an interesting lifestyle.'

Lucy listened in rapt attention.

'The female lays about 400 eggs at any one time, and when they hatch they have six legs. The mite then finds a host, feeds on it and when ready, it leaves. Interestingly, as the mite swims away it now has eight legs. The next stage of its life is taken up with eating other insects. When the time is right the water mite deposits her eggs on an aquatic plant, and the cycle starts all over again.'

Lucy's face was a treat.

With that a car could be heard in the driveway, Tony and Simon had returned from Norwich. Simon had been itching to spend some of his birthday money. Chris and Lucy went to meet the shoppers.

'You're a bit later than expected,' commented Chris.

'I know,' answered Tony, 'but we stayed for the annual charity duck race between St. Georges and Fye Bridges on the River Wensum.'

'There were loads and loads of yellow bath ducks,' added Simon, 'and some had been painted with faces.'

Simon then reached into the Range Rover and pulled out a big 150 piece gift bucket.

He had been given a Meccano set for his birthday and loved it so much that he wanted to add to it.

He showed Chris the container which had such things as wheels, axles, extra screws, bolts and brackets. 'And look, there is even a Meccano magazine!' he said waving the brightly coloured publication for all to see.

'Mmm, they're great.' She said suitably impressed. 'That should keep you quiet for a while!'

Meanwhile Tony was admiring Lucy's catches. She carefully pointed out each one to her daddy, naming the species. Tony was amazed at his daughter's knowledge. Lucy then emptied the tray into the water.

It was time for lunch.

⁂

By the end of May the twins had become experienced enough to sail the Optimist by themselves although, for the time being, they were either accompanied by one parent or both parents in canoes, especially when either of them was sailing solo.

It was Friday night and the start of the Whitsun half-term holiday. Tony and Chris had shooed the twins to bed early so they could finish planning an extended trip around the Broads. Tim and June, plus Ian and Ginger, were due to arrive the next day. They were intending to take the boats, plus *Bishy-barney-bee*, to Horsey Mere. Then the plan was to walk the short distance to the beach in order to see the seal colony. It was the first time in ages that the majority of *Spectrum* were together. It was a shame that not everyone could make it.

The doorbell rang. Tony answered it, and there standing on the doorstep were two very sun-tanned people in the shape of Mark and Sandra.

Spectrum was now complete.

'Where did you two spring from?' asked Tony in delight, as Chris came into the hall to investigate. While Chris was exclaiming her pleasure, two very bleary-eyed twins appeared at the top of the stairs. Mark looked up.

'Uncle Mark…..Uncle Mark….' cried Lucy as she ran down the stairs, Mark caught her. Simon followed his sister, for once sedately – he was still half asleep but it didn't last long, he soon pounced on his uncle. Chris glanced at them. 'All right you two' she said, 'five minutes with your favourite uncle.'

The twins eventually went back to bed leaving the adults to talk well into the early hours of the morning. Mark and Sandra could not stop raving about New Zealand, how there were so few people, how they had come across a traffic jam in South Island, a flock of sheep!

'Did you know a vast amount of New Zealand is national parks?' said Sandra. 'We visited Fiordland where the landscape is similar to Scandinavia. There we walked the long-distance footpath called the Milford Track.'

'Many years ago, whilst touring New Zealand and Australia,' commented Tony, 'I nearly walked that Track but ran out of time. I believe it starts at Te Anau, and don't you have to take a boat trip across a lake to begin the trek?'

'Yes,' answered Sandra, 'that's right. As you know, the track is about 33 miles long: it took us four days and three nights. We only had to carry our packed lunch and overnight clothes, everything else was supplied. Some of the suspension bridges crossing the rivers were only suitable for about three people so we had to take turns….that was fun! Unfortunately, we missed the spectacular waterfalls as there hadn't been any substantial rainfall for several weeks.'

Sandra was doing her usual, talking fast and without taking a breath!

'The views were amazing from the Mackinnon Pass, the highest point at 1,154m. Looking south we could see the stunning Clinton Valley, which we had just left, and to the north, Arthur Valley with our final destination Milford Sound in the distance.'

Mark managed to chip in.

'The bird life is basically similar to ours, as a lot of the songbirds were taken into the country by the nineteenth century settlers.

We did see a couple of endemic species though, for instance, the kea, which are the only Alpine parrot in the world. And talk about inquisitive! You have to protect your rucksacks or they'll be into them. The kea would also take any unguarded food, a bit like the gulls at the coast with chips! Furthermore, they are very partial to the rubber around car windscreens!

Then there is the weka, a flightless bird, a member of the rail family, also native to New Zealand. If you startle it on the trail it will suddenly run into the undergrowth. However, a short while later it will reappear and walk past you as if you're part of the scenery!'

'The panoramic views in Milford and Doubtful Sounds were like a picture book, it was incredible,' carried on Sandra. 'The still water reflected its surroundings as mirror images.'

So the pair of them continued to retell their various adventures until Tim called a halt as it was well after mid-night.

≈ ≈ ≈

By the end of the Saturday everyone else had arrived, and although two extra passengers had appeared on the scene, they still decided to take just *Spectrum, One, Two* and *Three*. Tim and family in his *Spectrum One*, Chris and Tony with the twins in *Spectrum Three*, plus *Bishy-barney-bee*, and the rest in Ian's *Spectrum Two* which was towing the rubber dinghy. The sail boards and single-seater canoe were split between the boats and carried on the cabin roofs.

Ginger was glowing and only too happy to show off her engagement ring to June and Chris; yellow gold with a round-cut diamond. 'It's beautiful' they both said.

Matt was at the quayside to see them off. Chris couldn't help noticing a look passing between Sandra and him. If that was what she thought then Mark might soon be without his best mate!

The aim was Hickling Broad by lunch-time where they were going to moor for the night before heading on to Horsey the next day. *Spectrum* still caused a bit of a stir when spotted along the waterways, especially with three in convoy. Simon and Lucy were used to doing a Royal Wave as they call it, but it was a bit of a novelty for Jamie and Jenny.

Nearing the mediaeval stone crossing at Potter Heigham several hire cruisers were moored waiting for the pilot to shepherd them through. *Spectrum* being experienced sailors sounded their horns and safely negotiated the low bridge. Still on the River Thurne the boats eventually turned into Candle and Deep Go Dykes.

Hickling was duly reached and once more the twins were let loose in *Bishy-barney-bee* with Tim, Jamie, Jenny and Tony accompanying them in the rubber dinghy. Ian, Sandra and Mark were wind surfing while the three friends, mugs of coffee in hand, sat in the cockpit of *Spectrum Three* having a good gossip and gaining Ginger's reaction of becoming a farmer's wife!

The next morning with the sun shining, they cruised the short distance to Horsey Mere. The car park by the National Trust mill was already very busy and the small café and shop were doing brisk business.

They walked across a couple of fields which had cows in them. Jenny moved closer to her mum for comfort – she didn't like these enormous four-legged creatures which towered over her.

The ground was crisscrossed with drainage ditches which the adults took in their stride. Not so the boys. Jamie and Simon had great fun jumping them until... you can guess, Simon landed in a puddle! All were splattered with droplets of muddy water!

'Oops sorry everyone,' he cheekily said, and then ran on after Jamie.

Now on the gravelled track, edged with low hedges and further farmland, they headed towards the beach. The dune system appeared in front of them, a natural defence against sea incursion. This barrier forms an important obstruction to prevent the sea flooding the Norfolk Broads.

Mark was teaching his niece a bit more about the natural world. Lucy was particularly taken by the dragonflies and couldn't believe her luck as one, a large red damselfly, rested on her sleeve. Her uncle explained that dragonflies could only start flying once they had warmed up and this was one of the reasons why the insect was so still. Then, as if on cue, with a quivering of the wings it took flight. Lucy's attention changed to the butterflies. She neared a lovely one with bright orange forewings and dark brown spots, but it suddenly flew off.

'Why did that happen?' she asked her uncle.

'Well' said Mark, 'like dragonflies, butterflies also fly better when they too have warmed up. That small copper was sunning itself but you unfortunately stood in front of the sun, casting a shadow, which is why it fluttered away.'

'Oh,' said Lucy.

Jenny's feet were dragging, she was getting tired, everything around her seemed so big, the cows, now the hedges, she started wining. Tim hoisted her up on to his shoulders much to her delight, probably, as far as he was concerned, for a bit of peace and quiet!

Soon they reached the beach, Simon and Jamie kicked off their shoes and socks and ran towards the water's edge. Ian couldn't resist following them, he was in his second childhood!

'Come on uncle,' cried Simon, as all three of them splashed around in the shallows.

Lucy joined them. Suddenly a grey nose with a whiskered moustache appeared in front of her. Startled she ran out of the water straight into her mummy's arms. 'What, what, **what** was that?' she cried.

'Don't worry darling, it is only a seal wanting to greet you,' answered Chris.

The boys thought this highly amusing until they appeared to be surrounded by further inquisitive seals. Now they weren't so brave and hid behind Ian for protection!

Chris gently turned her daughter around and pointed. The sight that met Lucy's eyes was awesome! Just to the other side of the groynes Lucy saw row upon row of grey bodies looking very much like rocks until a flipper moved. They had found beached seals sunning themselves. One gave a terrific yawn exposing its rather sharp teeth!

Lucy then looked at the wooden groynes, a form of breakwater preventing movement of sand to protect the coast from erosion. Around their basis were shallow depressions filled with water in which tiny crustaceans were swimming. She found this fascinating.

Jamie, trying out his new prowess of counting: 'There's more than 100,' he proudly said to his father.

Ginger was looking puzzled. The seals she had seen in the past at Pegwell and Sandwich Bays in Kent had always appeared to be grey or whitish with dark spots, but here, in front of her, and no mistaking it, there were orange ones! She questioned it?

Tim was the first to answer. 'I know they look a bit odd but actually they may have come from Essex.'

This was even more intriguing to Ginger.

'Essex? Why do you say Essex?' she queried.

Tim continued. 'Some seals from Essex can turn this eye-catching orange. Their fur picks up the colouration from the iron oxides contained within the mud which they have a habit of rolling in, usually at various river estuaries. These seals have been known to come up from the Thames.'

'Oh,' was all Ginger could muster.

Jenny, now at ground level, tried to run to the seals but June grabbed her T-shirt, 'No sweetie,' she said, 'just watch from here otherwise you'll frighten them.'

They ambled back along the beach. Chris was amused to hear a snippet of conversation as she passed a couple of ladies possibly in their thirties.

'I'm sure it is HIM,' said the one with long dark hair and wearing paisley bell-bottom trousers and a smock top.

'Are you certain, Sue,' her friend answered, who was dressed in a floral jumpsuit. 'We would look pretty silly if it wasn't!'

'No I am convinced. Come on let's see.'

'Excuse me,' said Sue, 'you wouldn't be Tony Dale, would you?'

Tony turned, a big welcoming smile on his face. 'Yes I am!'

'Wow!' said a gob smacked Sue. 'We saw your summer show in Yarmouth. We usually come to Horsey on Boxing Day to see their pups. But talk about luck! This is the first time we have visited at this time of the year. I can't believe it!' Sue was now gabbling. 'I can't believe I'm actually meeting you. I've bought all your records.'

Meanwhile Simon and Jamie had skidded to a halt. Simon raised his eyebrows. 'Here we go,' he thought, 'daddy's been recognised ..... again!' Simon didn't like it, but mummy had taught him and Lucy to expect it. However, he wished the fans would leave his daddy alone.

Tony felt chuffed that he had been acknowledged – once a celebrity, always a celebrity! He noticed a camera in Sue's hand and guessed the next question.

'Can Flo and I have a photo with you please?'

'Of course!' Tony was only too happy to oblige. Chris was just the photographer. She was so relieved that fans were no longer chasing after her and her brothers as *Spectrum*.

With a wave, and more profuse thanks, the ladies said their goodbyes.

Back at the boats, Meadow Dike was now very congested. They made the short hop to Hickling and by mid-afternoon were moored ready for the night. The children, still high from their trip to see the seals and a day in the fresh air, took a while to settle, but eventually the gentle rock of the boats lulled them to sleep.

Chris, Tony, June and Tim joined the others on *Spectrum Two*. While Sandra and Ginger cooked the dinner they sat in the cockpit drinking wine, the moon, in its first quarter shone in the starlit sky then, Ian asked.

'Chris, did Superintendent Devenport hear anything more about the threat from Jacob Wright?'

Mark's ears pricked up? 'Jacob Wright, wasn't he that man we helped to put away?'

Chris nodded and proceeded to tell Mark and Sandra about the warning received from the police.

'That's really scary', said Sandra.

'Yes it is,' replied Chris: 'but that was nearly two months ago, nothing has happened. We are treating it as an idle threat. Just relax, I'm not concerned.'

'Well darling, I'm still not comfortable about it,' commented Tony. 'He was vicious. The way he kicked you when you were down, was unforgiveable. I can only surmise that there must have been something in his past for him to act the way he did.'

'Tony, you can't keep your family locked up, and you certainly wouldn't be able to keep the twins restrained,' Tim added with a slight chuckle.

'True,' he said, 'but I still worry about it a lot. I just have a bad feeling.'

The next morning whilst Chris took the twins out for their daily sail in the Optimist, the others decided to stay on Hickling Broad, windsurfing. Tony was determined, under Tim's guidance, to become more proficient at the sport.

Ginger was now pretty much of an expert on the board and a member of a club in Kent close to where she and Ian lived. The pair of them had great fun in using the old piling in the middle of the broad as a make-shift slalom course.

Mark, Jenny and Jamie were paddling in the rubber dinghy on the broad. Sandra and June, although not as skillful at windsurfing as the others, sailed around the boat for the delight of the two children. Jenny and Jamie probably ever hopeful that their mummy, June, would fall in!

⚓ ⚓ ⚓

A gentle breeze helped the Optimist on its way, Chris paddled alongside in the single-seater canoe as the twins took turns to take the helm.

Martham Broad, a short distance away, was the target. The boats turned into the main river, and after a while negotiated the narrow gap between the supports for a swing bridge. This structure enabled the local farmer to access his land, which was surrounded by numerous dykes and ditches.

The crafts were now travelling along the navigational channel between two roped off areas of the broad's nature reserve where motor cruisers were excluded to avoid disturbance of the wildlife. Chris led the twins into one of the sections that, much to Lucy's delight, contained masses of mute swans. The majority of the cygnets sported speckled grey and white feathers which would gradually turn into their startling white plumage as they matured. However, one pair of adults, very protective of their tiny young, hissed at the boats as they passed.

With a sense of achievement, the twins eventually made it to the far end of the broad and Simon, as he had been taught, jumped onto the grassy bank taking the rope with him to moor *Bishy-barney-bee*.

Lucy looked up at the old mill standing towards the end of an overgrown path. The sun appeared to reflect off its dusty windows, almost as if there was something shiny behind the glass. The main thing drawing

Lucy's attention was the absence of any sails on its white domed roof.

Chris was busily pulling her canoe onto dry land. 'Mummy,' she called, 'why are there no crossed sticks on the top of the mill?'

Chris turned. 'The crossed sticks are called sails darling. Many windmills were built towards the end of the last century and their crumbling brickwork can no longer take the strain of the sails so they have been removed.'

Chris continued: 'Are you hungry?' she asked her twins – what a question for seven-year olds who were always ready for any sort of food.

'You bet,' the pair cried in unison, and then much to their delight Chris produced a small picnic.

Many of us have had a serendipity moment. Today was Jacob Wright's he couldn't believe his luck. Standing, just a short distance from him, was his quarry, *Spectrum*, whom he loathed to extinction. The glint from the window which Lucy had seen had been Jake's binoculars.

Halfway through her sandwich Lucy suddenly pointed: 'Look mummy,' she cried, 'there seems to be a nest in the reeds!' Chris followed her daughter's gaze. 'You're right, and can you see a bird all black, with white face markings.'

'Isn't that a coot?' asked Lucy.

'Yes, well done,' replied Chris.

Just then another coot swam into view from the opposite bank, trailing an extremely long reed. As it approached the nest, its mate took the stem and tucked it around the already massive mound.

Lucy digging into her memory: 'They're very territorial aren't they mummy?'

'Mmm.... clever girl, you remember everything I tell you.' To prove her point a pair of mallards inadvertently swam too close to the sitting bird. The other coot, lying flat on the water surface, shot across the broad at a rate of knots to chase the ducks away.

Chris continued, 'It is always interesting to see birds fly from a standing start on water. Some, like swans, seem to run along the surface before taking off whilst smaller birds, as you saw, just shoot straight up into the sky.'

Simon, not to be outdone, was also looking closely into the reeds and spotted another nest, this time, of a great crested grebe. He excitedly pointed to his mother.

'I didn't think grebes and coots got on?' queried Lucy

'No they don't,' answered her mum: 'However, nesting so close enables the birds to warn each other of any impending danger from a predator.'

For a moment all were quiet. Then a slight rustle caught the twins' attention.

'Mummy,' whispered Lucy, 'look, look a deer!'

Lucy then giggled as she saw the facial features. It had large ears, a furry muzzle and a black button nose. 'It looks like my teddy bear,' she said.

'It's a Chinese water deer,' said Chris. 'Interestingly, instead of antlers a couple of the male's upper teeth develop into tusks.'

'Wow!' exclaimed Simon. Probably visualising a sabre tooth tiger!

It was so peaceful and warm in the sunshine that soon, no doubt helped by their morning exertions, the twins dozed off. Chris watched over them, keeping an eye on the time and the weather. In the reed bed bearded tits flitted between the stems, giving their *pinging* calls. All very relaxing and a bit surreal!

Amongst the meadow flowers longhorn beetles were soaking up the sunshine, their yellow and black stripy bodies standing out against the white blooms of the chamomile daisies. Bright red cardinal beetles were at rest on the flat white petals of the cow parsley.

The marsh thistles deep pink flowers were just beginning to open. A beautiful yellow and black butterfly attempted to land on one of the buds only to find it wasn't ready to give up its nectar source. It was a shame her daughter had just missed the rare swallowtail.

Suddenly, without warning she was grabbed from behind. The attacker's hands dug painfully into her shoulder blades! She struggled!

Her startled cry woke the children.

'Got you!' said a gruff voice. 'I'll teach you to make me suffer and lose over twelve years of freedom.'

He spun Chris around and grabbed her by the throat.

She was now face to face with a bald-headed man sporting a scarred face. She smelt tobacco on his breath. Her attacker had to be Jacob Wright!

'I'm going to give you a taste of the same medicine! See what you think about being locked up with no real means of escape!' He threw her to the ground.

Chris was now terrified, especially for Simon and Lucy. 'Do what you want with me!' She cried. 'But please, please leave my children alone.'

Jacob Wright yanked Chris back to her feet. A couple of young lads seized Simon and Lucy. They were dragged to the mill and unceremoniously pushed into its cellar. The frightened twins ran to their mother. Chris cuddled them to reassure. Jacob had now produced a gun.

Although feeling battered and bruised her main priority was still the twins. She pleaded once more for their safety.

This fell on deaf ears. It was obvious from Jacob Wright's attitude he didn't care too hoots. Revenge was the only thing on his mind.

'What will your beloved pop star of a husband say when I demand a six-figure ransom for your safe return, not to mention his kids. And I don't need to stop there. The stealth weapon designed by your father will fetch a handsome price from some third world country,' snarled Jacob Wright.

'Yes, you will all make me very rich. I said I'd get even with you for what you did to me, and that is what I have every intention of doing!' He spun on his heel. The door slammed. Chris could hear the key turn in the lock!

Lucy was sobbing in Chris's arms. Simon looked at his mum, his face streaked with tears, trying his best to be brave.

'Mummy, what's happening?' sniffed Simon, 'I wish daddy was here.'

She looked around her. They appeared to be in some sort of storage cellar, with a tiny window near to the top of the high ceiling. This was the only form of lighting in the room. Here and there were some old sacks which still had grain in, and a couple of wooden packing cases. She stood on one of them and managed to see out of the window. Phew… it was at ground level. Fortunately, the boats were only a short distance away, and in full view of anyone coming up the channel.

As she watched, to her dismay, the two craft were moved by Jacob and his cohorts into deeper cover. The Optimist and canoe were now in direct view of the mill. Despite her situation Chris gave a wry smile, the idiots had left *Bishy-barney-bee* afloat! This gave her food for thought. Maybe there was hope for her children for a safe escape.

※ ※ ※

Back on Hickling Broad windsurfing was in full swing and a mini race underway on a figure of eight course. The beginning and ending point was Mark in the rubber dinghy with the two children. Jamie waved the starting flag. Sandra, June and Ginger began five seconds ahead of the men. Ian thought this a con. As far as he was concerned, Ginger was a far better boarder than he was, but he would never admit it!

When they finished, Jenny had the honour of using the chequered flag. The winner was Tony. Tim and Ginger tied for second. June, much to her surprise wasn't last, the wooden spoon went to a very disgruntled Ian who, at one stage, completely lost the wind and ended up becalmed!

By now it was mid-afternoon. 'Tony,' said Mark gazing at his watch, 'shouldn't Chris and the twins be back by now?'

Tony frowned: 'You're right Mark', he said.

'It's probably nothing,' said Tim. 'Simon might have egged his mother on to go further afield than anticipated. I think the original target was to sail to Martham Broad, wasn't it?' Tim was making light of the situation, but secretly he was as concerned as Tony!

'Yes,' acknowledged June, who had been party to the planning process.

Tony was now a very worried man. 'Tim, we'd better go and look for them in case something has happened,' he said.

'Right, we'll leave one of the boats here and use the other two,' answered Tim.

'I'll stay with Jamie and Jenny,' said June. 'There is no need to involve everyone.'

'I'll keep you company' added Ginger.

'Okay' said Tim, 'Tony and I will take *Spectrum Three* and head towards Martham. If the rest of you take *Spectrum Two* in the direction of Potter Heigham that should hopefully cover all eventualities. Don't forget to keep in regular radio contact.'

❧ ❧ ❧

Now, on the river, and out of earshot of Tony, Ian was the first to comment. He, like Tim, had also appeared unconcerned but, in reality, was rather apprehensive. 'Mark, are you thinking what I'm thinking?' Ian asked. 'It has to be Jacob Wright taking his revenge? Chris is far too conscientious not to have contacted us if something had gone wrong.'

'Mmm, I think you're right,' replied Mark. 'I felt pretty uncomfortable from the beginning after hearing of Jacob Wright's release. He was pretty vindictive at the time of the arrest. You could tell that retribution was on the cards from that evil man.'

'Well it is all too terrifying for words,' commented Sandra, shuddering at a possible outcome.

❧ ❧ ❧

Back in the storage cellar the twins, having calmed, glanced at their mother.

'Mum, what's going to happen to us?' asked Simon.

'Shush', she comforted him, 'Don't worry, your dad and uncles will come looking for us.'

'But what if they don't,' sniffed Lucy.

'They will,' said their mum. 'Your Uncle Tim knows this broad by heart.'

Chris was thinking. She knew there were several other creeks at the end of Martham Broad which had to be searched before they found their boats. *Bishy-barney-bee* was still close to the bank with its sail flapping gently in the light breeze. She then glanced once more at the window. It was too small for her, but the twins would probably squeeze through. Her plan was forming.

'What are you doing mummy?' asked Lucy.

'Hush,' whispered Chris. 'I don't want either of you two to make any noise for the moment.'

Chris was still surveying the scene when she heard steps outside the cellar door. She jumped off the packing case, quietly moving it away from the window. She rejoined Lucy and Simon on the only form of seating in the room, a wooden bench.

The door opened and in came one of the other men carrying a tray in one hand and a gun in the other.

She placed a protective arm around her twins, trying not to panic when she saw the firearm. 'Do you think that evil man will share any ransom money with you?' Chris said, hoping to create some reaction. 'I would be very surprised if he does!'

The man just gave a broken tooth sort of smile, which actually looked more like a snarl. He dumped the tray containing some refreshments, and left the room without uttering a word.

It was still early in the afternoon, and plenty of daylight hours left before nightfall. While the twins ate the biscuits and sipped the water, Chris worked away at the lock with a rusty piece of metal. She grunted with satisfaction as the window sprung open.

Chris turned to the twins. 'Now I want you both to be very brave and very quiet. *Bishy-barney-bee* is on the water's edge. I'm going to help you climb through the window, and then I want the pair of you to run to *Bishy-barney-bee*. You're both expert sailors now aren't you? But remember, no noise, no talking, don't call out to me, just go...'

'Yes, mummy,' said the twins.

'Can you remember the way we came?'

'We sailed along the river,' said Lucy.

'And then the length of the broad,' added Simon.

'Now I want you to sail down the broad and out onto the river and head in the direction of Hickling. Can you do that?'

'Of course we can,' said Simon.

'But what about you mummy?' cried Lucy. 'Why aren't you coming!'

'Only you can get through the window. I'll have to stay here, so that is why you both must be very, very brave.'

Chris checked the cellar door to make sure no one was about, and then lifted the twins one by one up to the window. They scrambled out.

'Now go and find daddy, and Uncle Tim, but shush, no noise.'

They ran down to the water's edge. Chris watched them, fingers crossed and hoping for the best. She saw

Lucy climb into the boat first and then Simon jumped in pushing the little craft away from the bank in the process. Fortunately, the wind was now behind the dinghy and very quickly and silently they sailed out of Chris's view. She smiled quietly to herself, despite everything the children even remembered to put on their life jackets.

Simon and Lucy worked together confidently which would have made Tony and Chris proud. In a very short time *Bishy-barney-bee* entered the main river and headed in the direction of Hickling. The twins were concentrating so much they missed a rare sight as a bittern, disturbed from its feeding, rose suddenly behind the little boat. It flew slowly across the river landing in the reeds on the opposite bank.

Storm clouds were now gathering, the wind growing in strength. On *Spectrum Three* Tony looked grimly at Tim, but no comment passed between them, the expression said it all!

Meanwhile, *Bishy-barney-bee*, which had been controllable by the children, became erratic as the wind changed direction and started to blow against the little boat. Simon was steering, whilst Lucy had control of the mainsail. The pair of them up until then had only sailed in fairly calm conditions. The Optimist suddenly swung broad side onto the stormy waters, and rocked violently. However, it was a sturdy little craft, and with Lucy spilling wind out of the sail, and Simon moving the tiller, they were once more pointing in the right direction.

Suddenly, there was a flash of lightning followed by a tremendous crack of thunder. The heavens opened. Driving rain caused the visibility to worsen. The twins, now soaked, were extremely frightened!

In the gathering gloom of the afternoon Tony suddenly grabbed Tim's arm and pointed. 'Tim, Tim! I think that's *Bishy-barney-bee*!'

'You're right,' he said. Tim eased the throttle and very carefully, much to the twins relief who had also spotted the boat, brought *Spectrum Three* alongside. By then the children were very tearful, but they still managed to throw a rope to their uncle who caught it, and tied *Bishy-barney-bee* firmly to the larger craft.

Tony leaned over the side and helped the children on board. 'Oh daddy, it was terrible,' sobbed Lucy. 'Men grabbed us and took us to a cellar and locked us up and they've still got mummy.' Tim picked up a couple of towels to wrap around the two very wet children.

Tony took them both into his arms. 'Hush,' he gently said. 'Now, where have they taken mummy?'

'We were in Martham Broad and up one of the creeks,' said Simon who was also sniffling but trying once more to be brave. 'Mummy opened a window and told us to come and look for you.'

Once more a look passed between Tony and Tim, both coming to the same conclusion, it must be Jacob Wright.

The children settled a bit. Tony took them into the cabin for a change of clothing and mugs of hot chocolate.

Meanwhile Tim radioed the Police H.Q. Brian Devenport was in his office, and immediately patched through. Tim relayed the twins' story.

'Superintendent, I think the mill mentioned by the twins is Thapes. It is situated at the end of Martham Broad's Navigational Channel,' said Tim. 'It was operational until about three years ago and I believe now up for sale.'

'Thapes Mill, you say, I know exactly where you mean. We have two police launches on the River Thurne at present. One is at Potter Heigham and the other at West Somerton. They will be able to investigate. Tim, please reassure Tony. Tell him we have everything in hand.'

Encouraging words or not from the Superintendent, Tony wasn't having it.

'Tim, we've got to go, I can't stay here doing nothing,' said Tony.

Tim also thought that some action on their part might help to calm Tony. They headed towards Martham Broad.

Ian on *Spectrum Two* and June, with Ginger, back on Hickling Broad were contacted and informed of the present position. Although relieved at the recovery of the twins they were now extremely anxious at the possible outcome for Chris.

CHAPTER NINETEEN

Back in the cellar Chris had climbed down from the packing case. She sat quietly on the bench bowing her head and clasping her hands together. Although not religious, Chris said a short prayer for the safety of Lucy and Simon.

Her peace was suddenly shattered by loud shouting. Her captors had realised there was a boat missing.

'At least,' thought Chris, checking her watch, 'the twins have had a good twenty minutes start and should be well on their way out of the broad, and onto the river system.'

It wasn't long before a clatter down the cellar stairs produced the appearance of a very irate Jacob Wright. He looked around the room. Advancing on Chris, yanking her by the hair, eye to eye, he spitted out: 'Where the *bloody Hell* are your kids?'

Chris grimaced in pain at the force she was being held. 'Obviously not here,' she replied, but muttered to herself, 'and well and truly out of harm's way.'

'If I don't have your kids, I still have you,' he cried. 'Your beloved might get his children back, but you are just as valuable to me, maybe more so!' He flung Chris away from him with such force that her head hit the wall, momentarily stunning her. She was brought back to reality when an extremely angry Jacob Wright slammed the door shut as he left the cellar. Chris burst into tears. It was all becoming too much for her.

※ ※ ※

Spectrum Three motored speedily down the River Thurne, eventually turning into Martham Broad. They headed straight to Thapes Mill. The twins had recovered enough to join their uncle and dad in the cockpit to watch proceedings. The rain had eased and the sun was peeping out from behind a cloud.

Nearing the end of the navigational channel they reached the mill. The prow of a kayak could be seen in the reeds. Tony leapt ashore with the mooring rope, and tied *Spectrum Three* to a convenient tree stump. The twins sat quietly in the boat whilst Tim joined Tony ashore.

'It's definitely Chris's canoe,' said Tony, walking around the craft. Suddenly, a roaring noise startled them. They looked up just in time to see a speedboat tear down the broad.

The twins jumped up and down pointing, 'mummy, mummy!' they shouted as the launch sped past them causing *Spectrum Three* to rock violently.

Tim leapt back on board and called up the Superintendent.

'Right' he said, 'the launches aren't that far away now so they should be able to intercept.'

※ ※ ※

Chris, in the cabin of the powerboat, a gun pointing at her and a wrist handcuffed to the bulkhead, looked on with relief, and a sense of motherly pride. 'The twins had made it to safety,' she thought. 'Well done!' But this didn't help her predicament as the launch, with Jacob Wright at the controls, zoomed down Martham Broad and out onto the river at a rate of knots.

Spectrum Three was in pursuit, but not making much headway. The channel in front of them was now blocked by a hired dayboat zigzagging from side-to-side, obviously an inexperienced driver! Tim and Tony could not pass! Towing *Bishy-barney-bee* didn't help either as it was also slowing their progress. All this was adding to Tony's frustration. Tim could see the panic on Tony's face. He had to calm the situation for the sake of the twins who were picking up on their dad's agitation.

'Simon, Lucy, could you get me a glass of water please?'

Whilst the twins were in the cabin Tim did much to reassure Tony. The twins reappeared with his drink. Tony was now doing his best to hide his emotions.

Chris, despite her plight, couldn't help but be in awe of Jacob Wright's driving skill. At the junction of the River Thurne and the opening to Hickling Broad, he did the most spectacular spin of which any powerboat racer on Oulton Broad would have been proud. This was backed up with another U-turn. He surged past the police taking them completely by surprise.

Now temporarily out of sight of his pursuers Jacob headed up a hidden creek, which Chris, with her extensive knowledge of the area, didn't know existed.

The two police launches now together, rounded the bend in the river and found their quarry had vanished.

They cut their engines listening hard for any noise which could point to the whereabouts of the missing speedboat.

Luckily, *Spectrum Two*, now on the scene, saw the manoeuvre. Guided by Ian, the police turned into the narrow waterway.

❧ ❧ ❧

Jacob Wright had such a good feel for the Broads and boats because of the early years spent with his grandfather George who had been a marshman. Throughout the year this band of local men was employed to maintain dykes and drainage mills and to keep the rivers free of any hazards so allowing boats, like the Norfolk Wherry, to transport their cargoes.

In the summer months it was trapping wildfowl, harvesting hay for fodder, managing cattle grazing on the rich marsh land and reed cutting. The cut reed bundles were then transported by a traditional boat called a reed lighter to village staithes, ready for thatchers to collect. The *Globe,* also benefited from the Norfolk reed, as every so often bundles were sent to London to re-roof this iconic theatre.

It was certainly a hard life for a marshman!

❧ ❧ ❧

At the end of the creek Jacob steered the boat into the bank and helped by Joe, his accomplice, pulled Chris out of the cabin and onto dry land. She was sandwiched between the two men. The revolver in Jacob's trouser pocket pressed uncomfortably against her thigh.

Reed beds can be dangerous places. The vegetation often conceals overgrown ditches. The underlying peat, similar to quicksand, can trap you in deep holes that are difficult to escape from. She wondered if her kidnappers had remembered about this quaking marsh.

Clear ground was reached, or had it? They were now faced with a coarse sandy bank alongside a dyke, which disappeared through some trees. Chris, hearing the sound of distant traffic, thought there might be a road just the other side of the wood.

Jacob and Joe, still holding Chris, walked onto this so-called smooth embankment. Chris, trapped as she was between the two men, could do nothing to prevent it. All too soon their legs sank into the bog. The men, attempting to lever themselves out of the mud, found no traction. They just sank deeper!

Chris, now free of her captives, knew what she had to do. She and Tim had been caught in similar circumstances a few years ago. Spreading her weight across the mire, she rolled to the edge of the reeds and into safety.

Jacob Wright, seeing Chris do this, attempted the same escape movement, but had struggled so much that he was in too deep. He still had his gun. He fired! Chris, now on firm ground, quickly moved into cover. The wayward bullet hit a nearby alder tree, splitting a branch in two, and showering her with splinters. A close call by all accounts!

Joe, hysterical and scared at his predicament was yelling: 'Help! **Help**!' at the top of his voice. The police had by now found the ditched speedboat. Following the sound of the cries they reached Chris. They were local, and only too aware of the dangers of the marsh. They called for immediate back-up.

Chris's assumption about a road had proved correct, as from the woodland came more police, this time with rescue equipment for the trapped men. The men were gradually freed from their holes. Jacob Wright for once, pale-faced, and downcast, seemed to lose all fight and went with the police without a murmur.

Chris was shaking, her ordeal was over. Would she ever get over the experience? Maybe, time would tell!

Brian Devenport placed a fatherly arm across her shoulders. He was as much affected by what had occurred as Chris. She looked up at him. His actions did much to calm and reassure her.

'Now young lady,' said the Superintendent, turning her around, 'let us get you back to Tony and the twins.' He helped her into one of the police launches and in a very short while she was at the mouth of the creek where the *Spectrums* were moored.

As soon as Lucy and Simon saw their mummy they ran to her. Chris knelt down, gathered them into her arms, emotional tears running down her face. Tony was close behind. He just held her tight, almost as if he was never going to let her go again.

All three Spectrums then made a leisurely return to Spindle. All thought that after the highly dramatic events a few more days of relaxation would be a good tonic. Communing with nature and the peace of the broads was a fine healer. Chris spent much of the return journey trying to blank out her experience. Tony and the twins helped a lot but she felt that it would be many months or even years for her to come to terms with it.

The *Spectrums* duly arrived back at the Hall. Sam and Grace were still abroad but Jessie, Frank and Matt were on the quayside to welcome them. No, Chris was not mistaken. Sandra headed towards Matt, arms outstretched he gave her a warm embrace. The others looked on in amazement. Mark took the greeting in his stride, as did Jessie and Frank. He was more interested in the bulky package in Matt's hand.

Mark was handed a thick brown envelope with a BBC insignia on the front. He tore it open and read. He looked at Sandra, who was still in Matt's arms.

'Were you successful Mark?' cried an excited Sandra.

A brilliant smile said it all. Sandra disentangled herself from Matt, and ran to him in delight and gave him a hug.

Chris, was the first to find voice. Looking from one to the other, she asked, 'What an earth is going on?'

'Whilst in New Zealand,' Mark said, 'we stumbled across the BBC doing some short films for the *Wildlife on One* series.'

Sandra butted in: 'You know what Mark is like in researching any wildlife we might come across on our travels, well he corrected them on some of their facts.'

'Not exactly,' retorted Mark. 'Well, I muttered to Sandra that the Presenter had quoted something wrong. I hadn't realised Phil Stamford, the Producer, was standing beside me. He asked me what I meant, and we chatted. The long and short of it all is,' waving the letter in the air, 'I've been offered a job with their Natural History Unit in Bristol.'

Now all were around Mark showering him with congratulations.

Chris glanced back at Sandra who was once more in Matt's arms.

'And,' Chris said, 'there appears to be something else about to be revealed.'

Sandra gazed at Matt, then at Chris, then the others.

'Well we had been corresponding for a while now, and Matt has been joining us abroad whenever he could get away.'

'...And, as they say, the rest is history,' said Mark, re-reading his letter.

ℨ ℨ ℨ

Nearly three months had past and as far as Simon and Lucy were concerned their ordeal was now a rather distant memory. It was Thursday afternoon and school had broken up for the summer holidays.

The twins arrived home and seemed to sense something in the air, and looked at their parents. 'Okay you two,' said Tony, 'go and see what's appeared by the quay.'

So the children ran down the garden to the Broad and there, bobbing beside *Bishy-barney-bee,* was a new member of the Fleet, *Bishy-barney-bee the Second.*

With a yelp of delight the twins, each taking an Optimist, sailed out on to Spindle Broad; Tony and Chris, arm in arm, looked on, with affection, in the evening sunshine.

The End

ENDPIECE

Spectrum is set towards the end of the nineteen sixties and although a story of fiction many of the landmarks and places mentioned do exist. Some dates have been changed to enable an even flow of the story. The names of Spindle and Teardrop Broads are obviously made up.

RAF Neatishead became a museum in the 1990s, and is well worth a visit. It has a unique history covering the period from World War Two through to the Cold War. *Aquillis* is a work of fiction and does not exist.

The Queen and Prince Philip's visit to open the new Ranworth Broad Information Centre was actually in 1976 and their visit to the Oulton Broad Motor Boat Club was in 1985.

The Norfolk Naturalists Trust was formed in 1926 and eventually changed its name to the Norfolk Wildlife Trust in 1994 to fall in line with the other County Wildlife Trusts. It is looking forward to celebrating its centenary.

Windsurfing eventually became an Olympic sport in 1984.

Much has been done to improve the marine quality of the Norfolk Broads and several Broads have been *mud pumped* and wildlife, including many rare species, is now returning to these tranquil waters. The comment about water quality improving briefly on Hickling Broad has happened on a couple of occasions. The most recent was in 2022. A wet winter followed by a drought killed the algae. The eventual rain stimulated lush aquatic plant growth causing an explosion of the tiny water fleas who feast on the algae. The abundant growth gives the invertebrates cover from their normal predator...... FISH.

Coypu were eventually eradicated from the Broads by 1989, though mink still exist in a few areas and are regularly trapped. On a plus for this family of rodents, otters are now spreading around the river systems and are regularly seen. Water vole numbers are also increasing.

The Norfolk Broads received the status of a National Park in 1988 and is the only National Park with a City in its midst.

www.ingramcontent.com/pod-product-compliance
Lightning Source LLC
Chambersburg PA
CBHW020940260626

47169CB00006B/1749